Rock My World

BY SHARISSE COULTER

ISBN 978-0-9888378-0-5

Chapter 1

Jenna saw the best in everyone. In sixth grade, she was voted "Most Friendly." Her table in the cafeteria was always full: a feat for any pre-teen. Then came high school, and she became "Most Likely to Ruin Her Life" in a less official, more viral poll of her peers. However, in the many years since, she'd worked hard to be a good friend, wife, mother, and daughter, priding herself on putting others first. That cheery optimism had served her well. Until today. Of course, she couldn't have seen it coming; and yet, a nagging little voice told her she'd known it all along. It's not every day something happens to turn your whole world upside down. But today, Jenna found herself standing on her head, and not just during yoga.

"CouCou!" Airika waved to Jenna as she walked up the path toward the frosted glass palace of Karyn C's studio. Jenna loved that Airika, born and bred in L.A., injected random French phrases into her everyday vernacular despite never learning a foreign language. She was so unaffected by other people's criticism, floating through life on a free-spirited cloud. It was refreshing being friends with someone so uninhibited. Someone so unlike herself.

"Hi!" Airika said, air-kissing Jenna's cheeks.

"I'm so excited! Thank you *so* much for arranging this!"

"Did you bring the album?" Airika asked, glancing up from her phone, fingers tapping away.

"Yeah, I brought it. Is Karyn C. a fan of my dad's?" Jenna asked.

"Who isn't?" Airika, knowing Jenna's discomfort with using her father's celebrity to garner favors, added, "She's so excited to dress *you* though. She told me you have the perfect body for her designs."

"Really?" Jenna knew she was being placated but secretly agreed the Karyn C. gowns she'd been seeing at award shows would accentuate her tall, athletic frame. She often felt mannish in gowns because they emphasized her shoulders, making her look like a transvestite. Karyn's draping and detail—quintessential to her designs—fell in perfect feminine lines, soft and flowing. Perfect for tonight's occasion.

"Come in, come in! I'm so glad you're here. Sorry it's so early," exclaimed a spritely Asian twenty-something, escorting them into the studio. "It is *such* a pleasure to meet you, Jenna. And a pleasure, as always, to see you again," she said, air-kissing Airika.

"I am in love with your designs, Karyn. I'm so grateful you'd open your studio for me." Jenna said.

"Oh please! You're Shawn Jax's daughter! *And* you were an amazing model! Don't even get me started on your yummy husband! Designers must throw themselves at you constantly!" Karyn C. enthused with a flick of her hand, as she bustled about, throwing garments on racks.

Jenna smiled, thinking Karyn seemed unbelievably young for someone with such a long list of accomplishments——she couldn't have been a day over 23.

"Not since I got knocked up and turned into a boring housewife," Jenna said. Karyn's brows knit together in confusion before she laughed politely.

"Oh, Jenna wanted to bring you a little something to say thank you," Airika said, diffusing the awkward moment.

"Right. From my dad." Jenna pulled the album out of her oversized shoulder bag. "Airika said it's your favorite?"

"Aww, that was so sweet of you," Karyn said to Jenna, setting it on a pile of paperwork on her desk.

"We wanted you to have these, too," Airika said, pulling out two front row tickets to Alex's concert tomorrow night. Jenna kicked herself for not thinking to do that herself. Good thing Airika always had her back.

"O.M.G.! OMG, OMG, OMG!!!! Oh, thank you, thank you, thank you! Oh. My. God. This is *amazing*, thank you! These tickets have been sold out since, like, forever!" Karyn squealed and danced around, clutching the tickets to her chest as though they were plated in gold. Her teeny frame wrapped the two friends into an impossibly strong bear hug, nearly knocking the wind out of Jenna.

"You're welcome," they said together. Jenna couldn't help but laugh.

Regaining her composure, Karyn picked out a silk chiffon one-shoulder dress, ending just above the knee, and handed it to Jenna. It was an almost nude pink that brought out Jenna's ivory skin tone without making her look naked. Her long chestnut hair flowed around her shoulders as she twirled for approval.

"Très magnifique! Like a haute couture harlequin heroine," Airika gushed.

Jenna didn't know what that meant, but felt feminine and beautiful and just *knew* Alex would love it on her. She thanked Karyn and left, fantasizing about his reaction when he saw her tonight.

Their daughter, Felicity, was staying with her grandparents for the weekend so that Jenna could plan the perfect weekend in. She stocked the fridge with Alex's favorite foods, even looking up his grandmother's recipe for Swedish meatballs and lingonberry pudding. Alex broke the stereotypical male mold in lots of ways, but the way to his heart was still through his stomach. And of course, what he sometimes called "dessert," which she'd been thinking about for weeks.

When their schedules allowed, Jenna and Alex loved being homebodies. Their idea of a great date night included a couple of rented DVD's and a homemade pizza, Alex's specialty. Jenna often joked that if the music thing didn't work out, he could make a killing as a private chef.

"I've got a crazy day today so I have to leave you, but good luck tonight!" Airika said, sashaying her way to the brand new Mercedes G-class SUV parked next to Jenna's Prius.

"Thanks for everything, Air! See you tomorrow!"

"I expect details. Ciao!"

Jenna loved hanging out with her best friend, yet relished the idea of getting a few hours to spend on her own today, and since the day started so early she had plenty of time to prep for tonight.

The happiness she felt for having an amazing husband and an incredible best friend was only slightly marred by the fact that they hated each other. Despised, to be more accurate.

Jenna painstakingly scheduled events so they always had a buffer (usually herself). She couldn't pinpoint the exact moment of their antagonism, but it started sometime senior year of high school.

Jenna suspected it had something to do with her. The first time she remembered noticing it was after she announced her pregnancy. Unexpected pregnancy is a breeding ground for teen drama and Alex and Airika were both fiercely protective of her.

Her brilliant modeling career and burgeoning Party Girl persona came to a screeching halt. The prom queen became the outcast as her friends and followers traded her in for a new queen bee while she transitioned from haute couture to maternity. They talked about her behind her back, saying things like, "She's gonna get fat!" and "Washed up before she's even legal!" and "Slut!" Alex and Airika defended her against the onslaught that semester while Jenna spent an inordinate amount of time in the girls' bathroom learning to cry silently. Through the humiliation and shame, she vowed to never again let anyone she loved lose friends because of her and her poor choices.

Before that, Jenna dropped her famous last name like ecstasy at a rave. She got into the hottest clubs, best parties, and backstage at any concert she (and her minions) wanted. Jenna toed the line of a perfect Hollywood cliché. As adults, those roles reversed. Airika, not born to famous parents, had styled her way into V.I.P. status, constantly dragging Jenna out to club openings and red carpet after parties. While Airika thrived in that party environment, Jenna knew she didn't belong there anymore.

After she and Alex married, Jenna swore to turn her life around. And she had. The picture of healthy living. She grew organic herbs in their yard. She worked out. She meditated. She drove a hybrid. She obeyed the speed limit (well, unless she was in a *real* hurry). She joined the PTA. She cheered Felicity on at every soccer game. She sacrificed having a career so her husband could achieve his dreams. She supported him while he toiled away in obscurity, with a little help from her trust fund. And finally, after all these years, the puzzle pieces were coming together. Her life was just like a commercial: all bright smiles and crisp clean living.

Chapter 2

The day began, as usual, in her meditation room. She went about her morning ritual of speed yoga (because she needed to squeeze in her cardio too), skipping the meditation pranayama at the end. She could never convince her thoughts to pass through her mind like clouds in the sky, as her yogi told her to do; they were more like tornadoes wreaking havoc and destruction, requiring immediate attention.

After yoga she blended her breakfast of spinach, tomato, carrot, pomegranate and wheatgrass into an anti-aging, energy-boosting smoothie. She called it gut-wrenching goodness; Alex called it compost. She split it between two re-usable steel canteens and hopped in the shower.

The day looked just like every other day in perpetually sunny Southern California. The sky was the cerulean blue of Jenna's eyes, the temperature perfectly warm with a cool ocean breeze. This fine February morning she put on a draped jersey tank with her new skinny jeans and jeweled espadrilles—sexy, yet comfortable.

She dropped Felicity off at school, listening to the usual teenage monologue.

"Seriously Mom, I don't see why I can't just get a ride from Trey. He's a better driver than you after only driving for a year."

Jenna smiled, and for the umpteenth time, reminded her sixteen year-old daughter that she would not be riding on the back of her best friend's motorcycle until she was mature enough to know not to get on it in the first place.

Though Jenna noticed a marked increase in the number of times they butted heads recently, she knew this particular outburst came on the heels of forbidding Felicity from any professional acting until she turned eighteen. Felicity had been offered a chance to audition for the director of a new biopic about her grandfather. Jenna knew better than to let her take that path. No daughter of hers was going to become a cautionary tale. One screw up in the family was enough, and Jenna claimed that title years ago.

She offered Felicity the smoothie she made, met, as usual, with a look of disgust, as if she'd offered her a steaming pile of something else. Felicity swept her golden copper waves up into a ponytail and Jenna bit her tongue, making a conscious effort not to ask her to leave it down. Those metallic colored locks, with her tanned face and blue eyes, made a gorgeous combination—one most girls would die for. Jenna wished she'd take advantage of it a little instead of dressing for soccer practice.

"Have a nice day!" Jenna said.

As the door slammed shut and she waited for the carpool line to start moving, she watched her daughter stalk off toward the high arched doorways of expensive private education, yearning for the days of timeouts and naps solving all behavioral problems.

Beep, beeeeeep! Beeeep! Her cell lit up with a text from Airika telling her when she could pick up her dress. She was grateful to have such a good friend, who always went out of her way to hook her up. She and Airika had been best friends forever. Since Airika was Erica. They met the summer before second grade at Jenna's lemonade stand outside her parents' house in Malibu. Even then, Erica could talk anyone into giving her what she wanted, and Jenna (along with everyone else) was mesmerized. Erica strutted up in her acid wash jeans, side ponytail and the bright white Keds Jenna had been eyeing for months, and said, "Man, it's hot! You wanna give me a glass of lemonade to cool off?"

Jenna did. She couldn't explain it, but she knew then, that this was the coolest girl she'd ever meet. From that day on, they'd been inseparable. Jenna's parents tried hard to instill in her a good work ethic, not spending much money on clothes or

private schools or unnecessarily expensive acting lessons
(which she desperately wanted to take). Jenna envied the trendy
girls whose parents took them shopping on weekends, to
auditions for commercials, and let them watch PG-13 movies.
Erica's parents belonged to that ilk. They thought her time was
better spent shopping at designer stores, enrolling in the most
expensive private school, and getting private gymnastics
coaching in case she stumbled upon elite-level talent.

Through recess games and first crushes; through Erica's
parents splitting up and her transition to Airika; through
sneaking out for the first time to go clubbing and getting drunk
off tequila—they'd been thick as thieves. They'd even stuck
together when Jenna got pregnant senior year, and all her other
friends stopped speaking to her. She became a social leper,
quietly getting fatter and fatter, the halls clearing quicker and
quicker as she trudged down to the delinquent wing where they
held remedial English, How to Pass the G.E.D. and Parenting
101, while her above-ground peers studied for the SAT's.

Airika was her only friend. Well, except her "baby daddy,"
of course. She was lucky to be one of the few people in the
world to meet her one true love in high school. To think that
now, eighteen years later, they would be preparing to celebrate
their anniversary as much in love as ever; it was more than she
could have hoped for, or deserved.

With the world against them, they conquered the odds and
escaped not only the Hollywood curse of doomed relationships, but the more common one (and less geographically
specific) of getting married too young and growing apart. Jenna
was lucky. No one could deny it, not even her.

And Airika, now fashion stylist to the stars, was still looking
out for her friend. Why else would she have booked Jenna's
exclusive fitting with the newest "It" designer, Karyn C? She
designed the most amazing red carpet gowns, having just
dressed Natalie Portman and Julia Roberts for this year's
Oscars. Jenna could barely contain her excitement.

Later on, Alex would be flying in from…where was he? Germany? Hungary? Japan? She couldn't keep track anymore. All she knew was he would fly in this afternoon to take her on a super secret date and she wanted to make sure she looked perfect.

It had been three months since they'd spent more than eight consecutive hours together. Alex was touring with his band to promote their new album, leaving her to take care of things at home. It took its toll, no doubt. But it was an amazing opportunity for Alex—the culmination of years of hard work to reach this point—headlining their first world tour.

Plus, she'd been able to convince him to hire Airika as his personal stylist, thus ingratiating her into the world of rock stars (her true childhood dream). Jenna owed her so much and it felt good to be able to hook Airika up. Airika came back early from the European portion of the tour, glowing with excitement. She had a beefed up roster of rock star clients hoping to replicate Alex's success for themselves. It was fantastic for everyone. Jenna was so proud of him and all that he had accomplished. And tonight, they'd finally get to celebrate.

***

Alex never got used to flying on private jets. Not that he minded. The food was amazing and as a light sleeper, being able to fully recline without some random stranger leaning their head on his shoulder was a bonus. Especially after playing shows almost every night this month.

He couldn't shake his discomfort that there were more staff onboard than passengers, catering to him. He tried to rationalize it as his own contribution to the nation's employment drought.

When they landed, a town car awaited his arrival, driver ready to take him anywhere he pleased. Fame meant a lot of things to get used to—entering establishments through side doors, traveling with security, paparazzi stalking him. Having someone else navigate L.A. traffic wasn't hard to enjoy.

"Hey Max," he said to the driver. "How's Shelly?"

"Good, boss. Thanks for asking. Where to?"

"Home."

"Home it is." Max said, pulling away from the tarmac.

A half hour later, they pulled up to a white mission style home on a quiet Santa Monica street. Its high archways lead into a Spanish tiled courtyard, opening up to an oversized red door. Alex opened it and breathed in a sigh of relief. No matter how nice the hotel rooms were on tour, nothing compared to home.

Their home was a perfect combination of his and Jenna's personalities. Bright and open, it was filled with photos and trinkets collected during their years together. The wall leading from the entryway into the living room overflowed with black and white photos of Felicity growing up. Looking at those pudgy baby photos gave him a twinge of nostalgia.

He loved returning home to the competing sounds of indie folk music blaring from Felicity's room—the antithesis of his own punk rock roots—and HGTV, which Jenna kept on 24/7 "for ideas," she said. She was constantly redecorating, but the style du jour seemed to be red and white nouveau-vintage-mod, or something along those lines. It was strange, returning to an empty house.

Before he could set his bags down, his cell phone rang. "What?" He demanded. "No, I told you I won't be able to be reached until sound check tomorrow. No. No. No. Bye, Simon." He shook his head at his overbearing manager and switched his phone off. He felt guilty about lying to Jenna, but needed time to pull off his big anniversary plan. The quiet of his empty house was overwhelming, especially in contrast to the gaggle of people who constantly surrounded him on tour.

The piece of home he missed the most was his backyard. Having grown up in apartments and high-rises his whole life, it represented adulthood. To have a backyard meant he was making his own way in the world—not slaving for a landlord or homeowner's association. Each house on their street was built in a different decade with its owner's style on full display. He loathed the idea of living in one of those cookie cutter communities where everything looks identical and no one can paint their house or forget to mow their lawn. Maybe it was the adult manifestation of his punk rock rebellion.

He slid on a pair of well-loved jeans and a white undershirt before heading out to his workroom. He wanted tonight to be perfect. His body craved the heat of the sun and the sweat of manual labor to transport him away from his professional problems and bring him back to where he wanted to be— home.

***

Airika Thomas left Karyn C's and headed straight to her office. "Good morning, Ms. Thomas," her assistant, Meg, said handing her a triple soy non-fat decaf sugar-free hazelnut macchiato. "Trevor called from the shoot and says they need more boots because the model is refusing to wear anything made from animal hide."

"Who the fuck does she think she is? Naomi-fucking-Campbell?"

Meg paused before continuing, "Jess says we're set on Martine's dress for the Grammys but we need her for a final fitting today. But you also have to go to Malibu to meet with Julia's niece who is going with the lead singer of Brands of Charlotte, who is slated to win Artist of the Year. Which do you want me to reschedule?"

"Neither."

"You won't have time for that and the photo shoot," Meg said, worried.

Airika rolled her eyes and looked at her assistant with pity.

"Um, also, Simon had this delivered a while ago. Phazee Crux are doing a behind-the-scenes DVD, and they need you need to sign this waiver."

"Call Martine, have her meet me at the office for the fitting.

I'll stop by the photo shoot on my way out to Malibu. And get me Gisele's selection for Milan so I can stop by while I'm out there. Do you think you can handle that?" Airika snatched the remaining messages from Meg, stomped in to her glass-walled office and slammed the self-closing door behind her, which took its sweet time clicking shut.

Today was turning into a total disaster, and it wasn't even lunchtime. What did these dimwits do when she wasn't here? She stared out her window at the oracle of the Hollywood sign she paid double the rent to look at, hoping it would offer the answers she sought.

She was leaving on tour in two days. There was too much to do and she didn't trust her team to keep up with her standards while she was gone. She had to go, though. And before then she needed to convince Jenna to let Felicity appear in the biopic about Shawn. The director fell in love with her from her headshot and offered Airika a producer credit if she could get Felicity Anders for the role, knowing it would lead to a massive boost in press for the film. Felicity approached her months ago saying she wanted to act but that her mom wouldn't let her audition. Jenna wanted Felicity to stay away from the spotlight until she was at least eighteen, preferably forever. And she didn't want her own daughter to go around exploiting her famous grandfather.

Prior to getting knocked up, exploiting her famous daddy was Jenna's M.O.; but now, in typical parental hypocrisy, she was above that sort of vapid name-dropping. Airika disagreed. She knew the power of fame in this town and intended to build her empire taking full advantage, dropping every name she had in her arsenal, casting the net as wide as possible.

"Cici Hi," Airika drawled in her Coolest-Aunt-Ever voice, pacing the floor. She hated leaving messages. "So look, Sweetie. Everyone is excited for your audition tomorrow at four. At this point it's really just a formality, but we'll need to get your mom to sign off on it. I'll keep working on her but maybe you can talk to your dad and get him to help us out with her. Kay? Bisous! Ciao!"

She hung up and opened a new email from her father's lawyer, Ira Stearn. Unconsciously she clenched her teeth as she read, her knuckles turning white as she thrashed out a reply on the keyboard.

She pulled a protein bar out of her fuchsia designer handbag, knocking over her macchiato. "No!" she yelled, grabbing the nearest paper, desperately dabbing in a vain attempt to save her brand new white jeggings.

"Is everything okay?" Meg asked, gasping in horror at the mud-colored stain oozing down her boss' leg.

"No, everything is not okay! Look at this! Uaaggh! Now I'm going to have to go home and change. I'll be on my cell. Get me Gisele!" Airika grabbed a silk sequined scarf from her office closet and cinched it like a belt, letting it dangle enough to cover the stain. She would die if anyone saw her like this.

Chapter 3

Glistening beads of sweat dripping from his forehead, Alex surveyed the wonderland he'd created. The lazy drooping pepper trees dotted with hanging candles, an antique wrought iron park bench below, and the white rose bushes lining the fence led his eye to the crowning jewel of his landscape design: the bridge. It was a little white bridge, simple enough, but in order to shape it, he'd spent time with an old boat maker learning how to curve the wood into neat little arcs, like the upside down hull of a boat. It was a near perfect replica of Jenna's drawing of the bridge where they first kissed. It looked over a small waterfall that wound down into a babbling brook, snaking around the oasis-like garden.

Paper lanterns were strung like a canopy and candles flickered on lily pads, giving off a magical glow. He installed rock-shaped speakers to blend into the surroundings for the reveal of a song he'd written seventeen years ago, but never before played for her.

He regretted the way they got married, and even worse, his proposal—or lack thereof. He hadn't been the best boyfriend (for which Jenna was all too forgiving) but he could have at least given her a proper proposal. Instead, while their parents sat them down, deciding what to do with them and their compromised futures, Alex blurted out, "We're getting married!" It had the desired effect: shutting their parents up. But Jenna didn't say a word. She looked down, hands on her stomach, silent.

When everyone finally settled down and came to terms with their impending parenthood, they went to the courthouse and signed the papers. That was it. All it took to become man and wife. It was quite possibly the least romantic proposal and wedding of all time, despite being on Valentine's Day.

That's why tonight was so important to him. He could finally give her the proposal she deserved, having realized the success they'd both worked so hard for. He intended to make up for everything he hadn't been able to give her all these years and get that sad image of her with her hands on her belly to stop haunting him.

***

Jenna strolled along the newly cobbled courtyard, its equidistant palm trees strewn with fairy lights. Lampposts draped with hanging flowers lent a vaguely European feel to the outdoor mall. She loved shopping for so many reasons, but her favorite thing was looking at window displays. Perfect mannequins dressed for every occasion transported her to alternate realities: a romantic gondola ride through Venice; a group of four best friends out for a fashion forward night at the trendiest hotspot you've never heard of; a single woman of eccentric yet chic taste, clearly in control of everything in her life. Each window promised that anyone could become an entirely new person if they only dressed the part.

The way the monochromatic whites played off the textures of colorful displays and bold accessories stirred in her a longing to be this store. In her next Zen meditation session, this would be her happy place, she thought as she perused rack after rack of bizarre accessories. On their own, they could look gaudy or garish, but paired just so, they evoked an image of a woman whose confidence allowed her to play with fashion, utterly unconcerned with labels and seasons of acceptability. She could be anywhere in the world, equally happy on her own or with a lover or friend. Jenna wished she could be her.

"May I help you?" a teenage salesgirl asked. Jenna smiled, reflexively about to refuse. Instead, she found herself saying, "This store is incredible! Do you sell shoes too?"

The young sales girl, glancing from head to toe at Jenna's haute couture ensemble, raised a skeptical eyebrow.

"Yes, the shoes are in that corner back there," she said

pointing to the other side of the store. "Let me know if you need help with sizes."

"Thanks! You know ... I'm not crazy. I just don't get out much." She said, feeling ridiculous to be swooning like a crazed love-struck schoolgirl.

She found the perfect pair of kitten heels to go with the dress she'd picked out; a large multi-stoned jeweled bangle to go with an almost-but-not-quite-matching pair of earrings; a too warm but amazing pea coat; and finally, a tiered chiffon dress perfect or Felicity. The way the fraying mismatched fabrics fell together into a soft silhouette seemed perfect for her daughter, who was anything but a "girly girl." Felicity hated when Jenna bought her clothes, claiming that she was trying to "impose an antiquated anti-feminist ideal" onto her. Those were her actual words. Where that vocabulary came from, Jenna would never know. Never mind. *She would look amazing in this dress!* Jenna thought as the salesgirl rung it up, folding it neatly into sheets of ivory tissue paper.

Outside the store, the velvety blue sky warmed her skin, which tingled with excitement at the mere thought that the day (and night) could get any better. A text from Airika ripped her from her reverie. "Beta Sushi, 10 mins." It read. *Uh-oh, what happened now*, Jenna worried.

Chapter 4

Twelve minutes later, Jenna pulled into the forgotten strip mall now occupied by the nondescript offices of an accountant, a travel agency and a second-hand sports equipment store. Beta Sushi was the only restaurant, and from the outside looked as though the health department should have shut it down long ago. It was dark and dingy and they served the best sushi in town. And it provided an anonymous low-light environment to bitch about major problems in the middle of the day. No self-respecting socialite, celebrity or professional would ever come here.

Jenna grabbed their booth at the back, tossed her packages on the seat next to her and waited, ordering their usual starter: sake and a rainbow roll. Ten minutes later Airika whirled in, layered straight blonde hair trailing her like a lightning bolt.

"Oh. My. God. You are never going to believe the morning I've had!" Airika said, plopping down across from her, taking a shot of sake. Jenna pushed half the rainbow roll across the table and waited. Airika ignored the food and launched straight in.

"So, I had a fitting with Martine for this afternoon, right? Huge, huge star who is going to win, like, all the Grammys and wear the clothes to every important after-party? So I'm getting ready when I get an email from my dad's lawyer saying he's being sued by my client. 'Fine,' I say, 'why is that any of my business?' He informs me that Martine's mom is suing him for malpractice! Uaargh!! And now she's going to ask me about it when I see her and I don't know what I'm supposed to tell her. Can you believe it? He's fucking up my career from 3,000 miles away! Who needs plastic surgery in Florida anyway? Who are they trying to impress, the Grim Reaper?"

With pitiable timing, the waiter appeared at the table. Airika glared at him. Jenna took pity and waved to the empty sake, indicating another round. He nodded and escaped without a word.

"Oh no," Jenna said, finishing off her half of rainbow roll. Airika fumed across the table and Jenna raised her eyebrows questioningly. Airika nodded in an as-if-I-can-eat-anything-at-a-time-like-this way before shoving the untouched plate across to Jenna, pouring the rest of the sake for herself. Jenna carefully navigated the minefield of Airika's emotional state. "What are you going to do?"

"I'm gonna throw him under the bus, if she asks. She's been better to me than he ever was. But I'm sure as hell not going to bring it up if she doesn't. This is why I changed my name in the first place."

When Airika was still Erica, her father, plastic surgeon to the stars, kept his family living in luxury. They lived in the most exclusive Malibu neighborhoods, updated their Porsches annually, vacationed at St. Barths, and enjoyed all the perks of stardom, albeit behind the scenes. In an unfortunate drunken moment, he once bragged to a hot young starlet he was lusting after the name of an A-list celebrity he worked on, hoping to impress her enough to sleep with him. Not only didn't it work out for him that night, but once word of his "indiscretion" got out, she, along with the entire female population of Los Angeles, ran him out of town.

Erica's mother, forced to downsize her life, reverted to her maiden name, Thomas. Erica took it a step further, re-spelling her first name too. The philandering husband wasn't exactly a shame-worthy story, but sabotaging a celebrity career for a hot lay was an unthinkable character flaw, obviously extending to his spouse as well. The socialites excommunicated her, shaming her into hiding. It was like something out of an Austen novel, with prettier people and uglier language. She never recovered. Though her parents remained married (he was still loaded, after all) they never saw each other again. The only contact she and her brother Zach had was an obligatory visit once a year during Christmas break.

"Maybe she won't know he's your dad? Then you don't have to throw anyone under the bus," Jenna said. Airika's mouth tightened. Jenna hurried to placate her friend. "Or maybe you can ask your dad to apologize?"

Airika rolled her eyes.

Jenna sighed and said, "Last time you fought with your dad he blocked your trust fund. For six months. Do you really want to do that again?"

"What? How can you, of all people, say that? It's my money, not charity! I've been supporting myself since I was seventeen, unlike some people."

"That's not what I...Sorry I said anything." Jenna said, throwing up her hands in surrender and blushing at the pointed critique.

The waiter took advantage of the silence between them to bring their sake and quickly scampered off. Jenna poured some for Airika, who pouted but drank it.

"And what about Cannes? Alex told me that was a huge success for you." Jenna said to change the subject.

"It was," Airika softened and told her all about her clients being on best-dressed lists and who was secretly dating whom and how her calendar was now booked through the rest of the year. She even took a bite off Jenna's plate, relaxing into a gossipy escape.

"And how about your love life? Anyone new on tour? Simon?" Jenna asked, playful once again. Airika had never been in a relationship, preferring a long string of one-night stands. Jenna wished she'd find someone who could change her mind, sure that it would soften the hardened edges of her personality.

Simon was Alex's manager and a little gruff on the outside, but a loyal teddy bear on the inside. He was as ambitious as Airika and came from a similar background, albeit the British version. Jenna knew he wasn't as handsome as Airika liked her men, but cute in his own way and she suspected Airika wouldn't mind being the prettier half of the relationship.

Excitement flickered across Airika's face momentarily, giving way to a bored shaking of her head.

"I wish you'd just open yourself up to the idea of it. You could be so happy. I know it." Jenna said.

"You just don't get it, Jenna. I don't want a relationship. I don't need a man like you do. And not everyone's life is a fairytale. Stop throwing it in my face," Airika said, getting up from the table, a blur of blonde fleeing the dark room.

Jenna sighed, wishing she hadn't said anything and paid the check before she left. She'd have to wait until tomorrow night to let Airika cool down. She'd always been hot-headed but that seemed excessive, even for her.

Jenna wondered what it would be like if Airika could just meet the right guy. Someone she actually cared about and wanted to plan a life with. Someone like Simon would be good for her. Of course, she probably wouldn't give him a chance because dating him wouldn't carry any cache. But maybe, if she just let herself, she'd discover what a lovable person she was through his eyes.

Before her dad left, Jenna thought Airika had a crush on one of Zach's friends. She never found out whom, but she saw a softer side during that time, proving to Jenna it was possible. Unfortunately, that person making a comeback was probably less likely than Felicity wearing the dress Jenna just bought for her.

Nothing could be gained by worrying about it now. Jenna, determined not to lose her pre-anniversary high, headed for her next fix: the farmer's market. Cooking provided her a daily escape.

That first scent of olive oil and garlic in a pan soothed her mind while whetting her appetite. She chose vegetables in contrasting colors—carrots, bell peppers, spinach, onion— to aesthetically satisfy her palette. She finished off with the earthy smell of freshly baked ciabatta, warm and soft in the center but still crunchy outside. She relished the challenge of timing it so the smells and textures drew the family in from whatever they were doing, sitting down to eat around the same table. It tricked her wheel-spinning brain into relaxing into the rhythm of the water boiling on the stove. She felt better already.

An hour later, she carefully balanced wine in one hand, an over-stuffed cloth bag weighed down by groceries in the other, and locked the car while struggling to find her house key. She pushed the door open with her hip, backing into her beloved living room. Then she turned around. Her world, like her fresh-from-the-farm groceries, fell to the floor and shattered, there, in that very instant.

Chapter 5

Stunned? Furious? Abject horror? There were no words to articulate what she saw. How would Ms. Manners have reacted to the sight of her husband and best friend kissing in her home, her sanctuary? The unholy cruelty of it was more than Jenna could process. She spun around and ran as fast as she could. Keys still in hand, she jumped in the car and sped off.

She drove on autopilot for what felt like hours, but must have only been about 20 minutes. She pulled into the familiar long gravel driveway lined with Birds of Paradise, sea grasses and rosebushes.

"Mom? Dad? Is anyone he-ere?" she called, her voice cracking.

"Jenna, is that you?" Anya said, making her way from the kitchen through the living room, finding her daughter just inside the front door. "Is everything okay? Oh, Jenna, what happened?" Anya enveloped her daughter in a hug and together they sunk into the couch. Jenna sobbed uncontrollably for many minutes before regaining enough composure to get the words out.

"It's over. My marriage. Alex. Airika. Saw. Kissing ... In our home ... " she sobbed. Anya stroked her only child's hair and let the tears soak her shoulder all the way through to the skin. When Jenna sat up Anya asked, "Are you sure? Do you think you could have misinterpreted what you thought you saw?"

"I saw my best friend's tongue down my husband's throat! How would you interpret that?"

"Okay, okay. What did they do when they saw you?" Anya asked.

"What? Nothing. I dropped the groceries on the floor and ran out."

"Did you see who kissed whom?"

"They kissed each other!" Jenna yelled, flustered.

"I'm only asking because it's important to know exactly what happened. This is a big deal and you wouldn't want to make a rash decision without all the facts." Anya said.

"How can there be another side? I came home to cook him dinner on our anniversary and he was kissing my best friend! What else is there?" Jenna shouted, shooting up from the couch.

"I'm sorry, sweetheart," Anya said, "I just don't want you to overreact. It doesn't sound like Alex ... maybe you should give him a chance to explain?"

Jenna backed out of her mom's embrace, speechless. She felt like the walls were caving in on her and all of a sudden she had to get out of there.

From the safety of her car, she glared at her parents' front door. She couldn't believe that the one person—who, more than anyone, should have been 100% on her side—took her no-good, cheating husband's side instead. Typical. She didn't do anything wrong. How could this be yet another example of her "overreacting?" Thoughts blurred into an incessant buzz inside her head. Or was that her phone? Yes, seven missed calls. She threw the phone onto the backseat and sped off again.

***

"What are you doing here?" Alex asked as Airika let herself into the house.

"Felicity told me I could find you here. I need to talk to you about something." Alex felt uneasy. He and Airika hadn't exactly been BFF's and he couldn't think of a good reason she would be here, seeking him out. Jenna insisted (despite his protestations) he hire her as the band's stylist for the tour. For the most part, he'd managed to steer clear of her and avoid her manipulations. She did her job and he did his.

"What do you need?" He asked in what he hoped was a

casual tone.

She took a step toward Alex, still in his landscaping attire.

"You," she said.

"Yeah? What for?" He said, organizing his tools, not looking at her.

She was close enough to smell him, the scent of manual labor mixed with cologne, and she became hyper-aware of his body, visible through his sweat-soaked shirt.

"You remember that morning in Barcelona?"

"Ye-eah," he said, not sure where this was going. The morning in question was seared into his brain. The producer of the music festival they were there to play made a pass at Airika and, by the time Alex happened to walk in, she was pinned with her hands above her head and her skirt shoved up to her waist as she yelled for him to stop. Alex pulled the creep off her, decked him, and took Airika back to his room to get her cleaned up and give her some space to calm down.

"Well, I wanted to thank you ... for being such a friend," she said, looking down at her hands.

"Sure," he said, thinking anyone would have done the same.

"Spending so much time together...it was nice," she said, finally making eye contact.

Alex gaped up at her.

"You know, I'm glad we've been connecting so much better these last few months."

Alex gulped and took a step back, wracking his brain for the right thing to say. He opened his mouth, closing it again as language failed him.

She paused, and then lifted a finger to his chest, traveling down his hard body, toward the top of his pants. It took a minute to absorb and react to this drastic departure in behavior. He grabbed her arm, and stepped back. She leaned in and kissed him hard, her tongue finding his, her arms wrapped around his neck. Before he could push her off him, the door opened and he heard a crash as Jenna saw them, dropping a bottle of wine and groceries to the hardwood floor.

He pushed Airika aside, running after Jenna, but she was already gone. Airika stood, paralyzed by both fear and vulnerability. When he came back inside, he wouldn't even look at her. "Get out of my house," he said quietly. For the first time in her life, Airika was speechless.

***

"Jenna? Please come back so we can talk. Airika came over out of the blue and kissed me! I swear that's the truth. Please come home." He stared at the phone, willing it to ring or transport him back a half hour in time. He couldn't comprehend this new version of reality—it was like he'd fallen through a wormhole into a hideous alternate universe.

Airika had always been a calculating manipulator, which is why he tried to stay as far away from her as possible. But she was also his wife's best and oldest friend, and what she'd just done seemed low even for her. He didn't understand why she did it and he wouldn't think about the possible repercussions if Jenna didn't hear him out. He couldn't imagine life without her. He pressed re-dial.

***

Airika sat, alone in her car, still parked across the street from Alex and Jenna's house. Her hands shook so violently that she dropped her keys. The bravado she'd felt earlier fell away, and a nightmare unfolded before her. Had she misinterpreted his signals? She was sure the sexual tension had been real between them. Why else would he have agreed to have her go on tour and then come in all knight-in-shining-armor to rescue her from that sleaze-ball producer? Guys don't just do that. She'd gone over all the details with Rose throughout the tour and even *she* had agreed that it sounded like he was conflicted, having feelings for Airika. So why didn't he have the decency to admit it to her when they were alone?

Insecurity didn't suit her so she called for reinforcement.

Her only other real friend, Rose McKenna, was her sole confidante in her pursuit of Alex. Rose was a journalist who started out in tabloids and, though professionally she'd moved on, found the gossip habit hard to break. She listened intently to every hashing and re-hashing Airika gave of each encounter between she and Alex from high school to, most recently, this morning. Rose encouraged her to "find out if he was The One That Got Away." Airika didn't think in terms of soul mates, but she didn't mind Rose's interpretation of her and Alex. After a review of the facts they came to the same conclusion: Alex was still in love with Airika, even if he also loved Jenna.

She dialed Rose's number.

Chapter 6

"Grandmother?" Felicity called, tossing her school bag over a chair in the foyer on her way to the kitchen. "Grandmother? You here?" She checked the kitchen before heading through the house to the back deck. There, on a wooden rocking chair, sat her grandmother, sipping tea, staring out at the vast Pacific Ocean.

Felicity stood for a moment, committing the sight to memory. She dreaded the idea of life without her grandmother's calming presence. "Hi, Grandmother," she said, plopping down into the chair next to Anya.

"Hi sweetheart," Anya smiled. "How was your day?"

"Pretty good. Nothing special. You?"

"Oh, just puttered around. Would you like to go for a walk?" Anya asked, standing up.

Afternoons with her grandmother, from as far back as Felicity could remember, were spent walking along the beach. They brought a bucket to collect treasures that, once full, signaled they head back. It was their tradition, their time to talk or be silent, and just be. Together.

Felicity kicked off her flip-flops, opening the gate that lead down eighty-four steps to the beach. When she was little she counted them. Funny, she thought, how some things stood out in her memory without any effort, while others slipped away like the tide.

The sand felt soft and damp, the tide was out, making it a perfect day for collecting.

"Cici, look at this." Anya said, holding a piece of iridescent glass up to the sunlight.

"Ooh, I like that one. Definite keeper." Felicity said. Anya nodded, slipping it in the bucket. They worked on a constant rotation of craft projects, using various treasures they collected to re-purpose into frames, lamps, or wall art.

It started out with shells and rocks haphazardly hot glued to any available surfaces; but over the years it became a little more sophisticated and specific like their current project: creating an ombre frame made of recycled glass for a mirror in Felicity's bedroom.

As the afternoon sun set over the horizon, bucket full, they headed home. Starting up the steps, Felicity saw a few flashes of light near the garage. "What was that?"

"Oh, I forgot they were coming today. Grandpa told me they're doing a photo shoot for that Rock n' Roll Hall of Fame induction."

"Cool. When's that?"

"March, after your dad's tour."

"Man, I so want to go but I'll still be in school. There's no way Mom will let me miss school," Felicity said, planting the seed for later harvest. In Felicity's room was an embroidered pillow that read, "If Mother Says No, Ask Grandmother." Words to live by.

Anya smiled and said, "We shall see."

"Speaking of your mom, have you spoken to her today?" Anya asked, affecting nonchalance. Felicity raised an eyebrow.

"No, but I talked to Dad. He was working on a big surprise. It's really sweet. He's going to have them renew their vows for their anniversary. He's got this whole elaborate plan."

"Really?"

"Yeah, he's been planning it for months and I've had to run interference to make sure she didn't find out. Why? Do you think she knows?" Felicity asked, hoping she hadn't accidentally let something slip. She couldn't think of anything. Unless her mom had been snooping in her room again.

"No, I don't think she knows," Anya said, more to herself than to Felicity.

Chapter 7

Red to green, green to yellow to red and back again, that's all Jenna took in as she drove aimlessly around. Her mind blanked, frozen in shock, unable to process this new warped version of reality. The streets wove their complex web around endless people, cars, buildings, hopes and dreams. They blended into a haze of nauseating brown, like all the colors had been stirred together on a single palette. Then the nausea took over.

She pulled over just in time to get the door open and hurl what felt like the leftover contents of the life she thought she knew over the edge of the canyon. Wiping her mouth, she was overcome with the urge to wash herself clean—this time both metaphorically and literally.

It dawned on her as she pulled into the valet that she'd never stayed at a hotel by herself before. And never stayed at a hotel in L.A, period. She chose the one hotel she'd always wanted to go to since she was a kid, because, like most little girls, the castle façade of Chateau Marmont stirred ideas of princesses and knights in shining armor parading the grounds. In the grown up version, Jenna liked the idea of a castle providing fortress-like protection over her fragile remains.

"Luggage?" the concierge asked, handing Jenna a key to a garden bungalow.

"No, just me," Jenna said, following the empty-handed bellhop.

"Here you are, Ms. Jax."

"Thank you," she handed him a generous tip, and walked past fragrant gardenias and lilies, that rose through the cool green ivy, snaking up to greet the sunlight filtering into the courtyard. In her zombie-like state, details flashed before her in a hyper-realistic fantasy, as though she were watching a 3-D movie.

Instantly, she felt miles away from the gritty streets of West Hollywood. The quaint, self-contained cottage reminded her of the little one-bedroom house she and her parents shared when they first moved from Australia to California. The Spanish architecture, with its open layout, led the way to a new life filled with larger-than-life dreams. But that was then, seen through the blissfully ignorant eyes of a child. How different it looked now.

She threw her clothes into the dry cleaning bag, stepped into the hot steam shower, and finally allowed herself to cry. The tears came easily as images of Alex and Airika's lips and bodies together played out in terrifying scenarios, projecting all around her in the steam. Her tears ran, indistinguishable from the pounding water rushing over her naked body. Once it started, she had no choice but to surrender, caving in to the pressure until she was on the ground, knees pulled tight to her chest, shivering in the heat.

The torrent of water and tears damned up the fears for her future, confining her to the horror of the present. Finally, after what could have been minutes or hours or days, the deluge ended. She turned off the shower, slipped on the plush hotel robe, and climbed into bed where she pulled the covers up and over her head, falling into a deep tear-induced sleep.

"Room service," came a voice muffled by the heavy mahogany door. Blinking, Jenna opened her eyes, adjusting to the dark. *Where am I?* She thought. Then, like an anvil on her chest, the truth knocked the wind out of her again.

"Ms. Jax? You ordered room service?"

She peeled herself out of bed and went to the door.

"I didn't order ... " she said, opening the door a crack. She stopped when she saw her husband. She slammed the door, turned on her heel and stomped inside, leaving her husband and a very confused butler outside. She heard voices and scuffling, followed by quiet. After another minute there was a knock.

"Jenna?" His voice sounded forlorn, muffled through the door. *Good*, Jenna thought, *Let him wallow*.

"Please let me in."

She wanted nothing more than to let him rot out there, but decided she'd have to face him sometime, and preferred to avoid a scene. Despite her inability to pay the emotional toll of his infidelity, her rational, possibly sadistic side appeared to be intact. Plus, her sense of morbid curiosity wanted to hear this explanation. There was nothing worse in this town than becoming the next tabloid scandal. She'd dedicated her adult life to evading that humiliating trap. She wouldn't fall in now.

"What?" She spat after they were safely ensconced in the room alone.

"Babe…"

"No. You do not get to call me that." Her vehemence knocked him off balance.

"I'm sorry, Jenna. Please, all I'm asking is for you to hear me out. Did you listen to any of my messages?" he asked. "She just showed up. I was in the yard and she showed up. She kissed me and you walked in. I swear that's the truth. It's not what you thought. What it looked like."

Jenna watched his face—the pleading in his eyes, the skin on his forehead wrinkling, aging him. She knew his every tell; every twitch in every expression; and she knew, with absolute certainty, that he was telling her the truth. But she wasn't ready to let him off the hook just yet.

"And if I hadn't walked in?"

"What? I pushed her away! It was completely one-sided! She used a stupid act of kindness as some kind of signal to come on to me. You know I think she's a manipulative bitch. I don't know what her game is but it has nothing to do with me!" He yelled, his deep voice cracking like a pubescent teen. He couldn't believe he had to defend himself. He never cheated on her, and he knew she knew him better than that. He stepped back from her, chest heaving.

She calmly sat on the edge of the bed, re-tying her robe, her eyes never leaving him. When the tension in the air subsided to a mere fog, she said, "What stupid act of kindness?"

He sighed and explained about Barcelona. When he finished she looked into his pleading eyes.

"I believe you." She said.

All the breath left him in one big rush of air and he stepped in toward her. She stood up to meet his embrace, letting her head fit neatly in the nook of his collarbone. The anger dissipated and made way for a sadness she couldn't quite place. Happy Valentine's Day, she thought.

Chapter 8

Gently, he pulled away, taking her by the shoulders, his face down near hers and said, "Happy anniversary, Babe. I love you." She smiled and felt her body surrender to the familiar warmth of his. Her anger melted away as it always did when she looked into his steady green eyes. She nuzzled into his masculine embrace, outwardly relaxing.

"Do you mind if we just stay here?" She asked, cringing at the thought of stepping foot in their house, now contaminated by a heinous act of betrayal.

"Of course. Whatever you want," he said.

He pulled away again and put up one finger. "I have an idea. One minute. Do you promise to let me in again?" He said, his cheeky confidence returning. She smiled and shrugged her shoulders.

"If you're lucky."

As soon as he was out the door, her smile faded. She couldn't deny the anger still brewing inside. She didn't want to discuss it with Alex, knowing he told her the truth, not wanting to start a fight and ruin what was left of their anniversary. She couldn't figure out which was worse: her husband cheating on her, or her best friend trying to steal her husband.

This morning, Jenna would never have believed Airika capable of something so malicious. There must have been signs, she thought, unable to come up with a single example. This wasn't the kind of thing that came out of nowhere.

Jenna knew Airika manipulated people and acted self-serving, but for the life of her, she couldn't come up with any agenda that made sense. She always thought things through. What could have compelled her to take such a big risk? Something was off and she couldn't place it. *Is Airika in love with Alex?* She wondered, disbelieving the thought as soon as it entered her head. No way was their antagonism masking attraction. Was it? She promised to contemplate that later, resolving to enjoy the limited time she had with Alex.

"How did you know where to find me?" She asked, as they sipped champagne and nibbled on the amazing spread of tapas that Alex returned with.

"Magic," he said. She raised her eyebrows. "The credit card company called to ask me to approve a suspicious charge."

"Oh," she said. "What's so suspicious about a hotel?"

"They said someone billed an unusually expensive room in a surname not matching mine." He smiled and popped a mini quiche in his mouth. Jenna blushed, thinking that using her maiden name to check in was neither stealthy nor warranted, considering. She tipped her head toward his, giving him a look that said, "Okay, you got me."

He raised his glass in the air, "A toast. To us. Eighteen wonderful years together and many, many more to come."

"To us," she said, clinking her glass to his.

The combination of champagne and heightened emotions, instead of making her feel vulnerable and needy as it normally did, felt empowering. The balance of power had shifted, and in this room she could be the woman she'd always wanted to be. Confident. Self-reliant. Assertive. She tapped into a raw sensuality neither of them had seen in her before. If she hadn't hated her at that moment, she'd have said she felt a lot like Airika.

The familiar feel of his gentle calloused fingers running along the top of her shoulder, down her arm, left a trail of goose bumps. She let out a low sigh, letting her head drop to one side. He kissed her neck so gently it almost tickled and, as their lips met, her worries drifted away.

She stepped back, slipping out of her robe, letting it crumple in a heap around her feet. He sat on the edge of the bed, looking on hungrily. She stalked toward him, disrobing his perfect body, and pushed him onto the bed below her. Their bodies undulated in perfect unison, each trying, with every wave, to get closer than was physically possible.

Jenna felt like an entirely new person. No longer passive and acquiescent. A woman in control, unapologetically taking and getting exactly what she wanted, when she wanted it.

"Wow," he panted, after. She snuggled into his chest, draping an arm across his stomach. "Wow," he repeated. "No seriously, Jenna, wow. That was … "

She smiled and rolled on top of him.

"I know," she said, "I was amazing." He looked up at her, his eyes wide, nodding in grateful agreement.

"Don't look at me like that, " she laughed. "You look like a little puppy on a leash, waiting for orders."

"Woof!"

Chapter 9

"Alex, mate! My favorite front man," boomed the husky voice of Simon Walker, self-titled Manager Extraordinaire. Women may have loved his British accent, but it didn't have the same affect on Alex.

"Hey Simon," Alex said. They walked down the hall, through the chaos of the nearly built stage toward the press room.

"Go do what you do," Simon said, opening the door for him. Alex strutted, all smiles, into the room full of journalists and bloggers who would inevitably ask the same questions he'd answered a thousand times before. Today he was ready to indulge them. He glanced up at the door and gave Jenna a sly smile, flashing back to their incredible night together, then turned and pointed to an eager college kid.

"Hey, Jenna. Look at you. How do you get more beautiful every time I see you?" Simon said. She rolled her eyes but secretly loved the compliment. "It's good to see you. Your man's doing great in there." Simon said, pointing in the direction of the press room.

"It's what he does," Jenna replied, grinning as she watched her husband win over the crowd of journalists. "How are you, Simon?"

"Great. Yeah, great! Couldn't be better." He said, mid-text, not looking up. "Can you excuse me?" He walked away before she could answer.

Jenna did a mental eye roll, and headed back to the green room to wait for Alex. Last night had been wonderful, despite the drama, and she wanted to linger in that little bubble as long as possible. It had been ages since she'd come to a show this early and hung out in the green room.

A big chunk of her childhood was spent in rooms just like

this one, waiting for her dad. They were all some version of the same: mirror, bathroom, something to sit on. But in all those years she couldn't recall a single one that was actually green. As a kid, she asked her mother why they called it a green room and one time, after a particularly relentless bout of questioning, Anya told her it was because performers turned green before they puked from nerves. The image of hundreds of performers puking in the same room before they mounted the stage haunted Jenna to this day. Since then, she'd spent as little time as possible in them.

In the early days with Alex, most green rooms were glorified closets, always dingy, usually shared with other bands and obnoxious groupies. If there was food (which often wasn't the case) it was half-eaten and cold—food poisoning guaranteed—and the bottles of beer (left over from the last band) were always room temperature—likely to have already been used as a spittoon.

She looked around at this room, with its clean modern lines, white leather couches, white velvet chairs in front of a gleaming marble vanity, flanked by tall white sconces. The sterility of the color did wonders for erasing the idea of people getting sick. *This lighting makes me look five years younger*, she thought, making a mental note to get something similar in her bathroom. Great lighting was undervalued as the best way to boost your self-image, even better than losing weight.

The buffet at the back of the room held neatly arranged platters of sashimi, bottles of water, still and sparkling, chocolate covered strawberries, and champagne chilling in a sterling silver bucket. Jenna smiled before she saw the folded card next to the champagne. They were all her favorites. It read, "Thank you. To more of the same."

***

Airika arrived early to meet her brother, Zach, at the backstage entrance. She would just drop off the band's clothes and bail; her brother there as an unwitting buffer of protection or distraction. He happened to be in town this weekend for the premier of his latest ski film. He was one of those guys into huck-yourself-off-a-cliff extreme sports and made little indie films of he and his friends doing crazy things. Airika didn't understand the appeal, but he did pretty well for himself, despite his über-monk lifestyle. She knew he lived in some sort of log cabin up at Lake Tahoe, but she'd never had time to visit.

When their dad left for Florida, they took very different paths toward their new identities. He'd gone the solitary introspective route while she'd created a successful business all about celebrities, award shows, and all manner of showy opulence. They couldn't be less alike. But right now, Airika needed her big brother. And he was here for her. Not that she'd told him why.

"I'll just be a minute," Airika said, wheeling the chrome clothes rack into the room marked 'Phazee Crux Wardrobe.'

"Need help?" He asked, grabbing the other side of the rack.

"Thanks."

They left the rack in the middle of the room, white paper labels attached to hangers, indicating which outfit was for whom.

"All set, let's go," she said, leading him back down the long hallway running the full length of the stage.

"You're not going to say hi?" He asked.

"No, they're busy. Let's go or we'll be late for your premier," she said, eyes darting back and forth.

Isolated mountain man he may be, but one thing Zach knew for certain was that his sister had never been on time for anything, ever. Her life was chock-full of drama, hence his desire to stay out of her business. He hadn't seen Alex in years, though in high school they'd been close. Their foursome had long since broken up, but whenever Zach came home or Alex passed through Reno, they made a point of seeing one another.

"We've got time to say a quick hello," he said, heading

down toward the press room.

"Fine. I have to get something out of the green room anyway. I'll meet you out back in a minute."

Airika was sure Jenna ran crying to her parents' and would still be hiding out. She would have taken the path of least resistance, as usual. In all the years they'd known each other, Airika had never seen Jenna stand up for herself or anyone else. Everyone catered to her delicate ego and handed her what she wanted on a perfectly polished silver platter. Airika too had been looking out for Jenna all this time. Must be nice, she thought. This time it might not be looking out for her in the traditional sense, but in a way she was doing her a favor, by forcing the inevitable. She knew she deserved Jenna's wrath, but the stubborn competitive streak in her wouldn't let go of the feeling that, just once, she deserved to get what she wanted and let Jenna be the one to suffer disappointment. It was petty—granted—but true nonetheless.

Her main reason for skirting around was that she couldn't face Alex yet. Not after the way he'd treated her. She knew his feelings for her hadn't been in her head, not after all the signals he'd sent. It was plain to everyone on the tour, not just her. She'd seen the knowing glances cast in their direction. The way people cleared out to leave them alone. It wasn't coincidence.

For now, she could hide out in the green room for a couple minutes and make sure the right clothes were sent over. After all, work was the one love in her life that didn't disappoint.

Chapter 10

When the door opened, Jenna stood up from the vanity, revealing her long lean figure in a short black negligee she'd picked up from the hotel's boutique while Alex checked them out of the hotel that morning. In a drastic departure from her normal prudish nature, she wanted to surprise him before the show. She felt a little naughty and like she wanted a reprisal of last night's performance. Her nerve endings tingled in anticipation. The last person in the world she expected to see was Airika.

"What. Do. You. Think. You're. Doing. Here." She seethed through clenched teeth.

"What are you wearing?" Airika asked, looking her up and down. Jenna closed the gap between them with a single step and repeated, "What do you think you're doing here? Trying to seduce my husband? Again?" Her eyes radiated a rage Airika had never seen before. Jenna stood up taller, puffing her chest slightly, towering over her former friend.

"Oh here we go. You're right. I'm a bitch. I kissed your husband." Airika wasn't one to stay on the defense for long. She stepped in closer, "Go ahead. Blame me. But just don't think you know the whole story."

"There is no story! You kissed my husband!" Jenna squealed.

"Yes, I kissed him, but it's not like it was the first time." Airika said, pleased to see her comment creating the desired effect. Airika on the offensive was unstoppable. Jenna stood speechless, mind reeling.

"Before you got knocked up, Alex and I were together. As in sleeping together. That summer when you were in Europe? We were dating. We didn't plan for it to happen but we just … fell in love."

Jenna's mouth moved but no words came out. Airika continued calmly, "We were going to tell you ... but then we found out you were pregnant." She let that sink in before she continued. "And I backed off. I held back all these years, letting you have him. But sometimes life's not fair, even for poor perfect Jenna. He made it clear he still had feelings for me while we were on tour together. And I'm sorry, but just once I'd like to be the one with the happy ending."

Before Jenna could muster a retort, Airika turned and left, leaving Jenna on her own, a black spot in the stark white room. There were a million things soaring through her mind, and she felt dizzy with information. Did Airika make that up? Why would she? Was it true? She didn't know which was worse.

"Jenna, are you okay?" Alex asked, entering the room two minutes too late. He hurried over to his wife, crumpled in a heap in the middle of the floor, nearly naked. "What happened?" he asked, forehead wrinkling in concern.

"Is it true?" she asked through a fog of tunnel vision.

"Is what true? Jenna, I don't know what you're talking about."

"I'm talking about you. And Airika. Dating. Did you sleep with her...ever?"

Her eyes scanned his face, watching it contort in agony. His eyes silently pleaded with her and he let out a heavy sigh.

"Yes. We dated briefly in high school when you and I were broken up. I never cheated on you." He steadied his gaze, letting that statement settle between them. "But Jenna, that was so long ago. It didn't mean anything. I chose you."

"You only chose me after you found out I was pregnant!"

She felt like she'd been punched in the stomach. His eyes widened, revealing the truth of her accusation. *Oh God.* "You were sleeping with both of us at the same time?" She felt nauseous at the thought. "And you never told me? You two have been keeping this from me. You've been lying to me for eighteen years!" She stood up to her full height, eyes ablaze.

He looked down at his feet and whispered, "We didn't want to hurt you."

She blanched at his use of the word "we."

"Did you love her?" she asked, closing her eyes in anticipation.

"No! I ... I ... cared about her, that's all," he stuttered.

"Well that's so much better. You're right, that doesn't hurt at all," she thundered on. "My best friend and husband were together behind my back and spent two decades keeping it from me? You're right. It's much less humiliating to find out now than in high school!" Adrenaline surged through her now, propelling her on, "Why don't I make this easy for you both. I'll just take myself out of the equation."

"Jenna ... " he said, reaching out to touch her. She pulled away. "I only want you. You're all I've ever wanted."

She glared at this stranger in her husband's body before storming out of the room, down the hall. When she reached the backstage entrance it dawned on her that she didn't have a car, or now that she thought of it, clothes. Before she had time to panic she felt the warmth of a jacket gently enveloping her shoulders. She jumped, spinning around. Seeing Zach's familiar face, she breathed a sigh of relief and fell into his open arms.

Chapter 11

Anya looked on with wonder, awed by her husband's patience and youthful energy. From the vantage point of her office, she could see into Shawn's music studio, set up over the garage, where he was giving an animated lesson to a scruffy teenage boy, a friend of Felicity's. She watched the young man strumming away on guitar. Shawn picked up a bass and let his head bob in rhythm as he plucked the thick strings. His back was to the window, but she didn't need to see his face to know that look. He was in his zone. When he created music, alone or collaboratively, he became an ageless entity existing in his own dimension. It was the purest state she had ever known, if only by proximity.

"How cute are they?" asked Felicity, plopping down on the window seat in front of her Grandmother's desk.

"Should we rescue Trey?" Anya asked.

"Are you kidding? He's in heaven right now. No, let's work on our own project. I have everything set up in the craft room."

Felicity felt guilty for keeping the audition she'd just been on secret, but she didn't want to elicit reproach if she didn't have to. If she got the part, then she'd worry about how to tell her mom and grandmother. Their irrational fear of acting perplexed her. For two women firmly entrenched in the music industry, they were abnormally distrusting of the film industry. The first time she told them she wanted to act they looked at her like she said she wanted to be a porn star.

Despite her guilty omission, she couldn't have been happier spending time with her grandmother. Even though they lived in the same town, their time together was limited. Her grandparents made regular appearances at industry events, took trips overseas, and even when they were home Felicity often felt overshadowed by her mother's demands on their time.

Once, during a home renovation project, Jenna showed up an hour late to Felicity's soccer final and took Anya away to sort out a "life-or-death" issue with a contractor. While they were gone, they missed Felicity's game winning goal.

Another time, Felicity had to call in sick (even though she felt fine), letting her stand-in deliver Juliet's lines in the opening night of her school's rendition of "Romeo and Juliet," because Jenna was certain they had ingested whipworms from their neighbor's dog pooping in their herb garden. After quarantining them all and bribing their doctor to do a home visit, the inevitable diagnosis came back—no whipworms.

So in these rare moments of uninterrupted time together, Felicity felt most like herself. Anya said Felicity was her greatest accomplishment—the one for whom she got to do things right—the one with the world in the palm of her hand. But when the front door flung open, clattering violently, Felicity wasn't surprised to hear her mother's voice.

The sight of her, however, was something else entirely. Jenna's normally smooth hair stuck out at odd angles in a disheveled mess. She wore something that may have once resembled fleece sweatpants and an oversized men's sweatshirt. The effect was alarming. She looked like a homeless person recently escaped from a mental institution.

"What happened now?" Anya jumped up, looking from Jenna to Zach. Zach stepped forward, steering Jenna inside, ushering her onto an overstuffed chair. She stared blankly at the wall as he spoke.

"I didn't know where else to take her. She and Airika had a fight. It sounded pretty bad." He looked over at Felicity, then back at Anya, silently motioning for her to join him out of earshot.

"What happened?" Anya asked, when they were far enough away. He hesitated, not sure how much to say.

"I heard them fighting backstage—she and Alex."

"I thought you said she and Airika had the fight," Anya prodded.

"They did. It was about Alex," he said, not looking up. Anya nodded, her fears confirmed. "Did she leave him?" He didn't say anything.

After a long pause he said, "I think she just needs space. I hope it's okay?"

"Thank you," Anya said, placing her hand on his. She appreciated his concern and could see his reticence to leave. "Would you like to stay for dinner?" she asked. He nodded, grateful for the invitation.

Felicity was tasked with taking her mother upstairs to help her get ready for dinner. She set out some clothes that she found in the closet, and sat on the edge of the bed as Jenna put them on. Felicity knew something awful had happened but couldn't imagine what. She felt like she was watching a sleepwalker to make sure she didn't go out in traffic.

"Mom?"

"Mmm?" Jenna mumbled, struggling with the buttons on her shirt. She wondered why people bothered with buttons at all. What a waste of time. She tied the shirt in a knot above her belly button instead, exposing a strip of tan midriff, playing with the loose skin that never quite got back to pre-baby tightness no matter how many sit-ups she did.

"What happened?" Felicity was nothing if not blunt.

Jenna looked her straight in the eye and replied, with uncharacteristic restraint, "Nothing you need to worry about, Sweetheart. Your father and I had a fight. A big fight. And I need some time away to sort through things. Can you understand that?"

"I guess so … " Felicity wasn't sure how to proceed with this zombie mother. She expected a tirade of exaggerations and more information than any child ever wants to hear about their parents, only to be shoved in the middle, forced to take sides. This calm, cool, calculating individual was like the Alternate

Universe Mom she used to think she wanted, but now wasn't so sure. What could she say?

"Where will you go?" Felicity asked.

Jenna hadn't thought that far in advance. She glanced around the room and saw a picture hanging up in the corner. It was a black and white photo of a pier in a lake. In small hand-written letters at the bottom of the matting, it read "North Beach, Lake Tahoe, by Jenna Jax, 1989."

Jenna pointed to the photo and said, "There."

Chapter 12

"Are you sure you know what you're doing?" Anya asked for the third time.

Dinner was a disaster, with Jenna drinking an entire bottle of red wine by herself, slurring incoherently at each person in turn. At one point, she turned to Anya, eyes narrowed, and said, "Y'wereright, Mom. I ended up jus' like you. Go ahead. Say it. Toldyouso. Say it! Juss like you said. Better seenthan heard. 'S all I'm good for. Look pretty. SAY IT!" She flung her glass around in front of her, eyes landing on Zach. "Do I look pretty to you?"

Anya watched, as though regarding an accident on the side of the freeway, and saved Zach from having to answer. Luckily Jenna passed out before dessert was served. Someone had the foresight to put a pitcher of water on her bedside table so that when she woke up, still drunk in the dark morning hours, she guzzled it and sat cataloguing every time she'd sacrificed something for either Airika or Alex. Every example she thought of, from the time she didn't buy the Calvin Klein prom dress she wanted freshman year because Airika had to have it to giving up modeling to stay home with Felicity so Alex could pursue his dream of touring around the country with his punk-rock band (who frequently found themselves ejected from venues before they got paid), made her realize she'd only ever played the supporting role. She'd never been the star in her own life's story. As she watched the pink glow of the sunrise, she made up her mind. No more stepping aside. Jenna felt certain for the first time in her life. She couldn't explain the transformation, but instead of sinking into a pool of self-pity (as she'd expected to), she felt alive and awake. She looked outside where the trees glittered green, and the ocean's blue saturated her core, connecting her to the world like never before.

Her life had flipped an illegal U-turn hurling her towards a new destination. Despite her still inebriated state, she couldn't help but go over logistics in her head. Felicity should stay with her grandparents (her preference, Jenna was sure), and now that the two people she ran everything by were the same two she wouldn't speak to again, she had no one left to answer to. Gone were the days of putting everyone else's needs, wants, and desires ahead of her own. Maybe high school Jenna had it right after all.

Pulling away down the long gravel drive, Jenna watched her mother and daughter wave, their eyes welling. Technically, she couldn't see their features from that distance, but she imagined they had tears in their eyes. She wished she could express to them how in control she felt. It was like she was a college student, leaving the nest for the first time, excited for the adventures awaiting her. As the house grew smaller and smaller in the distance, she knew it would never look the same as it did right now.

"Music?" Zach asked, handing her his iPod.

She smiled and put the iPod in the glove box. "Nope."

"You're the boss," he said, turning onto highway 395. The vast desert spread before them, broken only by sharp purple peaks dipped in snow. They drove in comfortable silence, taking in the majestic views. Joshua trees turned to pine trees, and the desert gave way to winding mountain passes as they traversed the ancient landscape.

"How you feeling this morning?" Zach asked.

"Hung over." Jenna looked over and had a vague flashback of telling him that all men are bastards when he said he needed to go back to his hotel. "I was awful to you last night, wasn't I?"

"Nah. I've seen worse." He smiled. "I've done worse too, without half the provocation."

She nodded, grateful to let it go. They settled into an easy mix of silence and conversation, keeping things light. The next thing she knew, they were outside the vacation home her parents purchased with her father's first big royalty check. It was a modest pale yellow cabin, set back from the street on the lake. The quintessential cozy mountain retreat, it still retained the original hardware and lovely built-ins.

She remembered it being bigger—the way adults often do, returning to places from their childhood. It was equally possible that it had been dwarfed by the mega-mansions flanking it on either side that sprung up since her last visit. Opening the door, she flipped on the light.

"Need help with your bags?" Zach asked.

"No, I'm okay. Thanks for the ride." She said.

"No problem. It was on my way," he smiled.

He stuffed his hands in his pockets to keep himself from helping her as she struggled up the two small steps to the door.

"Thank you, Zach. For everything." She put her hand over his and pulled him into a hug. In his ear, she repeated it again, wishing she could say more. He was the only one who'd been there for her when she most needed it and she didn't think she could ever thank him enough. He'd been so sweet to pack her bags for her when she couldn't face going home to do it herself. Thankfully he'd been able to avoid an awkward run into Alex, who was already on his way to the next gig. He squeezed her hand, got back in his car and reversed down the driveway, tires crunching on frozen earth. She stood for a long minute outside, watching his headlights disappear from view, leaving only the yellow orange light from the cabin spilling softly on her, beckoning her inside. Silence enveloped her and her hands trembled as she pulled out the handle on her toiletry bag. The cold hardwood floors creaked and moaned in protest to the thunk, thunk, thunk-ing of the bag's wheels as they hit each groove on their way to the master bedroom. Jenna looked out at the lake, moonlight dancing on its glassy surface, searching for the light switch. She flicked it on but nothing happened.

She tried again. Nothing. Great, she thought. She turned on the light in the bathroom instead. It provided just enough light for her to wash her face, brush her teeth, and climb into bed. The heavy down comforter swallowed her in its warmth, immobilizing her in its cocoon. Sleep had never felt so good or come so easily. Tomorrow she could think about what to do with her life, but for tonight, all she wanted was a dreamless sleep.

The sun rose above the mountains, illuminating the small room. Blinking, she opened her eyes to reveal a blue-bird day, the light spreading cheerfully across the white-washed pine walls of the master bedroom. She sat up, staring across the sapphire water. With a long yoga inhale, she breathed in the crisp clear beauty of her surroundings. Never one prone to introspection, Jenna had always opted to help someone else through their turmoil rather than dwell on her own. For the first time in her life, she was forced to sit, utterly alone with herself. I am me, she thought with Zen-like serenity.

The house, built in the early 1930's, had a lot of what people call "charm," which really meant that it creaked and leaked and was small compared to its contemporaries. It was like calling a woman "cute." Puppies, kittens and babies could be cute; women are either "beautiful" or "have a good personality." Cute is a passive way of calling a woman "not beautiful, but likeable nevertheless." No grown woman wants to be called "cute." Jenna surmised the cabin felt the same about being called "charming."

The Jax family had owned this house since the 60's, when Shawn's first single topped the Billboard Charts. They came here on their way to a tour date in San Francisco and got snowed in. Shawn ended up spending a few days learning to ski in this teeny resort town and fell in love. For the first time in his life, he could afford to splurge. So he bought a little cabin on the lake. Over the years, the other small cabins peppering the lake's shores were torn down and replaced by gaudy

monstrosities, but Shawn loved his little cabin in the forest with
its perfect lake views, private pier, and his very own boat
garage. Jenna adored her father's whimsy when it came to this
cabin and the mountain lifestyle he found refuge in, but now,
feeling the winter cold soar through the single pane windows,
she wished he had splurged on a few renovations. She padded
lightly to the kitchen to begin foraging for food and more
importantly, coffee. None. Anywhere. No coffee maker? No
toaster? What had she done? She pulled at her hair from the
roots and felt the first twinges of caffeine withdrawal coming
on. Sure, she needed some time alone, but not in lieu of
civilization.

"Hello?" came a voice with a little courtesy knock as the
front door swung open. Zach peeked his head around the
corner into the kitchen.

"Coffee? Breakfast burrito?"

"You're a lifesaver!" She said, nearly bowling him over with
a hug. He handed her a giant foil wrapped burrito, chuckling as
she devoured it.

"I'm lucky you didn't take off my hand," he said.

"Sorry," she blushed. "Thank you … again."

"I knew you didn't have a car," he shrugged. "And I figured there wouldn't be anything edible in the house—except
maybe some Twinkies from 1985. I'm heading down to Reno
to grab a few things. Wanna come?"

"Sure! She made a list (she couldn't give up all organization)
and let Zach run her all over Reno until every last item was
checked off. She got a toaster, blender, espresso maker, thick
warm-trapping curtains, bath towels, and even found an
organic supermarket to get her pesticide-free veggies, meatless
ground, tempeh and liquid aminos that she absolutely positively
could not live without. As she draped the last curtain over the
brushed nickel rod, she admired her progress. Things looked
better from up here. She made a mental list of things to ask
Zach (Best breakfast place? Best coffee? How to fix the lights?)

Once everything was neatly checked off her list, all clean and orderly, then she could tackle unpacking her emotional baggage. It was only logical to create a tranquil environment before battening down the hatches.

Chapter 13

"I need to take some time off," Alex said. Simon stopped his furious typing and looked up from his phone.

"Are you crazy, mate? The tour is completely sold out!" Before Alex could respond, Simon continued, "Look, in 6 weeks it will be over. Done. And then you can take as much time as you need. But it don't do well to dwell on it now do it? No. Tell you what. There were some nice girls backstage just waitin' to talk to you ... maybe you could go out with them. Get your mind off things."

"No. I'm done. I'm going to save my marriage. Tonight's my last show." Zach turned on his heel, striding off down the long hotel hallway.

Before the elevator doors shut, Simon jammed his stubby hand through. His face was different, the smooth salesman façade gone, revealing an angry Welshman who looked a brass knuckle away from busting someone's kneecaps.

"You listen to me. Listen good. You're gonna finish this tour. You're gonna go on stage every night and bust your guts up there. You're gonna do it whether you like it or not because if you don't, the label will drop you. If you don't, all the time and effort and money put into this tour to make your dreams come true will be refunded—out of your pocket. Or should I say, your wife's pocket. I'm telling you this for your own good. How do you think wifey's gonna like it when all this was for nothin' and she's the laughing stock for marrying a loser," Simon said, every muscle in his face tense. "I'm just telling you how it is," he finished in a softer tone.

Alex gulped and looked straight ahead at his warped reflection. "Fine," he said, feeling like a child caught in a tantrum.

"Look, mate, I'm just lookin' out for ya. You and me both know you can't afford that. Jenna wants you to be a success, so give her that. You owe it to her." Simon said, the tension in his face gone. "And you know what else you can't afford? Lettin' your fans down. And me. I been your number one fan for over fifteen years. You just gonna skip out on us now?" Simon implored, friendly again, betrayed only by the vein still bulging in his forehead. The elevator dinged. Simon held eye contact until the doors closed and Alex was finally alone.

Alex could feel every muscle in his body tense. His fists were clenched and turning white. He wanted nothing more than to tell the label what they could do with his contract. The anonymous backer behind the label that Simon refused to name was a real hard-ass. But Simon was right. This tour was the only way to pay back the label. And Simon. Simon had believed in his talent when everyone else wrote him off. He owed a lot to him, even if their relationship had turned antagonistic lately.

Short of winning a four million dollar jackpot in Vegas, there was nothing he could do. Most of all, he needed to prove to Jenna he could support them. And he would prove that all her sacrifices were worth it. There was no other choice—he had to finish the tour. Alex swallowed a mounting sense of dread.

He remembered the summer between their junior and senior years of high school. Jenna broke up with him shortly before school got out because he'd refused to get a fake ID to go out to some new club. The skeazy owner of said club invited her after she modeled for the grand-opening posters. Alex had barely controlled his rage when he saw the photos, so he didn't think it wise to be close enough to hit the guy.

"God, you're so boring," Jenna complained.

"I'm boring because I don't want to watch sleazy guys try to get in my girlfriend's pants?"

"Ugh! Not that again. Who cares if they want to sleep with me? I don't want to sleep with them. And what about all your stupid groupies? Huh? You don't think that's a problem, do you?"

"That's different! God, that's part of my career! Not just to prance around practically naked."

They seethed at each other silently. "Just do what you want, Jenna. I don't care anymore."

"Fine! And we're done, by the way. So you know. When I'm prancing around with some random guy, I won't be cheating on you!" She narrowed her eyes, hands on hips. "Oh, and modeling is a career too." She stomped off, leaving him alone in the quad with a slew of onlookers. Great, he thought, an audience.

***

During sound check, with the cameras rolling for their behind-the-scenes DVD footage, he went through all the motions, exchanged pleasantries, shook hands, signed autographs, and decided on the set list with his band. He watched himself from somewhere outside his body. He did everything he was supposed to do while his Real Self floated around the ether, trying to find a way back to his wife. He was desperate to wake up from this nightmare.

He knew she had a point. He knew he screwed up. But why did she leave? She had to understand he never loved Airika. Their brief romance had been prompted by his jealousy, and after Jenna went away that summer, it lasted longer than it should have. He never loved Airika the way he loved Jenna. Airika was just ... different. Fun and intense, more sexually daring and comfortable with her body than Jenna. She was a vixen, even then. He was a teenage boy with a broken heart. It wasn't hard to tempt him. But as soon as he saw Jenna in the airport, he knew. He would only ever love her. And he'd been faithfully devoted ever since.

She knew he wasn't just with her because he got her pregnant. Surely. If she'd just answer her damned phone maybe they could discuss it like adults. At first he thought she just needed time to cool down, but three days went by and she still hadn't answered any of his calls, texts or emails. It was beginning to feel a lot like high school.

He needed to know she was okay. Felicity was safely out of the line of fire at Shawn and Anya's, but other than a cursory call, the three of them were pretty tight-lipped. The open communication he was used to with Felicity now felt stifled, awkward. Worse still was when she gave him very parental sounding advice. "Give it time, Dad. Just give her some space right now. She needs it".

Great. Even Felicity was talking to him like a small child. All he wanted was to make things right and get his best friend back. He needed Jenna and didn't think he could act like everything was okay, knowing she wanted nothing to do with him. Was there someone else? He tried to bury the thought, but it resurfaced over and over, plaguing him with visions of her climaxing with some hot vegan yogi who owned an organic farm and mastered the ancient practice of Tantric sex.

His perspective felt distorted, reflected in a fun house mirror where he couldn't find his way out without her. He hadn't told her about his issues with his label or Simon's increasing secrecy because he wanted to show her he could take care of them. She didn't show any interest in the business, never asked questions or offered to help out, so he kept it to himself. He wanted to make her proud. It was humiliating for her to lose all her friends and see herself as tabloid fodder ("The Trappings of Celebrity: Teen Pregnancy", "Teen Pregnancy: Trendy?") and she deserved better—so much better. She was his moral compass and support system—the one he counted on to make him feel like he wasn't a loser who knocked up his girlfriend and ruined their lives. That he wasn't a bad guy. And she'd left him.

Chapter 14

After she'd hung every frame just so, stocked the fridge, cleaned the kitchen and bathroom, swept the deck and raked the sand on the beach, Jenna sat. She sank down into the couch, inert. Her body refused to obey her mind that was screaming at her to get up and keep moving. For a moment, she felt relief. Then, of their own volition, tears began to fall, glassing over her blue eyes, pooling on her cheeks, cascading down to her lap. She felt nothing. Nothing at all, except for the damp of the tears soaking through her pants to the skin underneath.

The one thing that propelled her was her sense of duty. She could feel a complete breakdown coming on and had one last thing to do for Felicity. She called Alex's voicemail to tell him where Felicity was so he wouldn't worry. She may not be speaking to him, but he was still entitled to know where his daughter was.

"Jenna?" He answered.

Crap! She thought, wishing she checked his schedule before calling.

"Hi," she said, unsure where to go from there.

"I'm so glad you called."

"I thought I'd get your voicemail."

"Oh," he said, frowning. "I know you're mad, and you deserve to be. I just ... miss you. You're the only one for me. How do I make this right?"

How indeed? She did believe him, didn't she? Yes, she knew he was telling the truth. That he didn't have feelings for Airika. That she kissed him. But still ... something niggled at her, making its way just under her skin.

"But you did sleep with her. And you dated her behind my back," she said in a bitchier-than-intended tone.

"That was so long ago. And I never cheated on you."

Technically, what he said was true. It didn't stop the deceit from hurting, though. She felt like all her memories of them together were now spoiled, like rotten fruit.

"After everything we've been through. All the sacrifices and hard times—we can't throw all that away for something so insignificant. Just when things are starting to go our way?" he said, voice wavering.

"Your way," she corrected, suddenly seeing things crystal clear. "I made sacrifices while you pursued your career. I was the one sidelined because I gave up my body for our baby. I supported you when no one else did."

He was stunned into silence.

"What have you ever sacrificed for me?" she asked, genuinely curious.

"I … " he started.

"Nothing. And you know what? It's my fault. I never asked you for anything."

"Jenna, I've done nothing but love you. I've been honest and faithful to you. I had no idea you felt you sacrificed so much for me. But you're right; you should have said something. I can't read your mind," he said, righteous anger piercing his normally calm demeanor.

She ignored it. "Well, I'm saying something now. I want you to get out of your record contract. Ever since you signed it, you've been different, distant."

"What?"

"You heard me. If you want to make this relationship—and our family—work, then we need you home with us. We need to know we come first."

"Jenna, you know I can't do that."

"You could if you wanted to badly enough. We don't need the money. But if you won't, then we don't have anything else to talk about."

"Please don't trivialize my career. You know it's not that

simple. I only have a month left. Are you telling me you won't wait one month?"

"I'm done waiting."

"Fine. I guess there's nothing I can do then."

"I guess not," she seethed.

"And I think I need to hang up before either of us says something we can't take back." With that, he hung up.

The silence felt heavy around her. Her hands shook with frustration, but she was torn because a part of her felt ... what? Free. Shouldn't she be sad? Shouldn't she curse his name? Bitch to girlfriends about him? Weren't there supposed to be pints of ice cream and chick flick marathons involved in this sort of thing? And then, that anvil teetering high above flattened her again.

It wasn't him, it was *her*. Yes, Alex was her best friend in the way that he was her partner. They shared a life together, and a child, a bond like no other. But really, a girl's true best friend was always another girl. It was like losing true North on a compass. Without her, everything else felt arbitrary.

It could be the girl she grew up with or the girl she met in college, or even the girl she met at work. It didn't matter where she met her—what mattered was that she had someone to share her inner thoughts with. Someone to be trusted with her inner demons. Someone who could take those demons and tell her she was "absolutely right" and that whoever wronged her was "just jealous." The girl best friend could be trusted with the kind of nitty-gritty talks she'd never share with her partner because she might hurt his feelings or he might take something out of context. Those sticky things that would flare up his insecurities made for easy, over-a-cup-of-coffee conversation with the girl best friend. That was what made her indispensable.

When teenage Jenna sunk to the bathroom floor with that wretched plus sign glaring up at her, telling her that life as she knew it was over, she called Airika. Airika sat with her, brought her food and magazines, painted her toenails, and told her it would all be okay. Jenna would have fallen apart left to her own devices. She probably would have walked straight over to the women's clinic and had the abortion she'd been contemplating if it weren't for Airika. She'd come bounding into Jenna's room the day after they found out, thrusting a teddy bear out in front of her. It wore a onesie that said, "My mommy's hotter than your mommy." Inappropriate, yes, but thoughtful too. She'd gone on and on about how cute Jenna and Alex's baby would be; and Jenna didn't take that trip to the clinic. Part of her felt forever indebted to Airika. So how could she reconcile those memories with this new information?

Her girlfriend was supposed to be the one who got her through this type of situation. To tell her everything was going to be okay. That he'd been an asshole and needed to do some serious sucking up. That in the end it would all work out. That girl wasn't supposed to be the reason for all of this! And, even worse than being the perpetrator was that she ripped her friendship out from under them both. Airika's actions negated every one of those conversations. Every bit of affirmation, of shared experience, of soothing comfort and inside jokes were now tainted with lies. Did she ever care, or was she only my friend because my dad's famous? Did she stand by me just to be near Alex? She felt lost in the sea of betrayal. The sense of loss was so overwhelming she couldn't breathe. Literally, it took effort to breathe.

They kept that secret for nearly two decades and she'd never known. Jenna had never even suspected it. What else hadn't she known? What secrets had she confided in this wolf-in-sheep's season-appropriate clothing? Airika knew everything about Jenna. Had she been laughing at her all these years? Had Alex? Did they laugh about her together?

The questions flooded her overloaded brain and her pulse quickened with rage. She hurled a pillow from the couch across the room. It wasn't enough. She grabbed her phone, inertly taunting her from the coffee table, and hucked it against the wall. It shattered into tiny pieces, Swarovski crystals plinking all around the floor, reflecting bits of light like prisms. Her chest heaved in satisfaction at her own destruction. She knew, of course, that she would be the one to clean it up, but the pressure inside her head was too much. The failsafe valve was fit to burst, messes and all.

When she looked around, instead of mocking herself for losing control, or feeling bad about destroying her brand new one-of-a-kind phone, she found herself dazzled by the flickers of beautiful rainbow light reflected all around the room. The juxtaposition of the old quaint cabin peppered in blinged out shrapnel seemed absurdly amusing. She didn't recognize that person who had time to apply multi-colored gemstones to a cell phone case, yet missed the fact that her best friend was harboring feelings for her husband for the last twenty years. A voice in her head told her to remember this moment—this anger—and to never let it happen again.

She ransacked the spare room looking for her old camera, having just destroyed her camera phone. It was an old Canon SLR that still had a roll of film in its back. Perfect. She set up the antique tripod she found in the corner of the room, set the timer, and glowered over her epiphany. There was a click, click, click followed by the sound of film being sucked back into itself.

She wanted to blow that image up in order to remember how badly she felt at this moment and to never ever let anyone make her feel like this again. Sadistic as it was, she found pleasure in the pain.

As she walked to the grocery store (the only place that still developed film in town) she felt an odd sense of self-satisfaction. Not ready to be fully articulated, it felt something like gumption. Being disconnected from the world seemed wildly underrated. No cell phone, no computer, no car, just herself. If she wanted to do something she wouldn't talk to anyone, consult anyone, or ask for anyone's help. She could just do it. How had it taken her thirty-four years to figure this out?

Later that night, glass of wine in hand, she ceremoniously mounted the poster size frame that would soon house her image of liberation. She envisioned herself looking calm, exuding intimidating confidence. Afraid of nothing. The good thing about hitting rock bottom was having so much less to fear. She couldn't say she had nothing to fear—she was the mother of a teenage girl, after all—but the two people she'd counted on to be her anchors, her pylons of strength keeping her from sinking in a sea of worst-case scenarios, had simultaneously abandoned their posts. And yet she was still standing. Figuratively speaking, anyway.

Somewhere around the third (or maybe fourth) glass this newfound confidence morphed into something akin to self-pity. The victim came out again. She hated that girl for being so damn whiny and pathetic. *But how am I not a victim?* She sniveled.

Maybe she shouldn't have finished that bottle off by herself. On a nearly empty stomach. This was why she busied herself with projects and shunned introspection. It was dangerous. And dizzying. Her cheeks were wet again too. The world spun so fast around her. She couldn't keep up. And then she passed out.

Chapter 15

"Your homework tonight, and every night this week," Felicity's teacher, Ms. Joy, addressed the class of high achievers as they shifted impatiently in their seats, "is to write a short, one-page vignette on a family member. They can be about anything … classroom appropriate," she clarified to the much too enthusiastic hands going up around the room. She paused for the collective groan of disapproval. "I want you to learn something. It'll be fun. It can be historical or gossipy or even abstract, but it must be written by you, from their point of view. Now is the time to get the dirt you've been wanting to get on your parents and get school credit for doing it."

As the bell rang, releasing their waning attention spans, Felicity slowly packed up her notebook. The class cleared out quickly. It was last period and everyone was in a hurry to get to practice, work, or just out of the classroom. "Is something wrong?" Ms. Joy leaned against a nearby desk, arms folded in watchful concern.

"No."

"Are you sure?"

"Yeah … no … " Felicity stared into her neatly packed book bag. "I was just wondering if it has to be about a family member. My parents are out of town so I'm staying with my grandparents … and they're really busy. I think I could write a more interesting paper on a stranger or historical figure instead."

Ms. Joy, accustomed to lying teens doling out outlandish excuses, teased out the line of truth. "Ask them. I'm sure they'd love to take the time to tell you stories. Grandparents live for that sort of thing. I think you'll be surprised." Felicity nodded.

"Okay, I'll ask."

"You have the second highest GPA in your class; I'm sure

you can write an interesting paper on someone in your family. It doesn't need to be scandalous, just interesting to you." Ms. Joy tilted her head, eyebrows cocked in that pitying look teachers give students who put too high expectations on themselves. Felicity, on the other hand, didn't appreciate being reminded that she was second to perfect miss Sadie. Dejected, she left the classroom and headed down the hall to her locker.

"Hey Trey," she said.

"'Sup?" he said, tilting his chin up in lieu of a wave hello. "You wanna go to the beach? Bonfire party tonight."

"Nah. I've got homework." She closed her locker and pulled her long hair into a messy ponytail. He followed her down the hall toward the parking lot.

"Can you give me a ride home?"

His eyebrows raised and he put a hand to his chest. "Would your mother approve?"

She rolled her eyes at him. "She won't know. I'm still staying with the grandparents."

"Nice. Will Shawn be home?"

She turned and gave him her most exasperated look. The last thing she wanted to do right now was talk about her family or listen to another conversation about the merits of this condenser microphone or that preamp. But it sounded better than talking about her parents.

Thankfully Trey left the other day before her mother burst in so he missed her meltdown. Felicity gave him a brief rundown, leaving out the gorier details. She worried because her mom hadn't checked in last night or the day before, and her dad was texting instead of calling, which was unusual on both sides. She still didn't know what happened between them but whatever it was had been enough to make her grandparents speak in generic clichés like, "give it time" and "they'll work it out" or the most annoying "these things have a way of working themselves out." It was disturbing, to say the least.

She slung her leg over the seat of Trey's dirt bike and unhooked the extra helmet. "Let's go to the beach."

His eyebrows shot up, but he nodded approval. "You said it."

She grabbed hold of his waist as they sped off, her sun-streaked hair whipping wildly behind them.

Good girl. Over-achiever. Athlete. These were the words frequently used to describe her. Today, she felt like being someone else. Someone who, for once, didn't do as she was told. Someone who went to parties and rode on the back of a motorcycle. Why shouldn't she let loose a little? She wasn't stupid enough to repeat her parents' mistakes. She'd done well enough in biology to know the odds of getting knocked up when you were a virgin without a boyfriend.

Sex held no interest for her. Not really. She had better things to do than worry about whether or not some guy was going to call her when he said he would. Sure, no one had shown interest, but that was beside the point. Her best friend was a guy and she loved him, but she couldn't imagine ever doing *that* with him. If she didn't want to do it with her best friend, why would she want to do it at all? It was illogical.

They pulled off the road, parking near an unmarked dirt trail that led down a bluff to a semi-secluded beach. Wafts of smoke and the unmistakable smell of fire reminded Felicity of barbecues on the beach with her grandparents and, for a second, she wanted to turn around and go home. Then she saw Trey, his messy blonde hair bobbing along the trail behind her, laid back as ever.

"What, you want to leave already?" He joked.

"Ha ha," she said, mad that he knew her so well. "Just checking to see if you can keep up."

"Oh-hoh! Game on," he said, sprinting down the path in front of her, flip flops clacking loudly beneath his feet. She ran after him, slipping along the path. She caught up with him just as they reached the mouth of the trail and jumped up on his back. Galloping in on piggyback wasn't exactly the entrance she'd imagined, but they certainly turned heads. There was some not-so-discreet whispering and then the obligatory teen head turn, as though nothing could be less cool than her existence.

"Wow, this sure looks fun," she said.

"It'll be fine. Look, isn't that Rachel?" He pointed to a brunette on the volleyball court. Felicity waved.

"She's coming over here. Be nice … " Trey warned, playfully elbowing her. "I'm gonna get a beverage. You want one?"

She glared back at him.

"Hey Rachel."

"What's up, Felicity? I'm surprised to see you here."

"Yeah? Why's that?"

"Uh, because I never see you at parties. But hey, we could use a fourth for volleyball."

"I'm in."

Felicity suddenly felt happy she'd come. It was nothing to stress about. She thought parties were all about drinking and smoking pot and people hooking up. None of that appealed to her, but volleyball—that she could do.

Spiking, bumping, diving across the sandy court: no problem. Making small talk with cliquey prima donnas and hormone infested boys trying to prove their manhood: a pathetic waste of time.

She and Rachel were paired up against two sophomores Felicity recognized from the volleyball team, but with whom she'd never spoken. They looked a full head taller than she was, maybe 6 feet tall, with shoulders most guys would kill for. If Felicity were the type to back down from a challenge, she may have been tempted.

"Hey, I heard your parents are splitting up. Bummer," someone said over Felicity's sweaty shoulder. She'd already thrown the ball in the air for her serve and it fell to the sand, untouched.

She whirled around to see her arch nemesis and general destroyer of good moods: Sadie. Their rivalry dated back to the second grade when, as the new girl, Felicity beat undefeated Sadie in the recess running races. After that, it escalated into full-on war. Spelling bees, science fairs, soccer, basketball, anything they could compete in, they did. And now, among other changes puberty brought on, their social rivalry had taken on a more malicious tone.

Felicity knew Sadie was trying to rile her up—that she had nothing to go on, because she couldn't know about the fight when even Felicity didn't know what happened, right? Sadie was the last person in the world who she'd want to know inside information about her family. Felicity glared at her, ignoring the game.

"You must be mistaking my parents for yours," Felicity retorted. Sadie's eyes widened for a moment, almost revealing real emotion.

"Oh really? Well, my aunt is with your dad now. At his hotel. I'm sure she'll clear it up for me. And you can read about it later." Sadie stalked off, her ebony cape of hair waving behind.

Felicity threw the ball in the air, serving three aces in a row, nearly decapitating her competition.

"Woah!" The unsuspecting girl on the other side of the net shouted.

"Sorry. I just remembered I have a thing. I've got to go." Felicity stormed off the court and straight up to Trey.

"Can we go now?" She said, shaking visibly. He gave her a worried look and grabbed their stuff. He didn't ask what happened as they wound up the trail in complete silence, his long legs not quite keeping up with her furious pace.

Chapter 16

I met with Alex Anders, front man of the multi-platinum band, Phazee Crux, at his hotel. The band is just over a month away from wrapping up their first worldwide sold out tour. Alex is the brains behind the music: writing, arranging and producing every track. Today, he's casual and down-to-earth in his jeans and t-shirt, eating a pizza, not looking concerned by the claim some are making that he's riding on his father-in-law's famous coat tails.

RS:

"So Alex, how does it feel to have your first headlining tour sell out?"

AA:

"It's awesome. The guys and I have worked so hard for so many years for this. It just feels like validation."

RS:

"It's got to be a nice way to answer your critics who said you only got here because you married Shawn Jax's daughter."

AA:

"You know, I try not to concern myself with what the critics say. I make music because I can't not make music. It's who I am. Not just what I do.'

RS:

"But you must have known what people would say when you included a cover of 'Speak'—Shawn Jax's biggest hit. Or was that just calculated controversy?"

AA:

"As much as I'd like to take credit for being so calculating, I have to admit the reason was a lot simpler than that. Shawn wrote that song about my wife, Jenna, and I wanted to pay tribute to them both. It was actually recorded as part of a documentary on him that will come out early next year. I thought it was a horrible idea to put it on the album, but the label, the band, and our manager outvoted me."

RS:

"Well, whosever idea it was, it obviously worked. Your album has sold over 11 million copies since it came out and you've been on a sold out tour ever since. What's life like on the road?"

AA:

"It's amazing. The difference between being on the road now versus when we were starting out is … night and day. Instead of sleeping on floors and in the van, we're in posh hotels, flying on a private jet. Life on the road is grueling but satisfying. We have the best fans in the world that, night after night, remind us why we do what we do. But we all have friends and families at home we miss while we're out and there's nothing like sleeping in your own bed. I think we'll be ready for the break when this tour wraps up."

RS:

"And the rumors?"

AA:

(Laughs) "Which ones?"

RS:

"That there's trouble in paradise? That you and Jenna are splitting up? That you've … found someone new?"

AA:

"What? I hadn't heard that one yet. Yeah, everything you read is true (scoffs). Tabloids these days sure are imaginative. And by that I'm being sarcastic. Just to clarify. I'd like to read a story where I get to be an alien put here to steal the secret of our survival on Earth and get to start an intergalactic war or something." (laughs)

RS:

"So you watch a lot of movies on the road?"

AA:

(laughs) "Yeah, I guess I gave away the big juicy secret."

RS:

"Thanks for taking time out of your busy schedule to talk to me. Good luck with the rest of the tour."

Alex stood up from the couch, shaking hands with his interviewer. She looked about his age, maybe a couple years older, with short black hair.

"Thanks, Rose. That it?" he said, hoping to keep this short. His natural wariness of reporters was heightened by the behind-the-scenes cameraman filming from the corner. He had no idea if the rumor she mentioned was an attempt to get a juicier story or if she'd heard something. He hadn't spoken to either Jenna or Airika since The Incident and he couldn't squelch his uneasiness with Rose's brazen leeching effort. She, on the other hand, wasn't hurried at all, casually gathering her things.

"I think my niece goes to school with your daughter," she said. He doubted it.

"Really?"

"Yeah," she said, surveying his expression, "I think they even have some classes together. Sadie. That's my niece."

Alex recognized the name but couldn't place her. He made a mental note to ask Felicity next time they spoke. From her tone he could tell she was inferring something more but he had neither the interest nor the patience to decipher it.

"Well it's a great school. I'm sure you're very proud of her," he said.

She lingered, a sly smile playing at her lips.

"Sorry to cut this short but I've got to get to sound check," he lied.

She seemed like the type to search his garbage as soon as he left the room and he had no intention of leaving her to it.

"Right, of course. Don't let me keep you," she said, still not moving. He had no choice but to pick up his jacket and head toward the door. She followed him to the elevator, slipping in just in time to ride together, leaving the cameraman out in the hall. When the doors closed, she slipped her card in his back pocket and looked him straight in the eye.

"If the rumors are true, call me." The elevator dinged and she strutted out through the lobby. Alex stood, mouth agape, feeling like the girl in one of those horrible sexual-harassmentin-the-workplace videos. He had a bad feeling he would see her again.

He rode the elevator back up to his floor, thinking about Jenna. He needed to talk to her. Her phone rang and rang. When she didn't pick up, he hung up without leaving a message. How could he fit everything he needed to say into a 30 second message? An open guitar case sat on the bed. He picked it up, sunk back on the bed, and started noodling around, playing nothing in particular. The chords and melody said what he couldn't articulate.

Chapter 17

Jenna woke up, barely registering the sound of the Weepies singing, "The World Spins Madly On" as the room started spinning around her in her attempt to get vertical. It was too much; the momentum forced her back into the warm abyss. *Where is that coming from?* She wondered. Then she remembered her impromptu solo dance party last night. She'd thought (hoped) that was a dream. She must have left the music on when she passed out. *Ugh.* This is why she didn't usually drink. At least none of her neighbors could have seen her through all the trees surrounding the cabin (or her fabulous new curtains). By the time the song finished, she managed to tolerate sitting upright.

Then it hit her. Again. Alex. Airika. The anvil was back, settled squarely on her chest. It allowed for the minimum intake of breath—just enough to keep her alive, aware of her misery and aloneness. She couldn't formulate the grief into actual thoughts. It was a completely physical reaction. Her body felt leaden, immobile from the weight of her burden. It had been three days since she'd left him, and during the handful of hours she'd spent out of bed, a nagging thought kept forcing its way into her head: *Who am I without them?*

The second the thought popped in, she pushed it aside, hating herself for allowing it in the first place. Of course she wasn't defined by her relationships. That would be pathetic. She was a twenty-first century woman, not some fifties housewife. There was so much more to her than that. Wasn't there? She was a mother, for one. *Felicity's doing just fine without you,* a voice in her head chided. She was also a daughter. It's not like she could help being the daughter of someone famous. Although that didn't help prove her point.

How did other people define themselves? She thought

about what people said when they introduce themselves. What it would say below her name on a Hi My Name Is _____ name tag. That's it!

All at once it hit her: she needed a job. Well no, not a job—a profession. Most people go to college and get jobs in order to make money. She didn't need money. She was a wife and mother by the time she graduated high school, so she'd never seen the point in all that in-between stuff. But now she saw there was another point: self-validation.

She'd spent her entire life surrounded by a crowded bubble of people who loved and cared for her, sheltering her from the big bad world. But now, those same people had popped the bubble just in time for her to feel the weight of the world crashing down upon her.

The thought was sickening, the introspective train too much for her hangover and severe lack of caffeine. She made a mental note never to drink again, before scavenging the cupboards for something greasy to eat. Nothing. Being a health nut turned out to be a terrible idea when in need of hangover food. The situation needed to be remedied—fast.

Twenty minutes later, she and Zach took their breakfast bagels, dripping in cheese and bacon, back to the car, and drove down to the snowy boat ramp. They parked, taking in the beautiful frozen landscape between bites.

"Thanks for picking me up," she said.

"I'm always down for food." He took another monster bite. "Dude, you're finished already?"

She blushed. Under normal circumstances she would spend the rest of the day at the gym burning off the countless carbs and fat she just ingested. *Ugh, the gym!* The mere thought of it made her stomach churn. Or was that the bacon?

"So how are you holding up?" He asked, making the kind of intense eye contact that always made her squirm.

"Fine," she lied.

Then, realizing that playing the role of the strong capable one who solves everyone else's problems was what got her into this mess in the first place, she decided to come clean.

"I'm devastated. I don't know who I am anymore. Without them, I feel like ... Like there's no reason to get out of bed. You know?" She couldn't bring herself to look at him. He stayed silent. She was sure he was trying not to laugh. Or else planning a quick escape from all the scary female emotions.

"Do you have any hobbies?" He asked. She thought about it.

"Not really. Everyone else thinks all I do is work out and shop."

Silence again. "What do you to shop for?"

The question surprised her.

"I shop for clothes for myself, or Felicity. And I love to buy home décor." He appeared to mull that over, his hand scratching the stubble along his jawline.

"What was your last job?" He asked.

She took a deep breath. She hated that question.

"Modeling."

"That's the only job you've ever had?"

She nodded.

"Well, there's your trouble."

She looked him over for signs of condescension, but he seemed totally serious. He must have sensed her confusion.

"If you've never really worked, then you've never had the chance to get a promotion, or a thank you from a boss, or the simple satisfaction of a job well done."

She laughed. "You can't say modeling isn't a job, but I get where you're going with this. Although I'm pretty sure my crisis isn't based on never being told 'thank you'."

He made a face that said, "How do you know if you've never done it?"

"Okay, here's your homework. When I take you home, you're going to make a list of everything you like to do. Anything that could be a profession. Then you're going to give it to me and I'm going to help you find a job. We're gonna put you to work, Jenna Jax!" His enthusiasm was infectious and she found herself looking forward to it. She didn't even wince when he used her maiden name. At least not visibly.

Chapter 18

Back at the cabin Jenna started her homework. She looked for paper but couldn't find any, eventually coming across an old diary in the spare room. She scribbled on a blank page near the back:

Job	Pros	Cons
Yoga Instructor	fun, stay in shape, work in very Zen place.	public speaking, certification and patience required
Interior Designer	lots of shopping	not qualified, no degree
Photographer	fun, creative, different every day	need lots of equipment and learn how to use it
A&R Talent Scout	listen to lots of music	family business, might not be taken seriously, reminds me of Alex

Looking over the list she'd made felt productive. She'd feared she wouldn't be able to come up with anything and now she had four legitimate possibilities. Ideas anyway. Discovering her employment ineptitude was disconcerting, especially in such a fragile emotional state. Most people went through this process at eighteen when they left home to go to college. Here she was, a thirty four-year old freshman in The University of Life. Pick a major.

In an attempt to procrastinate, she flipped through the pages of her old diary. She came across an entry from the summer before sophomore year. She read the words of her former self:

Dear Diary,

Today we went to Virginia City to watch the camel races. It was fun except that the camels were really gross. They spit! Ewwll!! But then we walked around downtown and tasted the fudge (yum!) and went on a tour of an old mine. I'm not normally interested in history but I was 200 feet below the earth, standing on a tiny elevator with my crush and his hand kept brushing up against mine. I don't know if it was on purpose or not, but maybe when we go to the movies later I can find out. I mean, even if he is interested it's not like he can be too obvious about it. Not with his sister around.

Jenna slammed the book shut in an attempt to stop the stream of suppressed memories flooding in. A photo slipped out, landing face down on the floor. She didn't want to, but couldn't help it. She picked it up. The three smiling faces, posing behind bars, belonged to none other than herself, Airika and Zach. She had forgotten how much of a crush she used to have on him. She'd liked him for forever. Until Alex. Nothing ever happened, of course. Their two-year age difference, insignificant now, was a gaping chasm then. When they were a little older, Jenna knew Airika would never have allowed it to happen so she kept it to herself.

She blushed, suddenly self-conscious he might find out about her crush, ancient history though it was. At least they didn't have his sister as a third wheel. "No!" she said out loud, hoping it would force her mind to stop wandering further down that path. The last thing she needed now was to add another layer of complication to an already convoluted Jerry Springer-esque problem. *Focus Jenna.* She shoved both hands in her pockets to keep them from delving further into the diary.

Inside her pocket, she found a piece of paper and remembered that her photos should be ready for pickup by now. They couldn't call her since she smashed her phone and didn't know the number to the cabin. Plus, she could get a better look at the shopping center now that it was light outside.

Her favorite skinny jeans were the only trendy item she could add to her otherwise hideous outfit if she didn't want to freeze to death. She dug in the second bag Zach had packed for her for something warm to put on. Unzipping it, she nearly keeled over from humiliation.

As he'd done with the other drawers in her bedroom, he dumped the contents of her nightstand drawer out on top of everything else. While she appreciated that he hadn't spent time going through her underwear drawer, she wanted to crawl in a hole when, glinting up at her, she saw the pink Rabbit vibrator she'd gotten in a gift basket from the Sex in the City party she'd gone to last year. *And it's not even in its packaging,* she thought, wondering if that made any difference at all.

She screwed her eyes up to try to banish the visual of Zach's reaction to seeing it and chucked on an unflattering puffy jacket, knit beanie (with tassel) and clunky snow boots. Not cute, but practical for walking around town and avoiding frostbite (and an excellent disguise when not wanting to be recognized by well-meaning friends).

"May I help you?" asked a perky salesgirl working the camera counter. Jenna smiled.

"Yeah, I had a roll of film developed. And an enlargement."

"Name or ticket?"

Jenna took the ticket out of her pocket, handing it over. The girl did a quick double take when she read the name, but was gracious enough not to say anything.

"Just a sec. The enlargement's in the back."

"Thanks."

While she waited, Jenna looked around. The grocery store

was much larger than she remembered, not quaint at all. It was fully modern and she could see an aisle selling books, another section for movies to rent or buy, and, on the other side, a sit-down bakery/café. It's funny how different a memory of a place could be.

"Here it is!" The salesgirl said. "Would you like to pay here or up front?"

"Can I pay at the bakery?" Jenna wanted to sit down with a cup of coffee to look through the photos.

"Sure!"

She took the photos and headed over to the café.

Cappuccino in hand, she sat at a corner table and opened the envelope. Nostalgia gave way to trepidation, remembering the diary entry. Who knew what might be lurking on this roll of film.

Chapter 19

The photos turned out to be mostly of them out on a ski boat. There were shots of she and Airika together, arms draped over each other's shoulders, making faces, Airika pushing Jenna off the boat where Zach swam around grinning, Jenna getting up on a wakeboard, and one of Jenna and Airika floating on a big inner-tube, their cheesy grins aimed right at the camera. Then there was a series of shots of the lake. An artistic close-up of the water after a pebble fell in, rippling the glassy surface. Another shot of a dock Jenna recognized from nearby the boat beach. The sun sank down below the mountainous horizon through the legs of the dock. It was striking—clean lines, good perspective and depth. *Did I take that?* She wondered.

The next series revealed sunsets full of pinks, oranges, reds, purples and a velvety navy sky taken from different parts of the beach. A sort of time-lapse panorama.

Finally, she got to the last shot, the one she'd had enlarged without seeing (against the sales girl's recommendation). It was different than the image she'd had in her head, but effective nonetheless. She was mostly in silhouette, exposing the sapphire blue of the sky and lake outside, but the little crystals glowed like the embers of a campfire, throwing light haphazardly around the room. The effect was half fashion editorial (maybe she still had some modeling chops, after all) and half horror film, with irregular up-lighting on her face and neck.

The longer she stared, the less she recognized herself. The image took on a life of its own. Her pose was angular and imposing. Her expression looked intimidating, even sinister in the harsh lighting—a look unseen in her daily repertoire. It frightened her to have that kind of anger lurking just below the surface. She was terrified she might be angry forever.

She quickly repacked the photos into the envelope and

braced herself for the cold walk back to the cabin. Big white flakes fell from the sky as soon as she stepped outside. She gave herself a mental pat on the back for dressing appropriately— the right choice in the battle of fashion versus function.

On the ground in front of her, littered by some rude passerby, lay a tabloid photo of her husband sitting at a table on a hotel balcony across from a woman with sharply layered blonde hair, exactly like Airika's, and a caption that read "Finding Love in Spain: Alex Anders out with another woman? Does Jenna know?" She stuffed it in her pocket, hating herself for not leaving it there on the ground where it belonged. She told herself not to give it credence. *Most stories are contrived and planted for publicity*; she heard her voice repeating the same monologue she'd often recited to Felicity, finding it wholly unconvincing. The snow whipped around, biting the skin of her exposed cheeks, thankfully giving her somewhere else to direct attention.

As she made her way toward the lake, the wind at full gale turned the blowing snow into a whiteout. It was like navigating a thick white maze, guided more by gravity than sight. She stuffed the photos inside her jacket to keep them dry. After a few slips and a close call with a snowplow barreling up the road, she made it back to the cabin, kicking the accumulated snow off her boots, jacket and hat.

Inside it was freezing. She flipped the light switch on to read the thermostat, only to realize the power was out. She couldn't bear the thought of freezing to death in this cabin, that tabloid being her last visual.

Flashlight, she thought, scavenging drawers and cupboards to no avail. She looked at the fireplace and noticed that there was wood already in it. She didn't know the first thing about lighting fires, but what better time to learn? Next to the fireplace was a pile of extra logs and butane lighter.

On TV they always lit some sort of newspaper or something first. She looked around. Nothing. A smile spread across her face as she pulled the tabloid out of her pocket, relishing each crumpling sound, placing it neatly between the logs. She took a deep breath and pulled the trigger. A small flame shot from the lighter and ... Poof! The paper caught fire quickly, black smoke filling the small fireplace. A few loud crackle pops followed as the flame spread across the ready-to-burn logs, stretching upward.

It seemed apropos that the tabloid smoke was black, but there was an awful lot of it. Was it supposed to fill the room? She spluttered a cough, covering her mouth with her sleeve. *Probably not.* She looked around for some sort of vent. A black wrought iron handle protruding from the rock seemed her best bet. She jiggled it until it moved, immediately sucking the smoke up through the chimney. "I did it!"

Jenna Jax-Anders—the girl who'd never been camping, whose idea of roughing it involved room service and down pillows—lit a fire to save her life. She assumed it was cold enough to freeze to death without one. Beaming, she rubbed her hands together, body and soul warmed by the fire.

The camera, still sitting on the coffee table, reflected orange light off its lens, grabbing her attention. She put in a new roll of film. This was worth recording. She took a couple shots of the flames in the logs and then set up the self timer, as though she were taking a silly tourist shot of herself in front of some famous monument, posing in front of her very first fire.

Her spirits weren't even dampened by the realization that all the other appliances were electric, and she had no way of cooking for herself. There was only one thing she could think to make, though she'd never done it before, but always wanted to. She found the ingredients needed (having conveniently shoved them into her basket on her earlier shopping expedition at Zach's insistence), including the wire hanger for optimal marshmallow roasting. Carefully laying out the graham crackers and chocolate on a plate, she speared a big fluffy marshmallow and stuck it right into the thick of the flames. It caught fire quicker than she expected and she extinguished it, the thin black skin sliding off its gooey flesh. Her second attempt was more of a golden brown bubbly effect: the perfect S'more.

With a belly full of the most delicious dessert of all time, and a roaring fire of her own making, she curled up on the couch, settled in for the night. Aside from paranoia about burning the house down if she left the room, there wasn't another heat source, making the couch the best spot in the house.

A week ago, if someone had told her this is where she'd be, she'd have had them committed. It was unfathomable that her whole world and sense of self could be flipped upside down so quickly. She'd had the perfect devoted husband. A loyal best friend. Her biggest concern was buying amazing one of-a-kind dresses and looking great for her anniversary, trying to make her husband happy. Even her teenage daughter was pretty perfect. She didn't have a boyfriend. She played sports. Got good grades. She was confident and capable, the opposite of her mother.

Chastising herself for having been so vapid and gullible, a conversation with Alex came back to her. It had to have been around the time Felicity started kindergarten, a particularly low point in Alex's career.

"I bumped into Ella Ryan today," she'd said, unloading groceries in the kitchen. Alex had looked up briefly from his laptop, grunting in response. "She mentioned a couple modeling jobs she thought might be perfect for me."

"Oh yeah?" Alex said, still not listening.

"Yeah. Maybe I should get some new headshots?" She grabbed the milk, turning to put in the fridge.

"Why would you want to go back to modeling? I thought you said it was a shallow industry, that you were basically an object."

"I did. No, I don't want to be a model. It just sounded like fun." She busied herself, turning everything in the fridge label side out.

"Jenna, I already told you, if you're worried about money, you don't need to ... " he started, sighing.

"No, no, that's not it. Never mind. You're right, it's shallow and stupid."

He looked up at her, concern etched into the creases in his forehead.

"I think I forgot something in the car," she said, excusing herself from the tension.

That was the last time she'd ever mentioned getting a job. She didn't want to work if it meant making Alex feel like a bad husband. But now the memory felt different. Now all the rules had changed. And she was changing too.

Chapter 20

It was dark when Trey dropped Felicity off at her grand-parents'. The silence chilled the air between them as they made their way up the gravel driveway. Felicity gave no indication of wanting to talk about what happened at the party.

"You okay?" he asked, his voice soft.

She pulled off her helmet and handed it to him, not looking up. "Fine." She slung her backpack over one shoulder, waved and mumbled something that sounded like "see you tomor-row."

She didn't look back, keeping her head down, looking at her feet hitting gravel on their way to the door. Before she reached it, it flung open. She jumped, momentarily forgetting her anger.

"Cici! There you are!" Anya said. Felicity adjusted her backpack. "I was worried sick!" Anya hugged her like she'd been returned by deranged kidnappers.

"I'm fine." Guilt for making her grandmother worry over-rode the anger she'd been stewing in. She should have called. It wasn't like her to take off and not check in. "Sorry."

"Are you okay?" Anya asked. It was the worst question to be asked when trying not to cry. She couldn't withstand her grandmother's imploring look and the tears started flowing.

"Oh Cici, what happened?" Anya hugged her, wrapped both arms around her like a small child, and kissed the top of her head. "Shhhh. Shhhhh. It's okay. Shhhhh."

"Is it true?" Felicity sniffed.

Anya took a deep breath and looked her straight in the eye. "If you're asking what I think you are, then, honestly, I'm not sure. I don't think we know the whole story."

"Why didn't anyone tell me?"

"I didn't think we should say anything until we knew if it

would blow over." Anya maintained eye contact with her granddaughter, carefully watching her face turn from anger to confusion to concern.

"I'm not a baby. I'm sick of being treated like I can't handle anything. I know a lot more than anyone gives me credit for."

"I know you do, Cic. I'm sorry I didn't tell you. I just wanted to protect you." Felicity thought about that. Her grandmother had always treated her like an adult from the time she was a little girl. The fact that she'd hidden it disconcerted Felicity more than the separation itself.

"It's been a week." Felicity said.

Her mom carried out a dramatic scene for a few hours, at most. She was always back and ready for the next round of theatrics before her perfect chestnut hair could fall flat. As over-reactive as she was, Felicity had never seen her move out, or even threaten to.

"Why hasn't my dad called?"

Now in full-on detective mode, she wanted answers. In the moment it took Anya to respond, Felicity regretted asking. Before she could hear the official answer, she preempted, "It was his fault, wasn't it? The fight?"

Anya nodded. "There are two sides to everything."

"Can't he just apologize?" Her voice cracked. The sad look on Anya's face told her all she needed but hoped she wouldn't have to know.

"You girls ready for dinner?" Shawn asked, poking his head around the corner.

"I'm not hungry. I'm going to bed." Felicity said, slipping past him up the stairs to her room.

"Suit yourself. If you change your mind later, I'll leave some leftovers in the fridge." His chipper mood couldn't penetrate the wall of tension he'd walked into.

After Felicity went upstairs and they heard her door close, Anya told Shawn what happened with Felicity. For a giant celebrity, he was still just a bloke from Woop-Woop, Australia.

He had a relentlessly optimistic outlook on life, and not much knowledge of the inner workings of the female psyche.

"Ahh, she'll be 'right."

Anya wasn't sure to which 'she' he referred, especially since he often used the same phrase after burning a sausage.

Shawn's musical career as a touring musician had been relatively short. He was on the road for five years before the band split up. By the time he ventured into his solo career (at Anya's urging), he was in a position, both leverage-wise and financially, to hit the summer tour circuit and add select dates throughout the rest of the year. It meant that he was around for most of Jenna's childhood, unlike Alex for Felicity.

Shawn's success came through smart use of his publishing royalties and by writing and producing for other artists. That's how he got to live out his childhood fantasy of creating a home studio (a feat far more ambitious in the analog days). He'd been able to make a good living off music with as few dealings with the dark underbelly of the industry as possible. His was not the usual tale.

Alex's career followed the more stereotypical path. He'd been in countless bands over the years, from punk to emo to rock, playing to drunks and a handful of fans, at every seedy bar and club around LA. He even did some solo stuff at one point that no one paid any attention to. His die-hard fans stuck by him while band members cycled out through drugs, alcohol and creative politics, but their numbers were never impressive enough to propel the band to that next level.

Fans attributed his not signing a record deal as his "fuck you" to the music industry. It gave him credibility that he'd been riding on for years, but as he watched his contemporaries sign record deals and sell out shows, he had to admit he was frustrated by his inability to get that kind of industry validation.

Success had only come recently, to the uproars and occasional death-threats from his die-hard fans. Some of the more virulent and outspoken ones (angry that his music had been featured on a soda commercial) blogged that he was the "worst kind of sell-out," "a pussy-whipped loser because his wife was sick of him living off her trust fund as he trifled in the shadow of his famous (and more talented) father-in-law."

Though Alex considered himself a pretty secure man, it wasn't easy to read that stuff, especially because at the heart of it was a grain of truth. Shawn knew the cruel realities of the industry as well as the dichotomy between his passion and practical pursuits of The Dream. He liked Alex. He'd never blamed him or held it against him that he hadn't broken in earlier, though of course he'd offered to help.

Alex wanted to do it on his own. Shawn respected that. He knew Alex's priorities were where they should be. And as a father, he appreciated the adoration shown his daughter, though the circumstances of their marriage were less than desirable, to say the least. This business with Airika kissing Alex seemed out of character, and Shawn was content to calmly wait for the truth to be revealed in time. Unlike Anya.

"Hungry?" He asked again. Anya smiled but it didn't reach her eyes.

"Famished."

They ate in comfortable silence. Their approaches to dealing with conflict differed, but they were united in parenthood.

Chapter 21

"Hi Dad, it's me. Again." Felicity stalled, not sure what to say in yet another voicemail. "Um, I just wanted to see how you're doing. I'm worried about you. Call me back, kay?"

She hung up, hating her whiny tone. For as long as she could remember, her dad had checked in with her at least once a day whenever he was on tour, even if it was just a quick text. It had been four days since his last text and that had been a photo of an old bookshop on a cobblestone street. He hadn't even attached a caption, let alone explained anything.

Felicity played the part of messenger in her parents' fights often enough, but typically they involved things like who was supposed to do the shopping, or the old standby: "I told you I had that thing to go to tonight. You just forgot." That always got Jenna in a snit and then Felicity would go from one to the other relaying messages until they made up or her mom cooled off, whichever came first.

But in all the years of mediating, she'd never seen anything on par with what was going on now. If she didn't know better she'd have suspected another woman. But he would never cheat. Never. She'd bet her life on it.

There must be a simpler explanation. Obviously it involved their anniversary, since that's when it happened, but Felicity helped him plan the whole thing—from the backyard winter wonderland transformation to the surprise renewal of their vows. She knew her mom would have loved it.

"Beeep!" She leaned out the window and signaled "just a minute" before running down the stairs to meet Trey. She shouted a quick, "Bye" over her shoulder and slung her backpack on as she shut the front door. Trey waved and handed her a helmet.

"You ready?" He asked.

"Sorry about yesterday. I didn't mean to take it out on you." Her cheeks flushed thinking about how she'd behaved.

"Yeah, what was that about?" He asked.

"Sadie was just being … Sadie. I shouldn't have let her get under my skin." Trey nodded, shrugged, and let the kickstand up.

"Shall we?" He asked.

She nodded and grabbed hold of his waist as they took off.

***

"Why is *she* here?" Alex said, glaring between Airika and Simon. Simon put up his hands.

"Mate, hear me out. She's under contract for the tour and we wouldn't want a lawsuit, would we?" He raised an authoritative brow. "Plus, didn't she do a great job for your last cover?" Another pause met with steely silence. "Yes! She did. The label loved it. I loved it. Everyone loved it. So this'll be fine. We're all big boys here." He glanced over at Airika. "And lass."

The sweet tone he injected into his gruff voice was like a girl scout selling cigarettes. Airika batted her eyelashes, eliciting a lascivious smile from Simon. Alex was trapped, and he knew that viper Rose must be lurking somewhere nearby, hoping to get a juicier story. *No sense spoon-feeding her material.*

He took a deep breath. "Fine, just do what I pay you to do," he said to Airika, glaring at Simon.

"Of course. I d- ," Airika started.

"Great, let's get to work then!" Simon cut her off, patting Alex on the back and steering Airika in the opposite direction. "Come with me doll, I'll show you the green room."

Once they disappeared from view, Alex couldn't stop the anger from boiling over. His skin crawled with frustration. What had he gotten himself into? He was so distracted he didn't even notice the cameras still following him.

He needed an outlet to relieve the tension, so he turned and punched the first thing in reach, which turned out to be a brick wall. The searing pain shocked him back to his more rational self, regret following quickly behind. *Ouch!* He shook his hand out, flexing his fingers to make sure it wasn't broken.

These outbursts were becoming more frequent and he knew, soon enough, he would end up doing something he couldn't take back. He needed to fix his issues with the label and get Airika out of his life in order to save his marriage, but as it stood, he could see just one way out of either situation: suck it up and finish the tour. By the end of the tour though, he may not have a marriage to save.

***

He tried Jenna's cell one more time, knowing that, like the last fifty calls, he would be sent straight to voicemail, just wanting to hear her voice. Before he could dial he saw a missed call from Felicity.

"Hey Cic," he said when she picked up. "What's up, kiddo?"

"Dad! Are you okay? What's going on with you and Mom?"

"I'm fine. Everything's fine. Don't worry."

She paused. *Not him too,* she fumed. No one trusted her with the truth.

"How's school going?"

"Fine," she said through clenched teeth.

"Hey, I had an interview with your friend's aunt the other day," he said, trying to lighten the mood.

"Really, which friend?" She asked, narrowing her eyes.

"Sadie? I think that was her name," he said.

Her jaw dropped.

"Hey kid, I gotta go now. Call you later?" He saw Simon heading his way and didn't want her to overhear their conversation. She and Jenna thought Simon would walk over hot coals for him and he didn't want to give her more to worry about. She didn't respond, but he hung up without noticing.

He dropped the phone to his side just in time for Simon's mouth to start running. The pep talk consisted, as usual, of shitty options doused in sweet honey. A way to make more money (and sell his soul). To be more successful (and further alienate the fans who'd stuck by him). To reach new fans (thereby rendering the die-hards unnecessary). Blah, blah, blah.

Alex wanted to scream. Instead, he forced himself to say, "I'm not interested in doubling down. I'm interested in making music. I took a loan; I'll pay it back. End of story." They stood, staring each other down.

For the first time, maybe ever, Alex was happy to hear Airika's voice over his shoulder. Simon looked away first. Alex turned toward his dressing room, trying to regain his composure before he had to be 'on' for the cameras. Wishing he were anywhere else, he decided to man up, reminding himself this was for his family and the only proactive step he could take toward getting out from under the weight of his contract. He suddenly yearned for the days of arguing with a club owner trying to scam him out of $20 off the door.

Chapter 22

"Hmmm," Zach said, walking around the photo, seeing it from different angles. He nodded, smiling, Jenna's job list in hand. They sat in companionable silence in the living room, glowing embers of last night's fire keeping them warm. Jenna's blown up photo sat framed and propped up on the mantle. Jenna smiled her first joyful smile since she'd left her husband.

"You like?" She thought it was good, but she was no expert.

"Mmmhmm ... Definitely," he said, standing up to get a closer look. "Can I show this to someone?" She raised her eyebrows, waiting for him to go on. "A portrait photographer. Mostly shoots pro athletes. She's been looking for an assistant," he said.

Jenna wanted to shout a resounding *Yes!* but her old friend, Insecurity, sat squarely on her voice box, stopping her. Just because she took a lucky shot didn't mean she knew anything about photography. Nor was she a sports enthusiast. Why would a real photographer want her? She'd just get in the way.

"Hey, I know it's not a glamorous job, but you've gotta start somewhere."

"No, that's not it," she said quickly, seeing his injured expression. "I'm just worried she won't want *me*. I don't have anything to offer." The joy she'd felt earlier was usurped by the demeaning voices in her head. She stared down at her coffee, fiddling with the lid.

He smiled. "That's the point of an internship. You go in not knowing what you're doing and learn on the job. For shit pay, or none at all."

Well, when he put it like that ...

"And you *do* have something to offer. A lot, actually. Look at these." He said, thumbing through the other photos in the sleeve. When he came across one of himself he paused, holding it up so she could see it. *Crap!* She forgot to take those out.

"When was this?" He asked. She felt her cheeks heat up.

"The summer after my sophomore year," she said, in what she hoped was a casual tone.

"Look at us," he said, flipping through the images of them jumping off the pier into the lake. There were shots of everyone, but in all the shots of him, he was shirtless. After a couple of family shots there was one of him pulling himself up the ladder, dripping wet. She blushed and looked away. "God, I look so young!" His eyes glazed over with nostalgia.

She was glad that's all he noticed. Her stomach did a little flip, remembering her crush on him and how much she liked him wet and shirtless. The image of The Rabbit flashed again in her mind and she struggled not to give away her embarrassment.

His face fell and he got quiet.

"What?" She asked, then remembered and felt awful.

"That was the last trip we ever took as a family." He said it so matter-of-factly. That was the summer before his mom left the family and his dad lost his medical practice. How self-absorbed to think his mood had anything to do with her. Apparently, she could check detective off her list of potential careers.

"I didn't mean to bring all this up for you. I'm so sorry ... " her voice trailed off.

"It's not your fault. Can I keep this?" He held up a shot of he, Airika and their parents smiling, bare feet dangling off the edge of the pier.

She nodded.

***

When Jenna finally worked up the nerve to call, Noelle, a lovely sounding woman with the hint of a French accent, invited her to shadow a shoot at her cabin the following day.

Jenna was a ball of nerves, hardly sleeping through the night.

Not only wasn't she qualified to be a photographer (or assistant), she was unqualified to be an employee, period. Teenagers had more work experience than she did. Maybe she should call and cancel. No, she couldn't make a fool of Zach.

***

Waking up, the cold morning was clear and beautiful, and a fresh blanket of snow sparkled in the sunlight. She layered up, opting for dark fitted jeans, with a silk thermal top under a cashmere wrap. Then she thought better, and added the puffy jacket. She couldn't bring herself to don the clunky snow boots in front of a photographer, instead opting for high-heeled suede boots.

The five minute walk along the slippery bike path to the address she'd been given had her slipping and sliding, feeling more and more foolish about her shoe choice. As she struggled up the steep driveway, the enormous home looming above her, she questioned whether she was in the right place. To call it a cabin would be like calling Mt. Everest a big hill. Huge pine logs graced the façade of a three-story mountain castle, complete with a stone turret on one side. Opulent without being gaudy, it resembled a hotel more than a home.

Before Jenna could change her mind and back (or slip) down the driveway, a white-haired woman opened the front door, waving her inside. At just under five feet tall, Noelle's child-size frame was juxtaposed by a chic blend of designer-meets-mountain wear.

"Bonjour! You must be Jenna. I'm so glad you found the place! You came highly recommended. From what I saw of your work, you've got a real natural talent!" Noelle's enthusiasm calmed Jenna's nerves enough to follow her inside.

"How do you know our boy, Zach?"

Jenna didn't have a chance to answer before Noelle continued, "I've known that boy for five years now and hardly heard him speak more than two sentences until the other day when he told me about you." There was a mischievous twinkle in her eye.

"We grew up together," Jenna said, hoping to avoid getting too personal.

"Oohh," Noelle said, dragging the word out. "So were you high school sweethearts?"

"No, actually I married his best friend." Jenna realized her mistake but it was too late.

"So…are you still married now?"

"Yes," Jenna replied. She didn't want to think about the state of her marriage. Noelle either sensed Jenna's discomfort, or got bored with the topic, thankfully dropping it.

"Follow me. The studio is upstairs."

Jenna followed her, amazed at this tiny woman's rapid pace. When they got to the top, the breathtaking view paralyzed her. The immense south wall, which could have added a fourth story, was instead covered in floor to ceiling windows, revealing a mesmerizing panorama of the lake and mountains. She had to force her eyes to look around the rest of the room.

On the opposite wall stood a twenty-foot wide seamless white paper backdrop, hanging from a roller on the wall, spilling onto the floor. There were two big lights on stands set up with light boxes. Jenna recognized the studio setup from her modeling days. She took comfort in the familiarity of being on set, and tried to keep the terror of failure at bay.

"Over here," said Noelle.

"Where are y-?" Jenna asked.

"In the closet."

The closet was the size of Jenna's living room at home. The only thing remotely resembling a normal closet was the shelving system covering three walls. Each shelf was packed with oversized chachkes and mismatched boxes. At first glance it looked like an antique store disemboweled. Slowly, her eyes adjusted to the chaos, revealing a surprisingly sophisticated labeling system, albeit highly personalized.

Jenna read the labels on the first shelf: "Birth Props", "Snowshoes from the 1900's" and "Faux Taxidermy: Regional Animals" handwritten on color-coded stickers. Her eyes lingered and she must have made a face.

"I'm vegan," Noelle said, as though that were clarification enough. She continued searching for whatever it was she'd come looking for in the first place. "Aha!" She said, holding up a small blue hatbox.

"Can I help?" Jenna asked, not sure she could. Noelle headed out of the closet and gestured for Jenna to follow. Jenna obeyed, walking back to the backdrop side of the studio. Noelle unhooked a rope ladder from the wall, which Jenna hadn't noticed before and looked up to see theater-type scaffolding running the length of the room, just wide enough for one person to crawl out on. Noelle deftly scaled the ladder, then reached her hands out to Jenna.

"Hand that to me," she said, adjusting knobs and light discs. She twisted a large light, angling it down toward the back of the room. "How do you feel about heights? I should have asked before."

"F-fine," Jenna said, handing up the box. Jenna didn't fear heights in general, but she was concerned about what she might have to do up there.

"Good. I'll need you up here sprinkling snow for at least part of the shoot today."

Jenna breathed a sigh of relief. Then she noticed the box's label read "Snow: Flakes (Large)." *See, nothing to worry about,* she told herself.

Noelle descended the ladder, explaining the concept for the shoot. By the time the stylist and make-up artist arrived, Jenna began to enjoy herself.

And by the time the model—a professional snowboarder—arrived, Jenna had already made herself useful. She helped move lights, set up props, and watched as Noelle directed each person on set, choreographing the day. Noelle talked non-stop, interrupting herself frequently to interject camera and lighting tips. She was so passionate, and Jenna couldn't help feeling awed, and a little jealous.

The shoot was for a book cover: memoirs of an X-Games champion. A couple of burly unshaven men lugged a full-sized chairlift up to the studio, hanging it from the scaffolding above. The complexity of the set astounded her. Jenna was in charge of the snow falling in the first setup. She hoped she didn't embarrass herself, or plummet to the ground from her perch. When choosing her footwear for the day, she clearly hadn't the foggiest idea what she'd be in for.

Noelle called for a reset, and Jenna came down, not gracefully, but without falling on her face either.

"Jenna," Noelle gestured for her to look through the camera. "See this shadow?" Jenna nodded. "What do you think we should do to get rid of it?"

"You're asking me?" Jenna felt like she was in Mr. Stone's sixth grade algebra class, unprepared for a pop quiz. Noelle nodded, folding her arms across her chest.

"Look," she said. Jenna took another look through the lens. She saw that the shadows being cast from the light above enhanced the model's deep-set eyes, making her look tired. She looked around the set. There was a round white light disc propped up against the wall. She gestured to it.

"Would that work?"

"Let's see." Noelle said as Jenna tilted the disc up to the light, just below the model's face. Click. Jenna leapt over a pile of cords to look at the screen, displaying an evenly lit face. Noelle beamed. Jenna smiled too.

Shot after shot, Jenna checked on how every little change, each angle, reflection and shadow affected the quality of light. She marveled at how subtle differences in lighting and framing changed the mood. She tried to see the light through the lens instead of with her eyes.

Her eyes brimmed with ideas, taking cues and direction

from Noelle, whose teaching process turned out to be the opposite of sixth grade algebra. For the first time in her life, Jenna was contributing. She was appreciated. She was addicted.

The trouble with highs, however, is their parasitic twin: low. The poor girl didn't mean anything by it. She was just getting her make-up touched up between shots. But when she picked up the trashy magazine she'd been reading and said, "Hey, is that you?" Jenna could swear she heard a metaphorical shoe drop. She was about to say "no" and brush it off when she glimpsed the photo of she and Alex at the Grammys with a sawn-through graphic separating them, next to a shot of he and another woman. Before she could look away, she realized she *did* recognize the woman pictured on a hotel balcony wearing a plush white robe and it definitely was not her.

Chapter 23

Airika drummed her perfectly manicured nails on the armrest of her seat. The plane sat, unmoving, as it had for the last two hours. This is why she hated commercial flights. She would definitely be getting someone to refund her money the second they landed at L.A.X. First class may as well have been steerage for all the difference it made in the standard of service.

A man across the short aisle looked up over his giant bifocals. "Do you mind?" He asked, staring at her hand.

"Uh, yes, I do." She said in a tone she hadn't used since tenth grade (or possibly yesterday).

She pulled her hands under her legs, which started bouncing against her will. Taking a deep breath like she'd been told to do in the bi-weekly speed yoga class Jenna had forced her to join, she pushed the button above her head. The flight attendant, barely masking her frustration, informed her for the fourth time, that they would be taking off shortly.

"You said that an hour and a half ago." They glared at one another. Finally, the flight attendant pulled out a mini bottle of champagne and a magazine.

"I apologize for the wait Ma'am. We would like to offer you these, as a token of our appreciation for your patience."

The only thing Airika hated more than waiting was being called "ma'am." "Ma'am" was the word used to describe Victorian women of a certain age, not hipper-than-the-moment celebrity stylists, still young enough to hook the hottest guy in the room without batting an eyelash. This stewardess clearly wanted to piss her off.

"What about me?" Bifocal Guy asked.

"Here you are, sir." The flight attendant said, handing him his own mini bottle. She leaned in, whispering conspiratorially, just loud enough for Airika to overhear, "You can't smoke it now, obviously, but here, just for you." Bifocal guy took the cigar, pursing his lips around it, gumming one end, rotating it in his mouth as though preparing to light up in the middle of the cabin.

The sound repulsed her almost as much as the smell. Returning to her yoga breathing, she swigged the champagne and flipped open the magazine. She beamed with pride when she saw one of her clients in the "Who Wore it Best" section. The next page showed a variety of gowns worn to award shows and her newest young country pop star client made the "Best-Dressed" list. For the life of her, Airika couldn't remember why she didn't have a subscription to this magazine.

There was nothing like a little professional validation to distract her from the unpleasantness of her personal life. The man she had secretly loved all her adult life apparently despised her. Her own brother had left her to deal with their father and his latest legal drama on her own, again. And her best friend hadn't so much as texted her since the fight and was off "finding herself" in some middle-of-nowhere cabin. At least that's what Zach told her when she called to ask him to come to Florida with her.

It had been six years since she'd seen her father in person, until 24 hours ago when she had knocked on his glass windowed front door. The heavy Florida air choked the pleasantries out of her as quickly as it released the unruly nest of curls she so avidly straightened each day.

"Erica!" Her father exclaimed, pulling her into a bear hug, as though this were a happy social visit. She pushed out a hand and walked past him, taking in the modern glass living room with its uninterrupted ocean view.

"It's Airika now." She said, over-enunciating the "air." His face fell. She pretended not to notice. "So what do I have to do this time?" She said, walking toward the clear wall, keeping her distance.

"Can you stay long?" He asked.

"This isn't a family reunion. We're not hanging out. Ira summoned me," she said, looking around for her father's lawyer. "What did you do this time?"

"I ... I didn't do anything, sweetheart. It's just a misunderstanding. That's all."

"Mmhmm, aren't they all," she said, her eyes never meeting his.

"How have you been? How's Zachary?" He asked, changing the subject.

"Don't pretend you're the concerned father type. It's condescending. What, exactly, do I have to do?"

As if on cue, Ira Stearn entered the room wearing a white linen suit, complete with Panama hat. All he was missing were a few gold chains and a henchman. As the most notorious attorney for the rich and famous trying to circumvent scandals, this little piece of business was mere child's play.

Ira set a crisp white piece of paper on the table in front of her relaxing into a plush leather armchair. He puffed a cigar. She scanned the letter, knowing she'd sign it regardless of its content. It wasn't her first time. For an absent father, the doctor had quite the collection of character references from her. If someone were just to read through them they would think theirs was an idyllic relationship. His probation officer probably thought she worshiped the ground he walked on. This time was different. In exchange for her trust fund (which kept her moderately successful business afloat) she had to convince her star client not to press charges against her father, who was accused of botching the star's mother's boob job. "Why sixty year-old women feel the need to bother, is beyond me," she said to no one in particular. That was beside the point.

Normally these little ready-to-sign letters came in the mail with a check and she needn't bother herself with the particulars. This time, however, it directly interfered with her life and she couldn't stymie the flood of memories. And resentment. If it weren't for a lifetime of these scenarios, Airika would still have a mother. For all the dirt she had on these two schemers, they better stop treating her like a child begging for her allowance. If they didn't start paying her some respect ... well, she'd finish that threat if she really needed to.

Blackmail wasn't the most endearing quality in a father, but she couldn't afford to give up her birthright because of his transgressions. That was the word her mother used to use. It was a five-dollar word for "whores," of which there were many.

"You have my money?" She asked in a flat tone. Ira indicated the kitchen counter with a flick of his cigar. Her father sat, like a naughty child, with his hands flat on his thighs, eyes on the floor. He couldn't even bribe her himself, she mused, sliding the thick envelope into her purse. That's the kind of father he was.

The roar of the engine pulled her from her contemplation and, as the plane sped down the runway, her champagne rattled dangerously close to the edge of her tray. She caught it just in time to narrowly avoid ruining her favorite silk blouse. She couldn't be sure but she thought she saw the flight attendant smirk as she buckled herself in for takeoff.

"Airika, doll, last minute appearance booked in Seattle. Need a consult ASAP. There's a car waiting."

Airika deleted Simon's message as she breezed past baggage claim to the uniformed driver holding a card up that read "A. Thomas." She handed him her bag, not looking up from her phone. He mumbled something to her, which she ignored, getting into the backseat of the Town Car.

She spotted Alex immediately, sitting alone at a table outside a trendy looking restaurant. As she approached the table, she noticed his posture tense, which both saddened her and turned her on (as his muscles became more pronounced through his thin t-shirt).

"Hey," she said.

"Hey," he said, not looking up at her.

"Where's Simon?" She asked, looking around before pulling out a chair opposite Alex.

"On a call. He'll be right back."

They sat in complete silence for many minutes until she couldn't take it any longer.

"Look, I know you hate me," she started, studying him for any sign of it not being true. "And you have every right to." He raised his eyebrows in agreement, still studying his menu. "But the thing is, I'm sorry. I'm sorry that I put you in this position. I'm sorry that I hurt you. I'm sorry that I hurt Jenna." She could feel her hands shaking and she clenched them together to keep calm. Alex finally looked up from his menu. He sat back in his chair, not saying anything.

"I can see now that I misinterpreted things between us. I just thought … after that trip to Barcelona … that you … felt the same about me." She forced herself to say it, and now it was her turn to avoid looking at him. When he didn't respond, she added, "Because I love you. I always have. And I wish I didn't, but I do, and I just don't know how to stop." She felt her face get hot and her eyes begin to sting as she took a shaky breath to keep herself from crying. She hated girls who cried in front of guys.

"Jesus, Airika," he said, shaking his head. She looked up at him, imploring him to go on. "I don't know what to say to that. I had no idea that's how you felt. And I don't know what I did that made you think it was reciprocated. I just … I dunno." He grabbed his hair, leaving it messier than usual. "I wish you hadn't jumped me in front of my wife. I could've sympathized if you hadn't told her about us dating in high school. You knew I always loved her, even when you and I dated for that half a second. You did this," he sighed in resignation.

"I know. I fucked it all up," she said.

They sat in silence until Simon finally joined them at the table, launching into a wordy detailing of tomorrow's interview, which she couldn't help but tune out. She'd just begun to relax when she noticed the cameraman in the bushes with his lens trained on them. *How long had he been there?* She wondered.

Chapter 24

Jenna slammed the door behind her, hurling herself face down onto the bed without bothering to strip off her layers of clothing. She screamed into the pillow, punching the mattress over and over again like a toddler throwing a tantrum.

Lucky. She hated that word. The next person to call her "lucky" would ... suffer a mean glare while she couldn't come up with a decent retort. She couldn't even think clearly enough to come up with a fictitious comeback. What was wrong with her?

She should have seen it coming, in some form or other. Airika had always been manipulative and self-involved, but it was usually directed at someone else. She should have known the odds were in favor of it happening to her too. Alex was a different story. Nothing could have prepared her for his disregard for her and, more importantly, for Felicity's feelings. *Oh God, Felicity!*

Jenna never expected Mother-Of-The-Year awards. She'd screwed up her fair share on that front. You don't get pregnant in high school, give up your entire social life and status, and not take out at least some of that frustration on the baby that's been crying for two days straight, despite your best efforts. But the one thing she'd always been hyper-vigilant about was keeping her daughter well away from the gossipmongers.

Sure, in high school, *she* coasted on the rails of the nepotism train, before the days of celebrity kids being famous from birth onward. She got into clubs, always had the best of everything, and got a modeling agent before she'd ever auditioned. But all that was small potatoes in comparison to the temptations and traps of the celebrity culture today. Celebrities' *toddlers* now appeared on best and worst dressed lists, for pete's sake.

The thought of paparazzi stalking Felicity at school to find out about Alex and Airika made the little hairs on her neck stand on end. She picked up the cabin phone and dialed.

"Allo?" Airika's fake accent grated on Jenna's ears.

"Hello Airika."

"Jenna?"

A pregnant pause spread between them. Jenna felt the anger well inside, making her teeth chatter. She gripped the phone tighter and willed herself to sound calm and steady.

"I want to know why."

"Why what?"

"Why *my* husband? Why are there pictures of you two in the tabloids? Why were you on a hotel balcony with Alex first thing in the morning?"

Another silence. Jenna refused to cave first. *Do not make this easy for her*, she told herself.

"Look, I know this isn't the politically correct answer or whatever, but I love him. The Barcelona thing is crap. Alex saved me from a guy that got out of line and let me cool off in his room. Don't be mad at him for that." Airika said. "Nothing happened," she added, almost under her breath.

Jenna exhaled, her shoulders relaxing slightly. Her grip loosened infinitesimally on the phone.

"But you know Jenna, you're not the only one whose life changed when you got pregnant. We were dating. You two had broken up. He cheated on me, not you!" She said.

Jenna inhaled sharply. She was speechless.

"We didn't mean to hurt you, but not everything is about you." Airika said, sounding dejected.

Airika breathed on the other side of the line, waiting. Jenna had no retort. She had absolutely no idea what to say. The word "we" clanged incessantly inside her head, compounding her worst fears. Airika was right. Technically, they hadn't done anything wrong. Technically. Girl World operated under a different set of rules though, and there was no question those rules were obliterated. Even if Jenna believed Airika's sincerity, so what? She had no idea what it meant to be married. The sacrifices, the love, the compromises. And trust. Airika knew nothing about trust. It crossed her mind that she sacrificed her career for Alex, not Airika. She made those life-changing decisions and divisions of labor with him, not her. Maybe it wasn't fair to put so much of the blame on Airika, and yet logic and emotion rarely went together.

***

"Mom?"

"Is everything okay?" Anya asked.

"No." Jenna's voice wobbled. "There's an article out. It's bad."

Anya listened as Jenna told her about it. When she finished, Anya remained quiet.

"Mom? What should I tell Felicity?"

"What do *you* think you should tell her?" Anya asked.

Jenna sighed. "I want you to tell me what to do." Her voice sounded small and pathetic in her own ears.

"Only you can answer that." There was that obnoxious calm again. Jenna didn't want to admit that deep down she knew her mother was right. But she had no idea what to do. Until now, she'd been taking a breather from her marriage. With this article and the inevitable press storm, she'd have to make a decision.

"I'm coming home." Hands shaking, she hung up the phone and sank down into the couch, staring straight ahead at the blackened fireplace. The sky outside was a steely grey, the color of armor.

Despite the warmth of the cabin, goose bumps covered her flesh. Half of her wanted to crawl under the covers and wake up when the whole thing had been resolved—preferably by someone else's decision-making. If only there were a highlight reel for relationships like in sports. She'd like to know the game-changing points all at once, rather than being bombarded by them, one by one.

Unfortunately, the world of motherhood was never so simple. She couldn't even get proper self-pity time in before her mommy alarm went off. She took a deep breath, wiped the tears from the corners of her eyes where they threatened to break through the dam of her resolve. *No, hold it together!* For Felicity, she would.

The image of Alex and Airika sitting on that balcony, looking like a pair of happy lovers assaulted her again, twisting the knife in a little deeper.

***

"Hey." She said, answering the door, seeing Zach on her doorstep.

"How was it?" He asked, oblivious. It felt like a lifetime ago that she'd been so excited and inspired. *Was that only a few hours ago?* She plastered on a smile.

"Noelle was great. Thanks for getting me the job."

"You're leaving, aren't you?" He sounded sad. It took her off guard.

"How did you know?" She asked.

"Your tone. You've got the it's-not-you-it's-me voice," he said. She laughed and told him she did need to go home but that she planned to come back.

"You're a good mom," he said. She blushed from the compliment.

They stood in the entryway for a long moment before her inner hostess kicked in.

"Would you like to come in? Coffee?"

He nodded and followed her inside. She went to the kitchen to start the coffee while he headed toward the couch in the living room. She sat on the large armchair next to the couch and let out a sigh.

"Is everything else okay?" He asked, brows knitting together in concern.

"I don't know anymore. I just got off the phone with Airika."

"Oh?" He shifted uncomfortably in his seat.

"Yeah, I just wanted to know why she did it."

"Did what?"

"Kissed Alex!"

Zach was stunned into silence.

"She said she was in love with him and that *I* was selfish."

The coffee maker pinged and Zach sprung up to pour their coffee. Her teeth started chattering again and she fought to calm down, tears pricking the backs of her eyes.

He returned, handing her a steaming mug. He sat down, instantly taking a sip from his own. She didn't want to talk about it either. But when she caught him looking at the diary she left on the coffee table, she smiled, longing for the simple days of having crushes and worrying about brushing hands in a movie theatre.

"May I?" He asked, picking it up.

"Why not?"

She had a pretty good idea what part he must have gotten to when he looked up at her with his big brown eyes. Instead of feeling embarrassed, she felt amused.

"You didn't know I had a crush on you?" She asked.

"Um, no. I thought I annoyed you. Whenever I came into a room you stopped talking and found excuses to leave." He didn't take his eyes off her.

"I was just nervous and awkward." She laughed at the thought of herself as a tongue-tied teen.

"I liked you too," he said quietly, studying his mug.

Chapter 25

After Jenna hung up on her, Airika felt particularly vulnerable, certain she'd just destroyed her relationships with both Alex and Jenna. Her phone rang, still in her hand.

"What?"

"Um … how are you?" Meg said.

"I told you only to call if there was an emergency. So?"

"I … I just got a call from Martine's rep. Her mom … "

"What?" Airika demanded.

"She fired us."

Silence.

"I tried to ask why … " Meg sounded near tears. Airika hung up without response. She clenched her jaw so tight she felt it turning into a headache. This was her father's fault. *That philandering no-good bastard!*

She headed down to the hotel bar. She only knew one sure-fire way to calm down: she needed to get laid. Some people turned to drugs or alcohol. She turned to orgasms.

When she saw Simon sitting at the bar, she sighed. *Slim pickings.* She strutted over and tapped him on the shoulder. He smiled that lascivious smile of his. *He better be good.*

"What's doin' doll?"

"Wanna fuck?" She said, straight-faced.

***

"Alex! Hey, wait up." Airika called down the long hallway. He turned around.

"What's that?" He asked, pointing to the magazine she held out to him. Her chest heaved as she tried to catch her breath. The pained look on her face made his heart sink.

"For fuck's sake!" He threw the magazine on the floor, slamming open his hotel door. He sunk onto the bed, head in his hands. Airika stood in the doorway, unsure what to say. He collapsed onto his back, pulling at his gold and copper hair.

"If it makes you feel better, I already told her you didn't do anything wrong."

"You what? When did you?" he stuttered, eyes open wide in horror.

"She called me." Airika said, gazing at the floor.

"Where is she?" He couldn't keep the hurt out of his voice.

"Tahoe. Don't worry, she's fine. She's with Zach."

"What do you mean 'with Zach'?" He sneered, eyes flashing.

"I mean, they're both there and Zach has been checking up on her making sure she's okay," she said, frustrated at the reminder that her brother was more interested in attending to poor Jenna's hurt feelings that helping his sister sort out a legitimate family dilemma.

"She went to Tahoe? With Zach?" He asked, eyes glazing over.

"Yeah. You didn't know that?" Her lip twitched in the hint of a victorious smile. *Maybe Little Miss Perfect has secrets too.*

"I gotta go. Sound check." He sprung up, grabbed a jacket off the back of a chair, and left her to let herself out.

***

His hands trembled as he pulled on his jeans, looser now than a week ago. He tried to warm up his voice but it kept cracking, hitting off notes everywhere. He hated being the last to know Jenna's whereabouts, let alone the fact that she was spending time with another guy. The irony was not lost on him.

Thunk! Thunk! "Five minutes!" the stage manager shouted through the door.

He made his way out of his dressing room, winding through the backstage labyrinth to the stage. He transformed onstage as the spotlight warmed him and the crowd's thundering cheers spread across the stadium, feeding his soul, bearing his burden. "Hello Portland!" They cheered to his pandering, tingling in anticipation. He lingered for a suspenseful beat before counting in. "Two, three, four." He thrashed his head, signaling the band as the crowd whooped and whistled, feeling the kick of the drum, and the first few chords of the song they all recognized—their first big hit. On a great night, it was the better than sex (almost).

Chapter 26

Felicity flicked through a pile of index cards in front of her, spooning giant mounds of cereal in her mouth. She loved studying in the morning. In the quiet breakfast nook the chill of morning dew evaporated with the rising sun. The salty smell of the ocean wafted up carrying with it faint hints of citrus and freshly cut grass. It smelled like home.

The warm fuzzy feelings did not, however, extend to the homework assignment she'd been procrastinating working on. The vignette. "Ugh."

Eventually she knew she'd suck it up and ask for her grandmother's help, unwilling to ruin her 4.0 GPA. She just hated the idea of asking questions she might not want the answers to.

Since the beach party, she'd been stewing over what Sadie said about her parents. Sadie, Queen of the Rumors, wasn't big on petty things like fact checking to stop the spread of juicy gossip. Even so, Felicity couldn't shake the feeling that there might be truth in what she said.

"Morning," Anya said, pouring herself a cup of coffee. She set a grapefruit on a plate and joined Felicity at the table.

"Morning," Felicity smiled and watched her deftly cut the juicy pink fruit in half, exposing its pulpy flesh momentarily before covering it in a thin layer of sugar. Vaguely, Felicity wondered how many days of her life Anya had done that. Would it amount to years if they were all added up?

Routine was a funny thing. It could be comfortable and reassuring—a sign that the world was exactly as it should be. Or it could be banal and mundane and make you feel like the walls were inching closer and closer until they would eventually flatten you into nothingness.

"What are you studying?" Anya asked.

"Organic chemistry. We have a test today. And this teacher makes it impossible to get all the answers right. There's always some obscure question thrown in, just to spite us." Felicity said, folding her arms across her chest.

"Do you have to get a perfect grade?" Anya asked.

Felicity tensed. Her grandmother had a way of making things look like the obviously correct answer was absurd. She sighed in resignation, aware that they'd already had the you-have-to-do-a-hell-of-a-lot-more-than-get-straight-A's-to-get-into-Ivy-League-colleges talk. No one understood. And now, apart from wanting to get into an Ivy League school, her more pressing desire was to beat Sadie for valedictorian.

"Oh, I meant to ask you, I have to write a vignette about someone in my family and I was wondering if I could write it about you?"

"Of course. That sounds like a fascinating assignment." Anya's eyes twinkled, a broad smile stretching across her face.

***

The sun lingered above the horizon that afternoon as Anya and Felicity sat on the large wrap around deck, their faces golden in the afternoon light. Felicity pressed record on her iPhone, nodding to Anya to begin.

"When and where were you born?"

"I was born in 1944, in a small town in Arizona, that's now part of Phoenix. My parents were from Kansas, where they were farmers. The Arizona land was too dry for crops, so my dad did odd jobs to support us. My mom ran a preschool out of the house."

"You have a brother and a sister, how much older are they?" These were heinously boring questions, she admitted, but Felicity comforted herself in the safety of questions she already knew answers to.

"Actually, I have a brother, Colin, who's three years older, and *two* sisters."

"Two?" Felicity tilted her head in confusion. Anya nodded.

"You know Lory, she's two years older than me. My other sister, Jennifer, died when she was two months old. SIDS, I believe. She died nine months before I was born. My mother never recovered." Anya stared off, a faraway look in her eye. "I always felt she was half-ghost, flitting between the present and the after-life, checking on all four of us. She went through the motions but her eyes always gave her away. They'd glass over when she went to see Jennifer." She shook her head, bringing her attention to the present.

Stunned, Felicity's mouth hung open. This was the first she'd ever heard of Jennifer. Anya, never the typical milk-and-cookies grandmother, surprised her in lots of ways, but this was truly shocking. Anya's spiritual beliefs lay somewhere within a Pagan, Christian, Buddhist sandwich with a side of Atheism—not exactly mainstream. Felicity, spiritually undecided, wondered if she believed in ghosts.

"So is that why you named Mom, Jenna?"

"Yes. It was the nickname I used when I talked to my sister. Usually I spoke to her when Lory or Colin took my toys or told on me and got me in trouble."

"When did you meet Grandpa?"

"We met when we were seventeen. His father got a contract to work with an American company for a year and dragged the whole family with him. Shawn was a breath of fresh air. He was funny, sweet, and talented. Not at all like the boys I grew up with. I knew I wanted to marry him by the end of our first conversation." Anya's eyes drifted upwards, remembering herself as young girl.

"When did you get married?" Felicity asked.

"As soon as we graduated. We were eighteen. We eloped in Vegas against our parents' wishes. Mine disowned me, his were just disappointed."

"Your parents disowned you?" Felicity asked, stunned.

"My father said I was a 'silly stupid girl', hanging my hopes on a man who would end up a street performer, begging for money. My mother never crossed my father so she didn't say anything. I think she was proud of me getting out of there, though. She gave me this as a wedding present." Anya said, fingering the jade and gold pendant Felicity had never seen her without. She'd had no idea there was such a story behind it.

"So off we went to Hollywood. Two kids with one big dream. I've never known anyone so single-minded as your grandfather. He knew what he wanted and went for it, wholeheartedly. You have a lot of that same quality, I think." Felicity blushed, and let her grandmother continue.

"Within the year he got a record deal and signed me on as his manager so that I could tour with him. He put together the band, rehearsed till his fingers bled, and recorded their first album. The rest, as they say, is history." Anya took a sip of her lemonade, lost in nostalgia.

"We toured for two years straight, taking every gig, sleeping anywhere from motels to couches and floors and, even once, under a blanket in Golden Gate Park. At the time I thought it was so romantic. Now, of course, I know it was just plain stupid." She looked at Felicity as if daring her to try it. Then her face softened. "And completely unsustainable. After that, the band did another world tour—year and a half of sold-out performances—with hardly any days off. By the end they were exhausted. Everyone went their separate ways, and we went back to Australia. We had your mom and made the decision not to tour anymore."

"Do you have any regrets?" Felicity asked.

"No. No regrets. But it's funny how sometimes the things you wish for most are the ones that turn out to be furthest from what you want."

"Hmm," Felicity crinkled her brows. *Why would you wish for something you didn't want?* She wondered.

Chapter 27

In a hurry to protect her daughter from the prying eyes of the paparazzi, Jenna didn't bother to think about logistics. The gossip hounds were out for blood, circling the truth without actually seeing it. Jenna couldn't bear the thought of Felicity figuring it out on her own, or worse, reading about it once the reporters closed in. The time had come for a mother/daughter chat.

She stuffed a few things in a carry-on and took the first flight out, heading home. Her parents' home, that is. Her own home was still off limits. She wasn't ready for that yet.

She tossed the cab driver a hundred dollar bill as she stepped onto the familiar gravel drive. The cab took off, leaving her alone in front of the quiet house. The What If's knocked around in her head, upsetting her sure-footedness. *What if Felicity already knows? Alex would have told me before he said something to Felicity, right? And what if she's blissfully unaware and I pierce that bubble of innocence unnecessarily? Would she want to live with Alex if we split for good?* She shook her head to quell the deluge, feeling that familiar anger bubble to the surface mixed with a chest-gripping fear, and reeling at the unfairness of it all.

"Mom?" Felicity asked, staring at her like she'd grown two heads. Jenna stood in the driveway, arms inert at her sides. An overwhelming feeling of love and affection rushed over her, bringing to mind the image of holding her daughter for the first time. She squeezed her, smothering her in a giant bear hug.

When Felicity finally extricated herself, coughing, she opened and closed her mouth in confusion. Her brows furrowed as she inspected her mother.

"Where are you going?" Jenna asked realizing Felicity hadn't come outside to greet her. She watched Felicity's forehead wrinkle again, as she swiped her golden coppery hair off her face. She looked just like her father. The anger she felt toward Alex lessened slightly, seeing him in their beautiful daughter.

"School."

"Oh, right. What time is it? I can take you." Jenna said in a casual tone, as though it were perfectly normal to appear unannounced waiting alone in her parents' driveway.

"It's okay, Trey's picking me up." Felicity said, gauging her reaction.

As if on cue, Trey's bike grumbled up the drive, crunching gravel beneath the tires. He flicked the kickstand down with his foot as he dismounted.

"Hello Mrs. Anders," he said, holding a spare helmet in the crook of his arm.

"Hi Trey. That's nice of you to take Felicity to school."

"Um, yeah, not a problem," he said, then turning to Felicity, "You ready?"

Felicity gawked at her mother for another moment, then nodded and took the helmet.

"Bye, Mom."

"Bye, sweetheart. Have a good day! Drive safe!" Jenna called after them, elated to see her daughter safe and normal. Maybe she could stave off the inevitable a while longer. Her mom would know what to do.

Anya sat in the breakfast nook, sipping coffee, reading the paper. It was a painfully nostalgic sight, reverting her to childhood. No matter how old she got, she always felt like a little girl in her parents' house.

"Mom?"

Anya looked up over her coffee, nearly spilling it when she saw Jenna.

"I didn't know you were coming back today." Anya said, looking her over, worry written all over her softly wrinkled face. *Checking for what*, Jenna wondered, *boo boos*?

She smiled inwardly at the thought. A warm wave of affection washed over her again as she plopped down onto the chair opposite her mom. She took an orange out of the centerpiece, tossing it from one hand to the other like a hot potato. Her nerves dissipated and she nearly forgot why she'd come in the first place. Nearly.

Anya demonized tabloids the way most mothers do strangers offering a ride. It was forbidden to bring one into the house. What was it she said? Something about words having power and not reading them protecting you from malevolence. Jenna never remembered the exact wording, though she'd heard it often enough. The nerves reappeared as Jenna tried to formulate an excuse for having read one and now coming home to attempt damage control. Seeing it through her mom's eyes, it seemed silly. Maybe she was overreacting this time.

Anya waited, not touching the partially eaten grapefruit in front of her. Jenna looked up at her mother, noticing the gray roots of her hair, the slight stoop to her once perfect posture, and wondered how long she had until she saw that image reflected in the mirror. Sighing, she decided to start at the beginning. There were enough problems in her life because of omissions and she didn't have the energy to add to that list.

When she finished, she glanced up, making eye contact for the first time. Anya looked away and Jenna couldn't be sure, but she thought her mom's eyes looked watery. Anya never cried.

"So what is it you'd like to do?" Anya asked.

Good question, Jenna thought. "I want the facts. I want to know all the information and get to make up my mind, without anyone telling me how I feel or omitting details for my protection." It escaped her lips before she'd thought it, but hearing herself say it aloud, realized it was exactly what she wanted. Her worst fears had come true. But she was still here. She hadn't collapsed or spiraled down the drain of despair. She was taking things as they came—one thing at a time.

"What can I do?" Anya asked. Jenna was taken aback by

Anya's uncharacteristic response. She'd expected resistance or challenge and not having to explain herself, she felt relieved. Her mom on her side felt like an army.

***

It was already dark outside when Felicity returned after school and soccer practice. Shawn, Anya and Jenna moved about the kitchen, chopping, cooking, and laughing. Felicity was sure she'd stepped into the twilight zone. The earthy, mouth-watering smell of garlic in olive oil wafting through the house summoned her to this alternate universe and she clutched her stomach in hunger.

She spent all day trying to convince herself nothing was wrong, that her mom letting her on Trey's motorcycle was a fluke. She knew something was off, but the happy sounds of her family cooking together put a smile on her face. If this was an invasion of body snatchers, it seemed a good trade. She could go along with happy.

"Cici, can you help me set the table?" Jenna asked, grabbing cutlery and napkins.

"Sure, Mom." Felicity said. Jenna smiled, handed her a stack of plates, and kissed her daughter on the head.

After dinner, everyone sated and sleepy, Jenna and Felicity sat alone in the cozy comfort of the living room. They looked at each other from opposite ends of the couch, feet up.

Jenna shifted in her chair, an indecipherable emotion flitting across her face. Felicity sensed a change in the air, and straightened up slightly. The jovial mood pierced by tension. Jenna knew it would be hard, but her maternal strength drew upon a well of faith she never knew she had. She could do this, for her daughter and herself.

"Sweetheart, you know your dad and I had a fight … right?" Jenna started.

Felicity's heart sank. She didn't want to hear this.

"Well, I needed to take some time to think about things. Decide what the next step was."

Felicity remained quiet, staring at her feet.

"An article came out." Jenna said, her voice shaky. "I'm afraid that kids may ask you questions about it and I don't want this to affect you ... or your schoolwork."

Since when is she concerned with my schoolwork? Felicity thought, not appreciating the condescension.

"What's the 'it'?" Felicity asked.

"It's ... about your dad and me ... and rumors of him with someone else." Jenna looked down at her hands as she spoke. Felicity gulped.

"You and I can spend the rest of the semester up in Tahoe. You'll be able to stay under the radar. You can start school next week. It's all set." Jenna looked up, gauging Felicity's reaction with great interest.

Felicity shifted in her seat, staring at the floor.

"Do you want to ask me anything?" Jenna said, trying to decipher the twisted expression on Felicity's face. Felicity looked as though she'd seen a ghost. The color drained from her face as she glared into her mother's eyes.

"You have no idea what's best for me."

"Sweetheart, I'm just trying to protect you," Jenna said. Her calm demeanor created the opposite effect on Felicity. Her pale face turned red.

"You actually believe this is better for *me*? This is all about you! It's always been about you!"

Jenna recoiled as though slapped. Felicity never shouted at her. She hadn't expected her to take this change lightly, but she thought she could at least be rational. Felicity continued, unperturbed.

"You're the one afraid of being embarrassed. Not me! I'm not going with you. I'm staying here. At *my* school with *my* friends. I know you don't get it. You don't know how to think about anyone but yourself. *I'm* not going to let my teammates down. *I'm* going to keep my commitments. *I'm* going to get into an Ivy League college and I'm not going to repeat *your* mistakes!"

"I-" Jenna stuttered. *Is this how my own daughter sees me?* She couldn't muster a retort. She studied the face of the little girl who used to love having her back tickled to sleep, who couldn't go to bed until she'd said, "I love you." The face looking back at her now wasn't a toddler throwing a tantrum. She was a young woman. Jenna alternated feeling hurt by Felicity's words and proud she'd raised a confident daughter unafraid to stand up for herself.

Felicity pulled her legs into herself, arms crossed protectively in front of her. Jenna tried to put herself in Felicity's position. Was it fair to ask a sixteen year-old to give up her life, her friends, and her sports in order to spare her humiliation she couldn't yet comprehend? *No, probably not.*

Jenna was acquainted with humiliation and the last thing she wanted was for her daughter to be isolated the way she'd been. Her job was to protect her child. She couldn't always be a friend.

"I know you're angry. It's unfair. But it's not up to you. It's up to me. I already spoke to your school. And we can stay until this weekend, after your last game."

Jenna stood up, desperately wanting to pull her little girl into her arms and make the pain go away, but she knew she couldn't. "One day you'll understand." She stood and headed up the stairs, leaving Felicity to sulk on the couch.

Chapter 28

Alex opened groggy eyes, adjusting to the ethereal morning light streaming through the windows. He checked the time: 9:15am. *Shit! Shit!* He shot up out of bed. The bus was set to leave in fifteen minutes and he hadn't packed yet. The post-show adrenaline buzz turned Alex into a touring insomniac. Between staying up late after shows and making it to early on-air radio performances, he felt like he'd been run over by a truck.

Conveniently, he'd fallen asleep fully clothed so all he had to do was brush his teeth and hastily chuck clothes in his old suitcase. Jenna tried to buy him a new one before the tour, saying that he needed something more durable for all the traveling. "I've had this suitcase forever, and I love it. I don't need a new one," he'd said to her.

Struggling with the old zipper caught on a piece of fabric, he thought maybe he'd been too quick with his refusal. Finally, he coerced the cranky zipper to bypass the clothing and stick to the teeth. He sat on the closed bag, pulled out his phone and was about to check his seven messages when he inadvertently answered a call already in progress. Though he didn't hold it up to his ear right away, he could hear Simon shouting and could picture him, red-faced, chugging espresso, pacing up and down in the lobby.

"Well good morning, Sleeping Beauty." Simon said. Alex could practically hear the veins bulging in his forehead.

"Yeah, I know. I overslept," Alex said. He couldn't force himself to apologize. He didn't forgive Simon for putting him in this predicament with the label. Seeing him flustered was the best vindication he could hope for at the moment and he'd take what he could get.

"We were about to leave without you."

"Keep your pants on, mate. I'll be down when I'm ready," Alex said.

"Ditch the diva act and get your ass down here. We've got a month left and we both know you're not going to fuck this up. Not unless wifey's gonna foot the bill. Is that what you want?"

A pompous blowhard Simon may be, but even Alex couldn't say he was wrong. As he packed up the remaining toiletries and double-checked the room for odds and ends, Alex thought about how different things would be right now if he'd just asked more questions.

He'd known the money was too good to be true. He should have expected strings. There were always strings. He'd been gigging around the greater L.A. area for over a decade without a single legitimate offer, and been screwed by promoters, stage managers, bar owners and other bands countless times. His father-in-law's label even tried to bribe him with a deal to get Shawn out of retirement.

Alex prided himself on not accepting charity or anything he hadn't earned. Plenty of musicians thought he was stupid—that he should take any offer, soul be damned. *They* would. Others whispered he could afford not to care because he mooched off his wife's trust fund. It was the same with the haters in the blogosphere. That was the hardest part to swallow because Alex couldn't completely refute it.

The fact of the matter was Jenna's trust fund paid their bills. How was an eighteen-year old father supposed to support a wife and baby by playing punk music? They needed help and her parents offered. After Shawn and Anya established the trust and bought the house, it was easy to maintain the status quo. In the back of his mind, he knew he'd pay it all back as soon as he made it big. But making it took so much longer than he thought.

He only used the money he earned from music to purchase equipment, fund tours, or pay for miscellaneous costs, though. That was an important distinction in his eyes, one that the gossip-mongers didn't feel inclined to mention.

Despite his youth, he was a good father. He loved hanging out with Felicity, teaching her to ride her bike, to surf, to play soccer. He was mesmerized by her strength of will and capacity for empathy. She was smart and beautiful with a good head on her shoulders. What more could a father hope for?

And with Jenna, apart from this stupid misunderstanding with Airika, the marriage was great. The last year or so had been crazy with all the traveling and recording, but they had a strong foundation and he went out of his way to do little (and big) things to make sure she felt loved by him—like the anniversary plan.

With everything to lose, why didn't he ask more questions about this anonymous donor wanting to fund his career? The world was full of what-ifs and he'd go insane entertaining them all, but this one thing—this one decision—if he could take that back … he'd love to know how different it would have been.

That day last spring began innocuously enough—just another sunny, seventy-degree day in Los Angeles. He'd gone to Simon's office to discuss a possible band deal. Inside the glass and leather conference room, he sat at one end of a too large mahogany conference table.

"Frank, how does it look?" Alex looked to his attorney, Frank Fitzsimmons, sitting across from him.

"Apart from the handful of phrases I've flagged, it is quite standard. I think the terms of renegotiation should remain open, but Simon and I disagree on that," Frank said, sliding a pile of paperwork across to Alex with little red flags poking out of a handful of pages. Alex flipped through the pages but couldn't understand most of what it meant. He felt like no matter how thorough he tried to be, it didn't matter—he had to decide whether to roll the dice.

Everything was set. The only detail left was Alex signing on behalf of the band. Simon had raved about the anonymous donor, heavily insinuating that it was a wealthy fan, just interested in tying some of his taxable income into a passion project. It sounded so simple.

The biggest lesson Alex should have learned was that in the music business, nothing was simple. Deals were done, not by men in suits sitting in offices like this, but in bars and after-parties, casually over drinks. Smiles and sweet-talk covered up the cutthroat reality of a say-anything-to-get-ahead business mantra.

In the end, Alex signed his life (and, more importantly, copyrights) over to this new "label." He and his band headed straight to the studio, their wallets fat with signing bonuses, hope lightening their steps, propelling them to creative genius. The band was elated. At the time he couldn't have named it— that prickle of doubt—but he couldn't match their enthusiasm.

Things started out simple enough. They finished recording, with very little creative interference, but just before the album dropped, he got the first call. Simon said the donor had asked that they do him a "favor" by playing a few songs and emcee-ing a book signing. "Sure," Alex had said. "No big deal." It was a memoir by one of those famous-for-being-on-a-reality-show wives. Not his cup of tea, but who cared? He played his part—handing out prize packs of free Botox treatments, silicon add-ons, and other injectables to women who would have been more beautiful without them—then got his check and went on his way.

The second "favor" was an appearance in a foreign com-mercial. He was promised it would never air in the States. It was for a food company in the Netherlands. This "favor" was going to make him enough money not to think about it. But then he got there and realized the food product was a pair of edible boxers. "I'm not wearing those," he'd said. The director threw his hands up, shouting French obscenities at his assistant director. He turned on Alex. "Putain! I told them non! Ameri-cans—they always too prude. Pain in my ass!"

From there, the relationship between he and his label deteriorated quickly. He felt like a snitch trying to escape the mafia life. The words "family" and "loyalty" were batted around like they'd been pilfered from a *Sopranos* script. The analogy cropped up in Alex's mind enough times over the following months that he started to do some research of his own. He never would have believed his findings if he hadn't seen it with his own eyes.

Chapter 29

Jenna, Anya and Shawn sat in the cold metal bleachers, watching soccer balls fly back and forth while the two teams warmed up. Felicity might not be speaking to Jenna but she couldn't stop her cheering her daughter on at the championship game.

Jenna had never been a big sports buff and didn't know much about the game. Felicity played keeper, making her easy to find on the field. Jenna watched a dozen teenage girls line up, rocketing balls at the goal, toward her daughter, which Felicity easily punched away.

Felicity crouched, hands up, dancing on the balls of her feet, ready to pounce the second the ball left the ground. Jenna marveled at her fearlessness. She leapt through the air, arms outstretched, body parallel to the ground, without the faintest hesitation. Jenna imagined the bruises that must be blossoming beneath her uniform.

An hour and a half after the ref blew the starting whistle, the hard-fought regulation time in its dying seconds, the score nil-nil, everyone seemed to have crept to the very edge of their seats. Jenna could practically hear the crowd holding a single breath, waiting for their girls to score.

On both sides of the field, coaches paced up and down, pointing and shouting things she couldn't quite make out. Felicity too, barked orders, pointing to gaps between defenders. "Who's on six? Someone cover her!"

The visiting team arranged themselves into some sort of set play, as a girl raised her arm from the corner, took the kick, and there was a collective intake of breath as the home team's parents all prayed for the ball not to go in.

"Mine!" Felicity shouted.

The other team's star forward—the one who had taken

shots relentlessly the entire game—jumped up above the defenders and headed the ball toward the lower far post. Jenna thought for sure it was going in and wanted to cover her eyes. Her hands refused to cooperate and she watched in horror as the ball soared through the air with inhuman speed. Felicity too, was airborne, heading straight for the post. Jenna watched, horrorstruck, as her daughter's body slammed into the hard ground, bouncing slightly before striking the post with the back of her head. Jenna gasped.

Felicity knocked the ball off its trajectory and out of the way of the goal. The ball bounced, making contact with the striker's hand as she tried to settle it and the ref blew his whistle, signaling the end of the game.

Groans of disapproval issued up from the crowd as both sides shouted about handballs and fouls. Felicity picked herself up off the ground and stooped, hands on thighs, regaining her composure. Jenna stood up, wanting to check on her, but felt a strong arm gently restrain her.

"She'll be 'right. Tough as nails," her father said, eyes sparkling.

Jenna shook her head, depressing every maternal instinct in her body to stay seated. She watched as Felicity stretched and jumped, literally shaking it off. She reset for overtime. The ref blew the whistle and anxiety rippled through the bleachers once again, but this time Jenna wasn't paying attention.

She couldn't stop staring at Felicity. She was amazing. For the first time in her life, she saw Felicity as an individual, not just her daughter. There was a lot for her yet to learn, but she was more capable than Jenna gave her credit for.

As the ball soared beyond the other keeper's reach, the home side erupted in cheers. Jenna jumped up with them, not because they won, but because she knew now what she had to do.

***

Later that afternoon, after the post-game pizza party, the

four of them returned home. Shawn headed out to his studio and Anya took her cue, heading upstairs to her office. Jenna made hot tea as a peace offering, handing it to Felicity outside on the deck.

She took it as a good sign that Felicity accepted the tea, and they sat silently watching the sun dip below the watery horizon, illuminating the clouds in shades of citrus and fuchsia.

Jenna broke the silence first. "It's up to you if you want to come."

"Is this a trick? Or some kind of warped Freudian reverse psychology thing?"

"No." Jenna took a sip of tea to hide her smile. She chanced a quick look at Felicity's stunned face. "It is what it is. You were right."

"Wha-? Who are you?" Felicity said, swinging her legs around to face her mother. The furrowed brows that were like her father's crept up her forehead all the way to her golden hairline.

Jenna smiled openly, a full-on goofy grin. She took advantage of the silence to deliver the speech she'd been practicing in her head all afternoon.

"You were right when you said it was about me." She said, cocking her head to one side. "You were wrong in that I *was* trying to protect you." She looked sternly at her daughter. "But I have to realize that you're not a little girl anymore." For good measure (and the wide-eyed smile on Felicity's face), she added, "You're not quite an adult though, either." Felicity's face fell slightly.

"I'm so proud of the person you're becoming. You carry yourself with confidence and poise. Today I realized I want to take a page out of your book. I want to be the mom *you* can be proud of. And for me, that means I need to spend some time away." She watched Felicity carefully, waiting for her to argue, but Felicity stayed quiet.

"You're probably going to hear a lot of things said about

Dad and me at school. But I trust you to decide how to deal with it. So it's up to you if you stay here or come with me." She stood up, turning to the sliding glass doors. "I'm going to pack, so let me know what you decide. Okay?"

Jenna went inside, not waiting for a response. She couldn't help sneaking a peek out the window though. Felicity sat statue-still on the deck. Jenna smiled to herself, realizing she made the first step toward becoming the mom she'd always wanted to be. It only took sixteen years and her entire life crumbling down around her. In this moment, it seemed a small price to pay.

An hour later, the expected knock came at her door. Felicity entered, not waiting for permission. She stood there, her long frame leaning on the doorway, and looked Jenna straight in the eyes.

"I'm staying." She waited for Jenna to challenge her. "I have responsibilities here I don't want to shirk."

Jenna bit her lip to keep from laughing at the wording.

"But I'd like to visit you during my break, if that's okay?"

"Come here." Jenna nodded and opened her arms, wrapping Felicity up in a big hug.

Felicity nuzzled into her mother's chest, noticing it was a bit softer than usual, cozier. Then, like a baby, she cried. It took Jenna by surprise, but she petted her daughter's hair, kissing the top of her head. Jenna hoped these tears were cathartic—the start of a new relationship between them. But she couldn't help worrying what the kids at school were going to say. How bad would it get?

Chapter 30

According to Wikipedia, Jackson Jones, nee Alexander Deshevka, was born in Russia and immigrated to Las Vegas with his parents at age sixteen. Lead guitarist in a rock band with dreams of making it big, his life detoured when his father was deported after his employer—a Russian property company—was implicated in a crime ring in the Las Vegas area. Deshevka struggled to take care of his mother and younger brother, Ivan, but found that no one wanted to hire someone with ties to a Russian Bratva ("brotherhood").

He dropped out of high school, changed his name to Jackson Jones and entered the only industry indiscriminate enough to let him in: porn. His success in the adult film industry allowed him to buy his mother a house and offer his brother a job, securing his family's future.

He started Flesh, Inc., the first XXX business to successfully transition into the mainstream, albeit through unorthodox channels. Little was known for sure of their exact holdings, though their estimated wealth was in the billions.

Christian conservative groups had been outing them every chance they got, most notably connecting them to a very large donation given to the Haiti relief fund. The charity that took their donation was forced to refund it after receiving thousands of death threats and enduring a smear campaign indicting them as a "destroyer of family values."

Shit. Alex snapped his laptop shut. Pacing up and down the room, he looked out at the Space Needle and the lush Seattle skyline. From the hotel's tiny balcony—just wide enough to stand on with his feet twisted to one side, he could watch the ferries traverse the Puget Sound carrying tourists and commuters across the grey expanse.

What do I do now? He'd sensed something was off before the

European commercial debacle. The creative freedom he'd been given, the generous per diems, the four star hotels on tour. It had been too good to be true. An alarm, like the one that goes off in a parent's head when their child takes it upon themselves to take out the trash, blared in his head. He'd heard it and ignored it.

When Jenna found out his funding came from a porn mogul with Russian mafia ties, she'd leave him for sure. It would do more than exacerbate the precarious state of their marriage; it would humiliate her. She'd be dragged through a media firestorm—they'd eat up the family-man-turns-to-porn angle. He couldn't stand the idea of her face when she realized she'd put her faith in a loser. His father had warned him not to be selfish, to put his family first.

He hit his head with the heel of his hands remembering how many times Shawn encouraged him to check the money trail. *Why didn't I hold on to my publishing?* From famous to infamous: it would be a scandalous dream come true. Combine fame, porn and stupidity with a side of presumed infidelity? The tabloids would hang them all out to dry. Jenna's nightmare would become reality.

She supported every creative decision he'd made, telling him to "be true to yourself and you'll get there." He thought she was too idealistic, having seen how easy it was for Shawn. He made it big quickly, toured for a few years, then basically retired and got to spend time at home with her. Of course she thought it would all work out; she didn't know any better.

Alex didn't get that lucky. It hadn't been easy. He often wondered if he deluded himself. He hated almost everything he heard on the radio these days and used to think it was because he had better than average taste. Other people were like sheep listening to anything played on the radio. But after all that time of thinking differently, could he be sure it wasn't just him?

Not everyone "got" his work. But music was subjective,

and he had fans that got him. That meant something—to him, at least. He'd read somewhere that for every one fan he knew about there were 100 he didn't.

Maybe, after all this time, all these years of playing thankless gigs at bars, cafes, bookstores and restaurants, his lack of success had nothing to do with being "unlucky," as his father-in-law put it. Maybe it testified to his complete and utter lack of talent.

His desk at home was piled high with business cards and numbers scribbled on napkins from people who'd seen his show and told him to "Call me!" They promised to be just a step away from realizing his dreams. Over the years, he heard the same message over and over again. "Shawn Jax is your father-in-law? Why don't you just go on tour with him?" Then they'd ask for an autograph (Shawn's not his), never to be heard from again.

So when a privately-funded independent label with major distribution wanted to sign him, how could he turn them down? If he did, he'd be admitting he was talentless—his failure earned—and that he let his family down through nothing but his own ineptitude. He didn't see a choice. He wanted vindication for all the dues he'd paid. He wanted to know what the view was like from the top, as acquainted as he was with the sidelines.

He wouldn't let this stop him. He resolved to find a way out of this mess, and to do it before Shawn's Hall of Fame induction ceremony. Even if she still refused to take his calls, he knew he'd see Jenna there. And she would avoid making a scene, giving him his best shot to talk to her. If there was any hope he could reclaim his life and save his marriage, he had to extricate himself from Jackson Jones' grasp. His puppeteer now named, he boldly took his next step toward freedom.

Chapter 31

"You're back!" Noelle said, leading Jenna up the stairs to her photo studio. Jenna had come by to thank her for being so understanding about her abrupt departure, hoping she might still have a job.

"You picked a good day to come back," Noelle said. Jenna opened her mouth to say she hadn't expected to be back to work so soon and then quickly shut it, drinking in the most extravagant set she had ever seen.

The entire floor had transformed into a Lilliputian-sized Parisian café, complete with building façades, umbrellas, tables, and purse-sized dogs. Off set a barista, brought in to make cappuccinos and lattes for the army of set-dressers, hair stylists, make-up artists and models littering every corner of free space, took orders as the espresso machine frothed and foamed away.

"Here," Noelle handed Jenna an intimidating looking camera, weighed down by its massive lens. Before Jenna could protest, Noelle bounded off, animated as always, gesturing to a hair-stylist, hands above her head, miming bigger hair.

Jenna turned the camera over in her hands, feeling its heft, trying to decipher the foreign piece of infrared technology blinking at her from the hot-shoe. She looked through the wide-angle lens and clicked, just to see what popped up on screen. As she depressed the shutter, two bright lights flashed in her peripheral vision. The two main strobes, set up on opposite sides of the set, flashed and the image simultaneously showed on the back of the camera and on a large computer screen sitting atop the only non-French piece of furniture.

Noelle's desk—made from an old wooden door, its chipping paint of decades worth of color changes—was covered by a thin piece of glass. It stood in contrast to Noelle's otherwise modern taste.

Scanning the room, Jenna watched the organized chaos coming together to create a single image. From her modeling years she would have guessed it was an editorial fashion shoot. Emaciated models looked bored in their chairs as make-up and hair artists primped and prodded them. They looked so young—like kids playing an expensive version of dress up.

"*Vogue*." Noelle said, with a wave of her hand.

Jenna nearly jumped out of her skin. "Wha-?"

"It's a *Vogue* shoot. Spring. Paris. It's cliché, I know, but you win some, you lose some, right? I tried to argue Moscow in spring, but alas," she flicked a hand toward the edges of the room, the floor obscured by metal racks of clothing and shoes.

"They're tying it into the release of some movie based on a Hemingway novel." Noelle said, rolling her eyes.

"Who's the actress? Is she here?" Jenna's eyes darted around the room, landing on a familiar face.

"Natalie something-or-other. Brunette. Cute."

"Primm."

"That's it! Oh, what are they doing now?" Noelle said. She bounded off, shouting something in French at someone near the wall of shoes. Jenna couldn't believe it. She had stumbled into the middle of a photo shoot for *Vogue*!

She recalled her long-ago dream of someday appearing on the cover of the infamous September issue. Though she hadn't kept up with the fashion world (except what Airika told her) she knew *Vogue* still represented the cream of the fashion crop.

She had underestimated Noelle. She made a mental note to Google her later. As she stood, quietly taking in the bustling scene around her, goose bumps erupted all over her body. Since childhood, she'd used what she called her "goose bump meter" as the physical manifestation of her intuition patting her back, telling her she made the right decision. She hadn't had goose bumps in forever, it seemed.

The shoot flew by in a whirl of creativity and heightened tension between strong personalities that were diffused time and again by Noelle's strong direction. Jenna watched, awed, as Noelle gave orders, not intimidated by anyone's title or tone. She executed her vision with unwavering confidence.

As Natalie modeled the gown, they encountered a problem. She was too short, even with heels, for the gown to skim the floor like Noelle wanted. The hem was too intricate to pin without sacrificing design. A vein in Noelle's forehead pulsed in frustration.

"What if we had her jump off the curb next to the cafe?" A stylist suggested. Noelle glared.

"Why don't we give her an umbrella and call it Avedon?" Noelle said through gritted teeth.

Silence settled over the set as they awaited further instruction. No one dared speak.

"What if we used the café chairs?" Jenna said. "We could have two guys behind her balancing the chairs, with the train draping over the front and have her feet spread apart on opposite chairs?"

A stunned crowd waited with baited breath for Noelle's wrath. Everyone stayed quiet, shifting their feet, awaiting instructions. Jenna was oblivious to the tension, trying to picture exactly how the angles and shadows would work.

"Let's try it." Noelle said, gesturing to two of the larger guys in the group. "You and you. Pull those chairs over and hold onto them as if your lives depend on it."

They snapped to attention and did as they were told. A flurry of activity followed as everyone reset for the new direction. Jenna stayed where she was. Noelle came over to her side.

"What are you doing?" Noelle asked.

"Nothing. I mean, just waiting for you to tell me what you want me to do." Jenna said, flustered by the commotion.

"Take the shot."

"What?" Jenna said. She must have misheard.

"It's your vision. You see it. You take it. Tell them what you need." Noelle gestured to the myriad assistants and stylists scattered around the room. Terror crept in, a cold sweat replacing the goose bumps.

"I'll be over your shoulder, making sure it works." Noelle placed a hand on her shoulder.

After a few moments of procrastination, Jenna held the camera up to her eye, trying to frame the shot. She heard herself direct people around the set, moving lights, adjusting angles. Even Natalie Primm was listening to her direction, adjusting accordingly. Jenna couldn't believe it. These people took her seriously.

She clicked the first frame and watched Noelle's face relax as she saw the image appear onscreen. She approved. She made a few suggestions along the way, but let Jenna take the reins. When Noelle saw exactly what she wanted, she pulled Jenna over to show her.

"See this angle on the chair?" Noelle asked. Jenna nodded. "See how her other arm goes in the opposite direction? And how the dress flows over the edge of the chair rather than just draping along it like in this one?" She pointed out another shot where the angle of the chair seat was visible through the dress fabric.

"Mmmhmm," Jenna nodded.

"That's the shot," Noelle smiled. Jenna's throat closed over happy tears.

Noelle yelled, "That's a wrap!" and the room burst into applause and happy chatter. Champagne flowed and hors d'oeuvres circulated, even passing the lips of a few of the more ravenous models.

"I've never done anything like that. It was ... amazing. Thank you."

"It's nothing," Noelle said, waving it off. "All I did was hand you a camera."

"No one's ever listened to me like that. I've never been so in charge."

"So? You in, then?"

"In what?" Jenna asked. Noelle raised her brows, in a do-I-have-to-spell-it-out expression.

"Yes, I'm in." Jenna grinned. *Jenna Jax-Anders: Photographer.* It had a nice ring to it, she thought.

Noelle smiled triumphantly and slapped her on the back. "Come," she said, dragging Jenna around, introducing her to everyone, whispering tidbits of gossip about each one. The glad handing gave way to evening and, by the time the set was dismantled, only Jenna and Noelle remained in the cavernous space, hunched over the odd desk, reviewing images.

Chapter 32

Another day, another city. Alex disembarked the rolling metal cage that transported him across the country. His neck, stiff from sleeping in the tiny bunk that was two inches too short for his long frame, cracked and popped as he twisted his head from side to side. He was grateful that his time on the bus this tour was limited, but it didn't help his mood this morning.

"You coming?" Asked Pete, his twenty-something drummer, slapping him on the back.

"I'm starving!" Bellowed Joe, the large Texan bass ingénue they recruited out of high school.

"Yeah, be there in a sec." Alex said, checking his phone for missed messages. None. He looked up at the truck-stop diner reeking of day-old grease at seven in the morning. The word "glamor" didn't exactly pop to mind.

The second bus pulled into the oversized parking lot, spilling hungry roadies into the diner. They moved in groups, talking and laughing. He'd never felt so alone amidst so many people.

He slid in beside Joe on the vinyl booth seat, and took a sip of the coffee in front of him. It tasted bitter, burnt. His face twisted in disgust. No amount of sugar could cut through the acrid flavor. He drained it in a single gulp. Joe and Pete bantered across the table but Alex didn't hear a word they said. The next stage in his battle for freedom was about to begin. He just had to figure out where to start.

Simon sidled up to their table, handing out sheets of paper with names and times written out. Every day he gave them a schedule and every day everything got done without ever adhering to the stupid thing.

"Did you hear me, mate?" Simon said in his best effort at a friendly tone.

"Sorry, no. Say again?" Alex said without looking up at him.

"You've got an in-station appearance in an hour and then I need you to call the other stations on your list and record station ID's. Keep it light. Keep it clean."

Alex nodded. *I know what I'm doing!* He wanted to shout. He yearned for the days of his hard-edged immigrant father lecturing him about applying himself in his work. "The most important thing", his father used to say, was to "take care of your family".

His father, a man's man by any account, spent years drilling the message of one's own hard labor being the only sure thing in this world into his son's young brain. He put his calloused builder's hands on Alex's shoulder, lecturing him.

"I work hard day after day to feed my family, and you will too. You do whatever you need to do. You understand?"

Alex's creative ambition clashed with everything his father stood for. He made it clear that Alex had disappointed his family and himself by pursuing a selfish career of "chasing fame". He frowned upon the frivolity he associated with creativity. Alex despised his father's cave-man attitude and denigration of the arts.

On Alex's wedding day, his father asked him what he planned to do now with a baby on the way. He told his father he was still pursuing a career as a musician. His father walked away, shaking his head. Alex hadn't seen him since. He'd never even met his granddaughter.

Alex excused himself from the table. He flipped open his phone, dialing the first number on his list.

"Hi, Alex Anders here and you're listening to KTKS, *your* station for yesterday's hits and today's favorites."

Was this success? Pitching sales for companies, traveling with a bunch of hygiene-challenged guys, glad-handing people with impressive job titles, left finding out about his own family through reporters who were more up-to-date? For the first time in his life, he felt like he'd sold out.

Chapter 33

"So? You gonna tell me what happened?" Noelle said.

Jenna squirmed. She wanted to run, to protest, but she was rooted to the spot under the weight of Noelle's gaze. And touched, too, by her concern.

"Where do I begin?" Jenna sighed.

"At the beginning." Noelle placed her small hand over Jenna's.

"I guess it started when we were kids." Tears fell as Jenna spoke, though her voice remained steady. She talked and talked, reliving the wretched sight of her husband and best friend kissing in her living room. When she got to the part about the article and her conversation with Airika, she slowed down.

"I snapped. I think I just … " she said, searching for the right word, "had enough. I don't know, maybe I overreacted. He didn't cheat on me, exactly. And I knew somewhere deep down that Airika had feelings for him. I ignored it. I guess I hoped it would just go away. I didn't expect to feel so … gullible." Jenna looked up, imploring Noelle to tread gently on her exposed soul.

"Did I ever tell you the story about how I came to America?"

"No," Jenna said, confused. They'd only had a handful of conversations, all work-related. And not to be selfish, but did she not hear the story Jenna just told her?

"The short version is: I ran away from my marriage."

"Really? Why?" Jenna couldn't help herself. She was nosy.

"He was a duke. You know, typical uptight royal upbringing. Private schools, polo star. He was the smartest man I'd ever met. The usual story. He swept me off my feet and when he asked me to marry him, I was sure my life had been made." Noelle sighed, her features softening, making her look younger.

"He wined and dined and romanced me until I suffocated from the stench of roses. My life—my being—became a dance of royal obligations broken up only by family obligations. My education, hobbies, interests and friends were relegated to the realm of trifles, to be entertained only when bored." Noelle mimicked a stuffy royal with a prim jut of her chin. "I was never bored. When you turn your back on your friends often enough, they stop calling. I couldn't blame them." Her eyes flashed from anger to sadness.

"So what did you do?" Jenna scooted forward on the chair, rapt.

"I did what women do. I suppressed my feelings and got pregnant."

"I didn't know you had kids." Jenna blurted. Noelle's eyes glassed over, like she was somewhere else. Jenna regretted saying anything.

"I don't. It turned out to be a tumor. I was told I had mere weeks to live. My husband wasn't equipped to give the emotional support I needed, so I called my friends. They tried to understand. But they didn't know what to say either. Too much distance lay between us and I couldn't muster the energy to bridge the gap."

"So what happened? I can't imagine … "

"It was a long time ago." From the look on Noelle's face, Jenna wondered if time had softened the grief.

"Anyway, I realized I was alone. And I decided if I was going to be alone, I better do something I loved with the time I had left. When weeks turned into months and I seemed to be improving on my own, the doctors were stunned. They called it a miracle. I knew, deep in my heart of hearts, it was a sign I needed to get out of that life and start fresh. So I took a job as a nanny for a family emigrating to America, and voilà, here I am."

"How did you get into photography?"

"In university, I'd taken a few courses and amassed a portfolio of portraits of my classmates. Hanging out, playing polo, some studio poses. Later, when many became important figures in the world—as children from prominent families do—my little student portfolio looked more important. I got a job assisting a fashion photographer in New York and one thing led to another."

"You make it sound so simple." Jenna said.

Noelle smirked. "Things sound simple when years of struggle are whittled down to a paragraph. Nothing worth anything is simple."

***

Jenna returned to the cabin late, still absorbing the day. Noelle's story reverberated in her head and heart as she thought about how brave she'd been. Jenna breathed in the pine of the walls. She took in the view, the moon sparkling upon the dark water. Then she picked up the phone and dialed without thinking.

"Hello?" The sound of Airika's voice pierced Jenna's softened heart. In equal parts, she wanted to talk to her best friend—to tell her about the *Vogue* shoot and Noelle—and also, if at all possible, cause bodily harm through her venomous rhetoric. Instead, she hung up.

Her heart clenched as though in a vice-grip. Her fingers itched to make another call, but her earlier bravado dissipated, giving way to sadness and self-pity. Bravery sounded so clear the way Noelle told it, uncomplicated.

Left to her own devices, Jenna couldn't mask the pain. Betrayed by her two best friends together felt like the universe kicking her in the gut and then disemboweling her for fun. If she believed in reincarnation, she'd have been certain she'd been a puppy-kicking, mass-murdering bigot.

She needed some air. From the driveway she looked up into the clear night sky, dazzled by the myriad stars, made more ethereal with her breath. Puffs of freezing smoke drifted across her vision. She walked to the end of the driveway to get a better look. She tripped over a box, falling to the ground with all the grace of a hippo on ice.

Sharp pain forced a scream from her lungs. She looked around, embarrassed. No one saw her fall. Suddenly she began to giggle. She giggled at her clumsiness. She laughed at herself being more concerned that someone saw her make a fool of herself than her own pain. She guffawed at the absurdity of the whole scene, of her life, of being in this place. She laughed until her cheeks were covered in frozen tears and her sides hurt.

Then she picked up the box. The label, written in familiar handwriting read: *It's time. -Zach.* Back inside the cabin, she opened it, revealing a brand new cell phone. She smiled, turning it over in her hand. He attached a case with a picture of a vintage camera and a packet of sticky crystals for her bedazzling pleasure. The card inside said:

Jenna,

> You've come a long way and now you're ready to make it back to the 21st century. Anya helped get your old number back. Hope you like the case. I couldn't bring myself to put those pink crystals on, but I know you love them.

Zach

She beamed. Like a kid on Christmas morning, she ripped through the packaging, assembling her new toy. The screen lit up as it came to life, informing her that her mailbox was full. She figured now was as good a time as any to clean it up. Since she wasn't ready to be on speaking terms with either Airika or Alex, she could at least hear their messages groveling for forgiveness.

Twenty minutes later, her smile faded, a dark cloud forming over her head. At least half the messages were from Anya or Felicity, usually hanging up quickly, remembering to call her at the cabin. The other half was from Alex. Most from the first day, asking her to talk to him, to hear him out. Later, they got more desperate and pathetic. The last couple didn't even sound like him. Part of her wanted to call and check on him, make sure he was okay. That made up the smaller part and she opted to let him suffer a little longer.

She was in no mood to soothe anyone. Airika hadn't called or texted at all. Not one message in two weeks. They used to speak at least twice a day. The longest they'd ever gone without each other was maybe a day or two. But even then, they usually emailed.

Her best friend hadn't so much as called, let alone apologized. *Bitch!* The only conclusion she could draw from that was even worse than what Airika did with Alex. Jenna realized, with a sinking heart, that if Airika wasn't talking to her, she was talking to someone else. Jenna had been replaced. As the thought settled in for the long haul, Jenna's mood plummeted. *Did my friendship really mean that little to her?*

All those sleepovers, the lemonade stands they'd run together, the partying and getting into clubs with their bad fake ID's, the endless talks about boys and clothes—had it been one-sided? She'd been a generic celebutante friend, a seat filler, no one special, except that she had a dreamy husband.

The truth of it shook her to the core. It was so clear. Occam's razor. Her legs felt like jelly. The couch swallowed her up as her life flashed before her eyes, like a person on the brink of death. But instead of the memories she thought she had, they flashed before her, rewinding the best friend parts, replacing them with images of her mortal enemy. How could she have been so stupid?

Chapter 34

Jenna awoke still feeling wound up. She thrashed around in bed for a while, to no avail. Thunk! She looked over the edge to see what fell. It was a frame she hadn't noticed before, an old photo of Alex and Zach on either side of her, sandwiching her. She set it face down on the nightstand.

Something else caught her eye in the open suitcase. *No*, she thought. But she needed an outlet, and she hadn't even worked out since she'd been in Tahoe. *It's not like I'm getting it anywhere else*, she thought, pulling The Rabbit out of the bag.

As she leaned into her pillows, starting to relax and enjoy herself, Alex's head popped in her mind. She didn't want to kill her momentum so she tried to focus, to think of something else to keep her in the mood. Zach's face appeared in her mind's eye, she envisioned his chest, wet and naked, like that summer. The memories turned into moving images in her head, as she mentally lived out her younger self's fantasy. He was so hot—strong and sensitive to her needs at the same time. Soon she felt herself heating up, getting close.

It took a minute for the sound of her new phone's ring to register. She picked up too late and voicemail got it first. She chucked it on the bed and tried to regain her happy fantasy.

"Jenna? You home?" Zach called.

Startled, she shot up out of bed, Rabbit falling to the floor, the sound of the vibration getting louder. She tried to find a shirt to throw on so he didn't burst in on her, naked. "Just a sec." She said, frantic to stop the damn thing. *Where is the off button?*

"I tried to call first," he said, getting closer to her bedroom door.

Running out of time, Jenna threw the convulsing creature at the hardwood floor with all her strength. It had a mind of its own, flopping around on the boards. The cruelty of being robbed of an orgasm by the threat of being humiliated sapped her ability to think straight.

She heard Zach just outside the door certain he could hear the taunting buzz. Before she realized what she was doing, it was silent. Bludgeoned to death by stiletto. Like a deranged, blue-balled Elmer Fudd, she had killed The Rabbit.

"You okay?" Zach turned the doorknob and she kicked The Rabbit under the bed, just in time. He poked his head in her room, frowning at the stiletto still in her hand. She looked at it, and shrugged. "Spider," she said.

She stood up and pulled the edges of her sleep shirt down with one hand while smoothing her out of control hair with the other. She suddenly felt light-headed and saw stars. Zach reached out to steady her. She took a deep breath and looked up at him. He took an appraising look and grinned.

"You wanna get some breakfast?" Zach said, smiling.

"Sure. Give me a minute to change and ... do my hair."

"Watch out for those spiders," he said, turning to head back to the living room.

She watched him go, trying not to pay attention to the way his shoulders filled his shirt or how touchable his curls looked. She definitely wasn't picturing the rest of him naked beneath those clothes.

What's wrong with me? She chided herself in the mirror, her flushed cheeks making her normally pale skin look even paler. Her blue eyes had a glassy look to them and her hair ... what to do with that rat's nest? She didn't want to take the time to flat iron her now kinky curls so she brushed and braided it, then added a beanie, for good measure.

She looked out at the platinum colored sky, threatening snow. She threw on some (mostly) clean clothes and took one more deep breath.

Zach was uncharacteristically chatty on the drive to the restaurant. He grilled her about Noelle, photography, asked if she'd gone skiing yet. She found his enthusiasm infectious and soon her mood, like the clouds, parted, revealing a beautiful day.

Their conversation was easy, relaxing. He told her about his latest project, the difficulties of shooting videos in the back-country where the weather was volatile and equipment failures ruin entire weeks' work. Despite his venting, it was obvious how much he loved what he did. At the restaurant, she asked him questions and he answered, illustrating points with his hands, occasionally jumping up from his seat to clarify or demonstrate. She laughed and lapped up Noelle's praise, delivered via Zach in the same manner.

Two hours later, full and happy, they drove back to the cabin.

"Coffee?" she asked.

"Sure."

As they sat down on the couch the atmosphere shifted. She became hyper-aware of his proximity, his smell, shampoo and laundry detergent, and wondered if the shift was in her head or not. She got up to make coffee. She raised her eyebrows, lifting a mug in his direction. He nodded.

"Sugar?"

"Yes, Love?" He said, affecting a terrible British accent. She rolled her eyes. "Looks like you're a popular lass. A message awaits your ladyship." He said, pointing to her new phone, vibrating on the coffee table.

She traded him his coffee for her phone, enjoying the flirta-tious banter, and sucked in a breath when his hands grazed hers in the exchange. She clicked the voicemail button to distract herself.

"What's the matter?" He asked, losing the accent.

"It's not important," she lied.

They drank their coffee in silence. Finally, Zach jumped up and held up one finger. He ran outside and she heard his car door open and shut. He came back inside waving a DVD.

"Yours?" she asked. She wanted to see the film he'd told her so much about, but dreaded the idea of hating it and having to figure out what to say.

He nodded. She grabbed it from him and popped it in the DVD player. They settled onto the couch, sitting just a little closer than was absolutely necessary. Or maybe that was her imagination.

The opening credits rolled over a montage of skiers hucking themselves off impossibly steep cliffs, tumbling down the mountain in a series of painful-looking crashes. An adrenaline-inducing rock song played over the top, one she didn't recognize.

"Who is this?" She asked.

"Me."

"No. The song."

"Me," he said.

"It's good." She paid closer attention to the hip-hop kicks layered with electric guitars with just the right amount of distortion: enough to avoid being douche-rock, but not so much to make it indecipherable noise. He smiled at the backhanded compliment, happy she liked it.

She watched intently, listening to skiers talk about waiting for snow and chasing the weather around the world on an endless search for the perfect run. She chanced a glance or two at Zach, looking away when he caught her.

She was struck by their passion. It was inspiring, how much fun they had, making the best of every situation, whether or not conditions cooperated. She envied their ability to enjoy life when things didn't go their way.

Not a skier herself, and not having spent much time watching extreme sports films, she was awed by how far these athletes were willing to go. They jumped out of helicopters, hiked up mountains with heavy gear, waited out storms, built jumps, and still managed to find new and interesting angles to capture their gravity-defying feats. By the end, she'd forgotten her earlier skepticism and said, without hesitation, "Amazing."

"You think?" he smiled, and she could have sworn he blushed beneath his stubble.

"Definitely," she said, nudging his shoulder with hers.

He turned to her, smiling, and leaned into her shoulder so that their upper arms were pressed flush against each other. She felt the warmth of his skin, and his forearm hairs tickled her skin where she'd rolled up her sleeves when she made coffee. Her pulse quickened and she felt nervous, not sure whether she wanted something to happen or dreaded it.

"Can I ask you something?" he asked, his face inches from hers.

"Of course," she breathed.

"Did you get the postcard I sent you? That summer you went to Europe?"

The handwriting! She knew it was familiar. But … that postcard was from Alex. It was his way of saying he wasn't over her. If she'd been wrong about that, then Airika had been telling the truth. As deluded as she was, she'd thought Alex and Jenna were broken up and she took her shot. They were together. The only reason he chose Jenna was that she got pregnant.

Her righteous indignation returned and as the what-ifs pummeled her, she suddenly wondered why Zach wrote to her.

"That was you?" she asked. He nodded. "Why?"

"I liked you." He said it as though it were the simplest thing in the world. And she supposed it was. She looked up at him, his eyes wide, earnest. She didn't know what to say. She gazed at him and felt the earlier excitement flood her bloodstream, igniting latent feelings she didn't know she'd suppressed. He leaned in, resting his forehead on hers, their noses touching. Her chest heaved, unable to normalize her breathing. She closed her eyes, savoring the feeling. She'd married her first boyfriend but she felt a pang of nostalgia for a life she could have led.

What would her life have been like if she'd chosen Zach? *You could find out now*, a voice said. She looked up into his brown eyes, and saw her desire reflected in them. Before she could stop herself, she kissed him—a soft kiss, with a closed mouth, lingering just longer than could be considered European.

She pulled away and the electric atmosphere changed again. Her body tingled with desire and excitement, her nerve endings over-sensitized. He stayed where he was, his interest evident, but he didn't make another move. Then, like a bolt of lightning, it hit her.

"Did you know? About Alex and Airika?"

"Yes."

Instantly she pulled away from him. Her mind reeled. *He knew! He knew and he didn't tell me!* Everyone claimed to care about her, to worry about her feelings, but not one of them thought she had a right to know what was going on. "Argh!" A primeval scream escaped her lungs and she grabbed her hair with both hands.

Zach's phone rang. He glanced at her and then at it, and seemed to decide she needed a minute. He answered it, excusing himself outside. As soon as the door closed, she started mentally listing all the ways she'd been wronged. All the ways they'd betrayed her. All the things that hadn't gone right.

So what? An annoying little voice in her head interrupted. *Excuse me?* She replied (surely, talking to herself wasn't a huge worry at this point). *What part did you play in it not working out?* This voice was really starting to piss her off.

It had a point, though. She could have asked more questions. She could have asked Alex what made him change his mind, what he'd done all summer. She could have confronted Airika when she'd acted weird or bitchy when she talked about Alex. And she could have told Alex she wanted to work. She could have done a lot of things.

But what had she done instead? She got mad and ran off.

Her train of thought drifted as she saw the time she'd been spending with Zach through Alex's eyes. He wouldn't have liked it. She hated the idea of him having the level of desire she'd just been feeling for someone else. *Oh God, I'm married!*

She'd had no trouble hanging on to the anger she felt for Alex and Airika, but in mere weeks, she'd been able to behave as if she was a single twenty something just enjoying herself and spending time with an old crush. She ran a mental inventory of all the breakfasts and talks and heart to hearts she'd had with Zach that, if Alex had been able to see them, would have been unacceptable.

Zach came back inside, lurking in the entryway. Jenna stood up, ready to apologize. Something in his demeanor stopped her.

"Everything okay?" she asked.

"Yeah. But you need to talk to Alex," he said, not looking at her.

"Why? Was that him? What did he say?"

"No. It was Airika. She said he's a mess and he needs to talk to you. He's your husband, Jenna. You should call him." He looked up at her, his jaw clenched. She couldn't tell what he was thinking. He was acting like nothing had happened between them.

She felt sufficiently shamed by her revelation, but the fact that Airika was telling her to call *her* husband ignited a fury that surpassed embarrassment. And why was Zach passing along her messages?

"No offense, but it's none of your business whether or not I talk to my husband."

"You're right. It's not. But I'm trying to be your friend. And as your friend, I think *I* should go and *you* should talk to Alex." He snatched his jacket from the couch, fists clenched at his sides. He took a deep breath and looked up at her. "We all made our choices, Jenna. There are always consequences." He looked like he was going to say something more, but decided against it. He turned and walked out, leaving her alone and reeling, more confused than ever.

Chapter 35

Jenna wanted to talk to someone—someone she could vent to who would hear her out, and offer sound unbiased advice. She ran through a mental friend checklist.

There was Stephanie Schroeder, but they stopped being friends in fourth grade when Stephanie moved to another school district. Jenna wanted to keep in touch, but Airika convinced her Stephanie would have been too busy with all her new friends. At the time, Jenna was devastated. Now, she felt Airika's knife twist a little deeper in her back.

There was Maggie Day, the other girl that got knocked up in high school. They'd had Lamaze together and took a class to prep them for motherhood. It was one of those classes meant to prepare you for the world of parenting and the difficulties you were about to face. It was mostly Reverse Birth Control: all fear inducing and wouldn't-it-have-been-smarter-to-just-use-a-condom talks. Genius.

At the time, Maggie and Jenna laughed at the ridiculous stories and compared notes as to why their lives would never be as pathetic as the guest speakers' were.

After Maggie's baby daddy left her to take care of the other girl he'd gotten pregnant a few months before the birth, they'd drifted apart. It got awkward to hang out because Jenna felt guilty about how great things turned out for her. She thought of how difficult it must have been for Maggie all those years ago. A pang of guilt ripped through her. She made a mental note to try to find Maggie and catch up with her again. Maybe all these years later it would be fun.

As Jenna continued to run through her mental friend list she realized the rest belonged to one of two categories: Airika's friends or Alex's friends. She couldn't think of anyone after high school that was just *her* friend. She'd taken for granted that she had a best friend and a husband. She hadn't needed to go looking for friends.

Suddenly, a name popped into her head. It surprised her, but Noelle was the closest thing to a real friend she had right now and maybe the only one able to give some much-needed perspective. And, though their last conversation was odd, she knew Noelle wouldn't sugarcoat her opinion.

Chapter 36

Most mornings Noelle took her coffee out on the deck. She'd worked hard to achieve autonomy in the world—a word she ranked higher than equality—and she chose to enjoy it. She preferred knowing she could take care of herself. She'd fought a tough battle to learn that lesson, and she respected it.

After 32 years with George they still lived next door to one another, rather than together. They chose not to marry and enjoyed a closeness of proximity, both geographic and emotional. They called on each other often without enduring the banality of picking out furniture or decorating to satisfy both their tastes, which really, was code for hating it equally.

They could say "good morning" and enjoy their ritual of reading the paper—hers the Herald Tribune, a habit picked up in Europe, his The New York Times—without the hassle of morning breath.

They read through the local paper once a week, which was all they could handle of small town gossip masquerading as news, discussed their plans for the day and met up for lunch, whenever possible. On weekends however, he was out early. He was what the locals called a "weekend warrior" working a couple days a week as a volunteer ski patrol at the local mountain. His job description primarily consisted of skiing all day, occasionally handing out Band-Aids and ice compresses.

Noelle, on the other hand, had no intention of retiring. She still booked shoots in Europe, taking half a dozen trips a year. She traveled for location work to see places at just the right time of year: Alaska in mid-April to shoot the Northern Lights, November in Koh Chang to shoot the synchronized mating of the fireflies, December in Puerto Rico to shoot the bioluminescent show of greens and blues in the aquamarine waters. If she'd been born a generation before, she'd have been an adventuress, relegated to spinsterhood. In the here and now, she was happy, and more than happy, she was content.

So she sat, contented, sipping her morning coffee at a leisurely hour, as was her Sunday habit, George, already up at the mountain, patrolling. She skimmed through a recent fashion magazine and looked up when she saw Jenna walking up her driveway.

"Up here!" Noelle called, leaning over the railing to wave at Jenna, who was ringing the doorbell. "Come on up." By the time Jenna made it up the stairs, Noelle already had a fresh mug of coffee sitting in the place across from her at the little table. There was still snow on the ground, but the dry air and sunshine made it feel warmer than just above freezing. The gas heater in the corner helped too.

"Thanks," Jenna said, sitting down, not taking her coat off. Her core temperature still belonged to the warmth of Southern California.

"Sorry to barge in on you like this. I should have called first."

"Not at all. Biscuit?" Noelle held up an American biscuit halved, yellow butter melting down the sides. Jenna shook her head.

Noelle shrugged and took a bite.

"Is it okay that I'm here? I mean, I can come back another time," Jenna said, backpedaling now that she was here.

"It's a beautiful day, isn't it?" Noelle said.

"Y-yes, it is."

"I thought I'd do a little snowshoeing. Care to join?"

Jenna's eyes widened. She'd never snowshoed before. "I don't know how."

"If you can walk, you can snowshoe. Come on, I have an extra pair in the garage."

Jenna followed Noelle down the spiraling stairs to the garage. The four-car garage was mostly covered in bamboo flooring, except one concrete spot for a car to park. The rest of the room seemed broken down into sections: one for sewing, complete with dress form, shelves of fabric, buckets of buttons, and more scissors and accessories than Jenna would ever know what to do with. Next to the sewing section was a jewelry-making center, with hundreds of pegs full of stranded beads, a table of bead boards, tiny tools, and a miniature kiln. The other two walls were covered in pegboard familiar to many garages, organized with tools, sports equipment by season, and accessories, and finally, a closet just for outdoor clothing.

Noelle went straight to the closet, pulling out lightweight waterproof clothes for Jenna, a pair of low Gore-tex boots, and a pair of snowshoes and poles. "Try them on in there." She motioned to a bathroom built into what would have been, in most garages, a utility closet.

Half an hour later, they were sweating, snowshoeing across a field of gleaming white. Jenna had already stripped down to her t-shirt, and started to take the idea of wicking undergarments more seriously. She never thought it possible to sweat so much in forty-degree weather.

Noelle set a grueling pace and Jenna, who thought she was in good shape, struggled to keep up in the altitude. Finally, they reached a low peak overlooking a valley below of soft brown mountains blanketed in fresh snow, sparkling in the sunlight.

"It's beautiful." Jenna said, panting.

"Mmm," Noelle agreed, the corners of her mouth turning up in a smile. "So, you ready to talk yet?" She looked over at Jenna.

Jenna fought her instinct to deny it. She leaned forward, transferring the weight onto her poles, looking into the distance, wondering how to begin.

"Do you have a best friend?" Jenna asked.

"You mean besides George?"

"Yeah, a female best friend."

"No."

"Oh." Jenna couldn't hide her disappointment.

"I did have one, a long time ago." Noelle said in a quiet voice.

"What happened?"

"A boy came between us." Noelle's jaw tensed as she said it. "The usual cliché."

"I'm sorry."

"It was a long time ago. I haven't thought about her in years."

"Really?" Jenna said, hopeful. "How did you get over it?"

"You make it sound like a break-up."

"Well, yeah. It kinda is, don't you think?"

"I suppose you're right. Different though. You can't go crying to your boyfriend about your best friend dumping you for another guy." Noelle said. They stood there, silent together.

"I'm so lost." Jenna admitted. Noelle didn't respond. Jenna plowed on, hoping she wouldn't cry. "For so long I thought I had it all figured out. I thought my job was to be a good wife, friend, mother, and daughter. I was good at it. I made sure everyone had all the love and support they needed. I gave them everything I had. And now I have nothing to show for it and no one to turn to. It's not fair."

"It's not about life being fair." Noelle said, without a hint of cruelty. Whatever Jenna had hoped to hear, that wasn't it. Noelle saw her stricken face.

"It's about what you do with the life you're given. It's about you being the best version of you," she said. Jenna didn't reply, she felt stung. Noelle tipped her head in a gesture that said "take it or it leave it" and started the trek back to the car. The weather hadn't changed, but the sweat on Jenna's body turned cold and she sped up to get her circulation pumping again.

The bitterness she'd felt quickly evaporated through the exertion of stepping and pulling the bulky snowshoes in and out of the slushy afternoon snow. By the time they reached the car, they were both exhausted and sweating.

They stripped off their layers, throwing their equipment in

the back of Noelle's hybrid S.U.V. Noelle pulled out two thermoses and handed one to Jenna.

"Hot toddy?"

"Yes, please."

They sat on the back bumper, sipping their thermoses, looking out at the lake.

"How do I know if my marriage is over?" Jenna asked.

Chapter 37

Alex Anders sat alone, in another anonymous lobby of a five star hotel somewhere in America. The marble floor was cold. A chandelier hung in contrived grandeur. He faced the front desk, sitting on the only couch not looking out through the wall of windows. He wasn't there for the view.

He tapped the keys of his laptop furiously, face obscured between a baseball cap and the top of the screen. He wrote a daily travel blog for his social networking fans full of all the crap they wanted to hear; regaling them with anecdotes about the terrible food on the road, the more interesting banter between he and his band mates, their mustache growing competitions and bizarre superstitions, leaving out the unpalatable things like the bet between Joe and Pete to see who could sleep with the most skanks per zip code.

Alex did as he was told. He went through the motions, but to what end? He didn't know anymore. That was the worst part. He created for the sake of creating, because he had no choice. Not because some rich puppeteer got off on it, but because making music was how he knew he was alive. *Well then why not just make music in your garage and call it a day?* His father's voice sounded in his head.

What else could I do? Could I be happy without music? He knew the answer to that. No. He didn't want to face what that meant, though. Could he choose between music and his family?

"Is that him?" whispered a teenage girl from a nearby couch.

"Ask him!" said the girl sitting next to her. They giggled, unaware that Alex could hear everything they said.

It was just like being on stage. As soon as he was on stage people acted as though he was in a bubble, impervious to sound. Like he was a hologram, visible yet somehow oblivious to their whispering or throwing things or taking flash photos right up in his face, making him feel like a caged animal at the zoo.

The first girl chickened out of talking to him, and though she kept stealing long glances, he knew it was the second one that approached him, even before he looked up from his laptop.

She looked like one of Felicity's classmates, dark brown hair with unnaturally yellow highlights, styled to look much older, wearing shorts too short to suggest anything she should mean to, and a pair of tall shearling boots made popular by surfers. The look was more Lolita than fashionable, he thought.

Unlike her shy friend who squirmed on the opposite couch covering her mouth in delighted horror, Lolita strut right up to him, forcing him to look up from his screen. She tilted her head up in a "what's up" gesture, without speaking. Alex raised his eyebrows, amused by her audacity.

"You're Alex Anders." It was a statement, not a question, and he kept his face neutral. She took his silence as confirmation and plopped down next to him, not-so-subtly glancing at his open screen. He snapped it shut. She shrugged, inching toward him.

"Could you please respect my space?" he said, moving as far over on the couch as the loveseat would allow. He was aware of the hotel clerk watching them, probably with a camera phone at the ready. He set the closed laptop between them as a buffer.

She turned to face him. "I don't even use Myspace," she said, pulling a rolled up magazine from her impossibly small back pocket. "Can you sign this for me?"

"Sure," he said, keeping his eyes up.

This girl made him grateful they were in broad daylight in a populated space. He took the magazine from her, flattening it on the table. He recognized the photo on the opposite page as being one of the shots taken for the *Rolling Stone* article, which he assumed is what he must be holding.

"Do you have a pen?" he asked.

"Sure do," she said, standing inches away from him, her crotch at eye level. He looked down at the magazine. She set the pen in front of him, brushing his hand as she pulled hers away. He scribbled quickly, not asking to whom he should make it out. He shoved it out towards her, mumbling, "Here," under his breath.

She took it, but stayed where she was until he chanced a glance up at her.

"So ... is it true?" she asked.

"Is what true?"

"Are you screwing your wife's best friend?"

He didn't know if he felt more uncomfortable because of her language or the accusation. He narrowed his eyes, mentally giving her a lesson in where her behavior was leading and encouraging her to find some self-esteem. "Do you believe everything you hear?"

"That's not an answer," she said, shrugging.

"No," he said, his tone harsh.

"Geez, okay. Don't get all defensive. You could do better anyway." She said, turning around to leave slowly enough to give him the reverse view while he picked his jaw up off the floor. He made a promise not to let Felicity ever hang out with a girl like that.

The encounter shook him up so much that it wasn't until he got home from that night's concert that he realized he hadn't heard about the *Rolling Stone* article coming out. He checked online. No emails. It wasn't on their website. He didn't want to talk to Simon if he didn't have to so he called his publicist, Mindy.

"Hey Min, sorry to bother you." He never knew what time zone he was calling from so erred on the side of caution that he'd just woken someone.

"Not at all. What's up?" a perky voice answered.

"Just wondering if I could get a copy of that *Rolling Stone* interview."

"It's not out yet. It comes out next week. I can ask though."

"No, that can't be right. I signed a fan's copy today," he said.

"I just spoke to Kelly and we're supposed to get a proof tomorrow. It's not out. Maybe it was an old edition?" She asked, not at all perturbed.

"Maybe." A knot wound itself up in his gut. "Thanks, Min. Talk to you later."

He hung up, the knot tightening. He couldn't articulate why, but he had a sinking feeling he was right about Rose McKenna.

Chapter 38

"Are you going to the game tonight?" Trey asked Felicity as they walked down the long hallway, lined with lockers on both sides. She spun the dial on hers, clanking it open and draping her backpack over the bottom hook.

"Yeah, I thought we were going together?" She said.

"Just checking." He grinned.

"How'd you do on the Chem quiz?" She asked.

"Meh," he said, leaning back against the closed locker bank. He smiled. "Let me guess, you're pissed because you got an A minus."

"No! Okay, yeah, but it's only because that last question was total BS!" She hated when he made fun of her perfectionism. It was pointless to stay mad at him when he was so cute and playful, though. "Meet you here after last period?"

He nodded, pushing his lean frame off the metal lockers. His broad shoulders acted like a hanger for his worn t-shirt, his scruffy caramel colored hair brushed a pale strip on his tanned neck where, Felicity noticed, he'd recently had a haircut.

A driver's ed class and a history test later, they sat, cross-legged on Trey's living room floor. Felicity loved how homely his house was—unlike her own. With all her mom's design obsessions, everything was always shiny and new, unsullied by the normal messes incurred by living in a home. Trey lived in a small two-bedroom house in urban-suburban Silverlake.

His mom, a nurse who worked nights, got the house in the divorce long before it became a trendy neighborhood, and she'd furnished it piecemeal over the years. Nothing matched but it was comfortable and Felicity felt at home there.

They began their pre-game ritual of ordering a pizza and watching B-grade horror flicks on mute. The tradition started in junior high when Trey invited Felicity to watch a zombie movie and, when she caught her first glimpse of the gauze-wrapped-fake-blood-soaked zombie, she screamed and ran out of the house, terrified by nightmares for months. She didn't speak to him for two weeks.

The next time they hung out he challenged her to be scared while watching a horror film on mute. She hated the idea but didn't want him to think she was chicken so she took the bait. When they got to the part where the actress' head got chopped off and ketchup launched itself from her decapitated body, Felicity got the giggles so bad that milk shot out her nose and Trey doubled over laughing at her laughing at the movie. And just like that, no more nightmares.

If Trey hadn't suggested watching on mute, she would never have seen another horror flick. That's what she loved about Trey—he wasn't like everyone else. She grinned up at him and he gave her a suspicious look in return as he handed her a slice of artichoke/pineapple/Canadian bacon pizza (her favorite) and popped in the film du jour.

"I don't know how you eat this stuff," he said, shoving half a slice down his throat. She smiled. He always complained about it, yet ordered it every time without asking.

"You know you love it," she teased, pulling out a slice with cheese stretching between the box and her plate.

"Mmmm!" he exaggerated a look of ecstasy like an actor in a food commercial. She mock laughed back.

"Have you made any plans for prom yet?" he asked, his voice much quieter than before.

"No, I hadn't thought about it yet."

"Oh."

"Why?"

"Well, I thought if you wanted to go, maybe we could go together?" he said, the words strung together as one. His aquamarine eyes shone in his tan face. She cocked her head like a puppy, confused.

"Yeah, sure. Let's go," she said, amused by his awkwardness. It occurred to her she'd never noticed how attractive he was, objectively speaking, of course.

"Cool."

"Cool," she mimicked, poking fun at his sudden serious-
ness.

Later that night, under the fluorescent lights of the high
school gymnasium, they sat together on the bleachers, legs
nearly touching, paying little attention to the basketball jumping
across the court in a flurry of limbs vying for possession. They
didn't say much. After the final buzzer, their side of the gym
cheered the win and people swarmed all around, making plans,
giving high-fives, cracking jokes. Trey and Felicity stood up,
arms at their sides, close enough to but not quite touching.

Breaking the electric silence, Trey said, "Don't look now."
Felicity looked up. She saw Sadie strutting across the court,
heading right for them, her banana highlights peeking out of
their ebony cage. Felicity swore under her breath. Trey grabbed
her hand. She squeezed his. It would have been sweet if it
hadn't been for Sadie.

"I saw your dad yesterday. My aunt flew me out to Aspen
to meet this producer who's dying for me to be in a band he's
putting together," Sadie said, rolling her eyes as if she couldn't
care less.

"Super," Felicity said.

"Yeah. Anyway, it sure looks like your dad's having a *great*
time on the road," she said, emphasizing "great."

"Is that what you came to tell me? That my dad's enjoying
his sold out tour? Thanks. Update complete. Buh-bye," Felicity
said, waving Sadie along like an annoying dog. Sadie was not so
easily thrown off course.

"I just wanted to check on *you*. It must be so hard on *you*
now that your dad is sleeping with other women."

"You're pathetic, Sadie. Seriously, don't you have anything
better to do?"

"Oh, it's not me. Everyone knows about it. It's even in *Roll-*

ing Stone," she said, triumph spreading across her face.

Felicity's bravado fell away and she snatched the rolled up magazine from Sadie. Instantly, she recognized her dad's signature and the photo of him climbing a wall of amps, guitar dangling from his back. *No, she's lying.*

Felicity had no idea what Sadie was still yammering on about. She could have been speaking Swahili for all she cared. She forced her eyes up from the pages, which, no doubt held the answers she'd been trying to get from her mom and grandmother. *Be careful what you wish for,* she remembered.

She looked up to see a satisfied Sadie spin around and leave, flanked by her gaggle of minions. It would have been comical if not for Felicity's family's business being plastered across *Rolling Stone* magazine. Her mom warned her.

There it was. In black and white print, the soft flowing script promising entertainment to the rest of the world and disaster for one insignificant family. The title read, "Love Knows No Bounds: Exclusive Interview with Alex Anders and his New Love."

She couldn't read it. It wasn't that she'd never seen a tabloid with a story like that before, but this was *Rolling Stone,* the magazine that broke the story that got a general fired during a war. They didn't waste time with unsubstantiated stories. This was bad.

Trey coaxed it out of her hands, slipped his arm around her lower back, steadying her enough to escape the crowded gym. They didn't say a word until they got back to his house. His mom was still at work, and half a cold pizza sat on the coffee table where they left it. The congealed grease sat atop the cheese, like petrified tears of lard.

"Hungry?" he asked, moving around in the kitchen.

She shook her head, staring at the wall. She looked so hard she saw a corner of wallpaper curling up, revealing a previous owner's taste below it—faded ugliness. She knew how it felt. A wall, held together by a flimsy paper façade, peeling off to reveal its deepest darkest secrets.

Trey made her a mug of microwaved water with a packet of chamomile tea. She put it to her lips, taking the smallest of sips. It tasted horrible. The lukewarm water hadn't quite absorbed the tea, and a hint of something else she couldn't quite place— probably whatever had been in the mug before—remained. Trey wasn't known for his domestic skills.

She thanked him. He watched her carefully, making her feel self-conscious.

"Do you want to read it?" he blurted.

"I can't." She struggled to find her breath. "Will you?" she looked into his beautiful turquoise eyes. They widened, but he nodded.

He opened it slowly enough to give her time to change her mind before his eyes scanned the page. Her agony intensified during his silence, as she was simultaneously desperate to know and not. She couldn't take it any more.

"So? How bad is it?"

He shushed her with his hand, turning the page. After what felt like hours, but was probably only a few minutes, he closed it and set it down.

"Are you sure you want to know?" he asked.

"Yes!" she said, louder than she meant to.

"Okay, but…"

"Just tell me. I'll find out anyway."

"It's Airika—the other woman," he said, looking at his hands.

"What!" she screeched, snatching it from him.

'*…The feelings were always there, waiting for the right time. We knew it would be painful whenever it came out, and we really didn't want to hurt anyone. But the truth always comes out. And in the end, love wins.*'

"I can't believe this," she stood up, pacing around the small living room, palm pressed against her forehead. Trey looked down at his shoes. His own dead-beat dad was off raising someone else's family, barely deigning to pay enough attention to foot the bill for his private education and extravagant birthday gifts every other year. He was familiar with the male-bashing session he presumed would imminently follow. He braced himself.

"How could my mom not tell me? I feel awful. I've been such a brat. I was blaming *her* for being a drama queen. How could he do this to us?"

"Maybe it's not true?" he said, testing the waters. Now that she was acting off-script, he wasn't sure how best to proceed.

"But why would they print it?"

"I dunno. I just don't think your dad is the cheating type."

She didn't know what to say. Collapsing onto the couch, she didn't think so either, but what other explanation could there be? Every scenario she imagined seemed less plausible than the first.

Trey put his hand out, halfway between them on the couch. She reached out, squeezing it. He interlaced his fingers between hers, the warmth of his hands radiating up her arm. An unfamiliar twinge of excitement ran through her body. She hadn't yet identified it when she felt his full lips press against hers. The kiss was soft, affectionate. He pulled back, looking carefully for a response. She closed her eyes, kissing him again, this time pushing her tongue toward his.

They kissed and kissed, bodies unmoving on the couch, hands linked together, cutting off the circulation to her fingers. She didn't care. The most surprising part was how natural it felt. Before tonight, she could honestly say it never crossed her mind to think of Trey like that, but she found herself wondering how she could have missed it. Her brain told her it was an inappropriate time to be kissing someone while talking about her parents' marriage collapsing, but her body didn't seem bothered. The evening was full of surprises, horrifying and electrifying in equal measure.

The sound of a key twisted in the lock. They shot apart,

sitting on opposite ends of the couch.

"Hey Mom."

"Hi Mrs. Parker," Felicity said, running her hands over her hair.

"How was work?" Trey asked, getting up, taking the pizza remnants up to the kitchen counter. Mrs. Parker raised an eyebrow, looking from one to the other of them. She sighed and pulled a Tupperware container of leftovers out of the fridge and popped it in the microwave.

"Fine. What were you two up to?" she asked.

"Nothing," they said in unison.

"Mmm, hmmm." She turned her back so they couldn't see her smile.

"I should go. My grandmother will be worried."

"Okay, sweetie. Trey, honey, take my car so you can make sure she gets home safe."

"I will," he gave his mom a peck on the cheek, grabbed her keys, and followed Felicity out the door to his mom's Mini Cooper, parked in the driveway.

"That was close!" she said when they were safely inside the tiny car.

He turned to say something, changed his mind, and turned the key in the ignition. As they twisted their way down the narrow streets, bumping shoulders, their every touch excited her. The trip to her grandparents' was quiet. She wanted to say something, but needed time to sort out how she felt. She wasn't in any position to make life-altering decisions after the night she'd had.

He pulled into the long gravel drive, turning the lights off before killing the engine. They sat, unmoving. A million different things ran through her mind at once. She looked over at her best friend. Without thinking, she kissed him. He kissed her back, this time moving his hands around her shoulders. When they finally pulled apart, he was smiling.

"What?" she grinned.

"Nothing," he said. She punched him on the arm. He pretended it hurt.

"See you tomorrow?" she asked.

"See you tomorrow."

She floated up the steps to her room, forgetting, for the moment, about the demise of her family unit. That could wait. She flopped onto her bed, happy.

Chapter 39

Can we talk?

Jenna read the text message blinking on her phone's screen. It was from Alex. She sat up on an unfamiliar bed, worried before remembering where she was: Noelle's guest bedroom. They had a good old-fashioned sleepover, grown up style: wine, bread, cheese and chocolate. It had so refreshed her that without thinking, Jenna replied: *I'll call you in an hour.*

As soon as she sent it, fear gripped her heart. She hadn't spoken to Alex since their fight and she didn't know what to say or what he wanted to talk about. She didn't know if she was ready to talk. In a panic, she got up, throwing her clothes on, hardly noticing that they'd been washed, dried and folded for her overnight.

Noelle seemed miniaturized sitting at the giant breakfast table, bathed in early morning light. Her snow-white hair was perfectly coiffed and she exuded sophistication even dressed in her pajamas.

The table, set for two, reminded Jenna of the tea parties she and Airika used to throw for their dolls when they were little. Noelle ate a bowl of oatmeal, a newspaper open in front of her. Jenna didn't want to be rude.

"Good morning," she said, joining Noelle at the table.

"Sleep well?"

"Yes. Thanks…for last night," Jenna said.

Noelle didn't look up. She just made a "pfshhh" sound, flicking off the compliment with a wave of her hand.

"Eat! Manja!" Noelle pushed a basket across the table, piled high with croissants, muffins and bagels—a veritable feast of carbs. Jenna looked from the feast in front of her to the lonely bowl of oatmeal in front of Noelle. Noelle waved a hand again.

"My old body won't let me eat like I used to, but at least I can take pleasure in watching someone else eat my favorite foods."

Jenna hesitated, part of her already pushing the calorie-ridden foods away, knowing how long it would take her to burn off just one of the offending tempters. She could hear Airika shrieking that one bite would add ten pounds and at least as many cellulite dimples directly to her thighs. She used to listen to that part of her.

Instead, she smiled and picked up the biggest blueberry muffin of the bunch. She took a satisfying bite off the top, her favorite part, relishing the airy texture and sweet fruity flavor. She followed it with a gulp of cappuccino. Noelle watched, approving, and flipped through the paper. Jenna ate the muffin, watching out the window where a squirrel stripped a pinecone with its tiny hands.

Its movements were quick, methodical, purposeful. She studied it, transfixed by its determination not to waste anything. *I wish I were so certain.* She was jealous of a squirrel's purpose in life. That couldn't be a good sign.

"I have something for you," Noelle said.

"What?"

Noelle pulled a hatbox up from where it sat unnoticed on a nearby chair. She pushed it toward Jenna, gesturing for her to open it. Jenna pulled at the large ribbon, lifting the oval lid. Inside the box was a very large, very cumbersome looking camera, just like the one she'd used the day of the *Vogue* shoot.

"For me? I can't accept this!"

"Of course you can. Every photographer needs a camera. Plus, now I get to make my stipulation." Noelle's face exploded in a huge grin, alluding to how she must have looked as a teenager.

"Yes, this is purely selfish," she continued. "You must take photos every day and you must use this one, prime lens. The 50mm is considered the most honest lens—the closest to approximating the human eye—and I want you to record something every day. No frills, just light and shadow. That's how you'll learn."

Jenna opened her mouth, speechless. She picked up the camera with its tiny lens dwarfed by the massive camera body. She looked through the small viewfinder, finding Noelle. The frame was only large enough for her head and shoulders. Jenna clicked the shutter, capturing Noelle's pleasure and surprise. The soft light pouring in through the window lit everything else in the frame, allowing Noelle's sharp brown eyes to pop, silently conveying their message.

"I will. Thank you," Jenna said, turning her lens out the window to the squirrel, still working on its pinecone. She looked at the image, frowned at the blurry shapes, then adjusted the shutter speed and clicked again.

"Ah, voilà! A photographer is born," Noelle said, beaming.

***

An hour later Jenna sat on the corner of her bed, phone in hand, working up the courage to call Alex. She felt like a teenager, dialing the numbers she knew by heart, stopping, and hanging up. Finally, she took a deep breath, dialed all the numbers and waited for him to answer.

"Jenna?" he said, answering on the first ring.

"Hi."

"Hi."

"You asked me to call. I'm calling," she tried to keep her voice from shaking.

"Yeah, thanks. It's good to hear your voice. I miss you." His words sounded formal, foreign. She was used to his easygoing confidence. *Why is this so hard?*

"How are you?" he asked.

"Fine. What do you need to talk to me about?" She asked, not at all sure she could stay strong if they fell into their usual banter.

"I wanted to warn you about an article that's coming out." As he said it, her body stiffened. She didn't say anything.

"It's in *Rolling Stone*. I did the interview a couple weeks ago, just days after ... you left," he said. "I thought I recognized the girl interviewing me, but I didn't put it together. Do you know Rose McKenna?"

Oh shit, what did she do now? Rose McKenna had insinuated herself into Airika's circle of influence through her job as nanny to one of Hollywood's A-list actors. Her charge was nine at the time. Somehow or other she got Airika the styling job when the mini-celebrity got an Oscar nomination and, ever since, a bizarre friendship had blossomed between them.

Jenna hadn't trusted Rose from the first time they met, when she had the gall to ask if she could get a signed guitar from Shawn Jax. When Jenna said "no," she replied, half joking, "Relax, I'm not a stalker fan or anything. I just wanted to sell it on eBay."

Jenna gripped the phone, holding her breath, waiting for her husband's voice, wishing he were going to say something she knew he wasn't.

"I know Rose."

"Well, I guess she spliced my interview and then did a separate one with Airika. So it looks like ... but Jenna, I swear, it's not true ... "

Jenna's mouth went dry. Her heart thumped in her ears. Her breathing became choppy and Alex's voice muffled.

" ... It looks like we did the interview *together*." He sighed, sounding defeated. The only audible response was a sharp intake of breath and a small squeaking sound Jenna assumed must have come from her. She was outside of her own body. *This can't be happening*, she thought. *But it is*, said another, more annoying voice in her head.

"Let me get this straight. You did an interview with Rose. Airika did an interview with Rose. And then Rose cut them and pasted them together to look like you did the interview *together*?"

"Yes," he said in a small voice.

"And that's the absolute truth?" she asked.

"Yes."

"Okay."

"Okay?" he asked.

"Has the issue hit newsstands yet?"

He was having trouble comprehending her line of questioning. He expected her to rail about how stupid he was to do an interview without Mindy there and that nothing was ever really off the record. And he would agree and then they'd make up and go back to their isolated bubbles. But something was ... different.

"I don't think so. I haven't even gotten the mock-up," he said.

"Have you told Mindy?"

"No."

"Call her. Tell her what happened. Then call Frank."

"Frank?"

"Your attorney," she sighed in exasperation. "Give them the details. Let them do their jobs. If it hasn't shipped yet, we can still salvage this."

She heard the assertive tone in her own voice. She felt a surge of power coursing through her body as she gave him orders. Her whole life she'd been passive and let other people do things for her—fix things for her, protect her. For the first time, she took charge of her own life. A smile crept across her face, the wild thumping of her pulse steadied into an anthemic rock beat.

"Thank you," he said, his tone unfamiliar.

"Call me when it's done." She hung up, feeling a rush of adrenaline. Without giving herself time to think, she dialed Airika's number.

"Why did you do it?" Jenna spat as soon as Airika picked up. It was a loaded question and she didn't mind how Airika took it.

"Jenna?"

"Why did you do it?" Jenna repeated.

"Didn't we already do this?" Airika said.

"I'm talking about the interview. With Rose."

"What interview?"

"Your interview in *Rolling Stone* with Rose McKenna. You can tell me what you said and help me fix this now, or you can talk to our attorney later. Either way you're going to have to explain."

"Look Jenna, I can tell you're mad. I honestly don't know what you're talking about. I never did an interview with Rose."

Jenna hated to admit that she believed her. Airika may be a conniving, backstabbing, atrocious friend, but she never out and out lied. This assumption was not based on Airika's innate integrity, it was based on the fact that Airika was a terrible actress.

"Why did you pretend to be my friend all those years?" Jenna asked, surprised at how calm she sounded.

"I wasn't pretending. You're my best friend." Airika said.

"Then why did you try to steal my boyfriend and then lie to me and then do it again all these years later?" she asked, surprised by the lack of anger in her tone.

"I ... I wanted to know what it was like."

"What it was like to kiss Alex? You found that out in high school." There may have been a little venom in that one.

"No, I wanted to know what it was like to be you."

In a million years, Jenna could not have been more flabbergasted by any single response.

"So you don't have feelings for Alex, you were just jealous of me?" Jenna asked.

"No, I do have feelings for Alex. I'm in love with him. I just ... I've always envied you. Especially after you started dating the only guy I'd ever had feelings for," Airika said.

Jenna fell silent. Airika breathed on the other side of the phone. Jenna's mind swirled with years of memories rewinding and replaying, as if shot from an entirely new angle. She couldn't decide if this revelation angered or depressed her. Suddenly, as if hit by the biggest "aha!" moment of her life, Jenna felt a new emotion on the matter: sympathy.

Their friendship hadn't been a farce. The emotions were real. The perspective just got skewed. Airika was born to have it all. But her parents split up. Her dad disgraced the family. And despite finding professional success, romantic love, and most importantly, happiness, eluded her. Jenna had the things Airika wanted most in the world——not Alex, per se—but a loving family and a husband who was her best friend and partner. All this time Jenna envied Airika's style and self-confidence while she envied Jenna for her own reasons. Jenna felt … free. Free of anger and hurt. Free from the conspiracy she thought formed against her.

"Thank you."

"What?" Airika squeaked.

"Thank you for showing me how lucky I am," she said without a trace of irony.

Airika let out a garbled noise, choking on her instinctive retort, uncertain how to proceed.

"I forgive you," Jenna said, hanging up the phone. She felt light as air. The switch, now flipped, couldn't go back. She was a new woman.

Chapter 40

Airika held the phone in her hand, mouth agape. Many minutes later, she couldn't come up with a cohesive thought. Jenna sounded sincere. But she couldn't have been. How could anyone forgive her for what she'd done? Terror gripped her heart as she thought about what Jenna might be planning.

If Jenna was that shrewd, however unlikely it seemed, Airika knew she had to take an offensive strategy. She called Rose.

"What did you do?"

"Hey Air," Rose said, sounding bored.

"Did you fake an interview with me?"

"No."

"Well, that's what Jenna thinks. Why does she think that?" Airika said. Rose smiled over the phone.

"You gave me an interview." Rose said. Airika could practically hear her filing her nails and rolling her eyes.

"No I didn't." Even as she said it, Airika knew it was pointless. She knew that Rose considered everything "on the record." Like everything else in her life, she expected those rules didn't apply to her. Suddenly every conversation she'd had with Rose about Alex flashed back through her memory. *She wouldn't!* Airika felt the walls closing in on her remembering their conversation from Alex and Jenna's driveway ... after The Incident.

"She *knew* she was trapping him!" Airika had vented. "Jenna was so selfish to keep the baby. Denying him his right to adolescence—what was she thinking?" Airika's stomach twisted as she heard herself go on and on about Jenna's wrongdoings and misdeeds. The memory of her words spewed back at her, unrelenting. "He was always checking me out. You know, like he was looking back at what could have been if it weren't for her selfishness. It was only a matter of time before the tension grew too much and we had to see it through. In the end, love always wins."

Airika hung up, feeling sick. She had turned into her father. She had turned the personal into a professional catastrophe. There wasn't anyone she could blame but herself. She was alone. Unlovable, wretched, and utterly alone in the world.

Chapter 41

"Thanks, Min." Alex said, hanging up the phone, taking his first full breath since this whole thing started. He couldn't get over how different Jenna seemed. Whatever caused this shift in her, it was sexy. He couldn't admit it to her, of course. He'd followed her directions and two hours later, crisis averted. "Rose has been taken care of," he was told. It turned out to have been a mock-up that hadn't even been approved for print. He lucked out.

He should have felt emasculated by his estranged wife telling him what to do, giving him orders. He didn't. He felt … grateful. Grateful and loved. And a little guilty. Guilty that whatever changed her, made her this new empowered woman, wasn't him. That after all their years together, he not only hadn't noticed those strengths, he'd prevented them from surfacing. He hadn't understood her anger about not working before, but now it was clear that his insecurities about his own manhood affected her too. And she'd never held it against him. He felt a sudden awe for her devotion to him over the years. He didn't deserve her. And now she knew it too—or would soon.

The thought was more than he could stand. He knew he needed to tell her about his anonymous backer and everything he'd discovered, but first, he would try one last thing to fix it on his own. Jenna had enough to deal with and he didn't want to burden her with another one of his stupid mistakes. Not if he didn't have to.

Chapter 42

"Cici?" Anya called from downstairs. Felicity grabbed her backpack, checked her reflection in the mirror, changed shirts, and sprinted down to the kitchen. Her cheeks were flushed when she reached it and Anya looked her over, eyes narrowed.

"What have you been up to?"

"Nothing," Felicity said, trying and failing to stop smiling.

Anya raised a brow, but let it go. She handed Felicity a bowl of cereal and motioned for her to sit. Felicity poured a glass of orange juice and tried to sip without smudging her lip-gloss.

"I got a call from Grandpa's agent today, saying they found someone to play the part of the young me in his biopic."

"Really, who?" Felicity asked, twisting her hair around her finger.

"You." Anya looked at her, disapproval spelled all over her face. Felicity felt a tightening of her insides. She hated lying to her grandmother. She especially hated getting caught.

"I ... Airika said I should just audition. It wasn't a big deal. I didn't think I'd get it," she said, knowing it was a flimsy excuse. Hearing herself say Airika's name—knowing she'd betrayed her mom—made her feel so much worse. She looked down at her bowl of untouched cereal and pushed the soggy flakes around.

Anya didn't say anything for a long time. Finally, she stood up from the table and fixed her eyes on Felicity. "You'll tell your mom today."

"Okay," Felicity said.

Excitement usurped her guilt as she lingered by her locker, waiting for Trey, hoping he'd make it before the first bell rang. She ran out of legitimate things to do so she re-organized her books for the third time, hearing the bell blare through the halls.

She jumped as he edged next to her, a giant smile spread across her face. He grinned back, leaning in to give her a little kiss. It was nice but it lacked the passion of last night's kiss. She scolded herself for wishing for more when they were in the middle of the hall, surrounded by classmates hurrying along. Not that she cared what anyone else thought. He walked her to her first class, their hands entwined, not letting go until she was across the threshold.

All day she struggled to pay attention, waiting for the bell to ring, for Trey to hold her hand, and sneak in a kiss between classes. They fell into an easy pattern of him picking her up from her class, holding hands to her locker, walking together to her next class. She was sure he'd been late to every period today. By last bell, she knew she'd find him outside her classroom, his hand ready for her to take, like this was how it had always been.

She hopped on his motorcycle, grabbing his waist, enjoying the contact all the way home. She handed him her helmet, making small talk as they loitered in front of her grandparent's house. She desperately wanted to invite him inside but hadn't told her grandmother about their kiss and after this morning she didn't want to be thought an even bigger liar.

She wanted to keep him separate from everything else happening in her family. He was the one good and reliable thing in her life at the moment and he made her happy.

He tangled his fingers in hers as she stood facing him, their hips close.

"So … " he said.

"So … "

"You gonna invite me in?" He smiled.

She looked into his brilliant turquoise eyes, hungry for more time with him. She flipped her hair over her shoulders. "Yeah, just give me a minute. Kay?" She bounded up the steps to the house.

"Grandmother? Grandpa?" she shouted. No answer. She ran into the kitchen to find a foil wrapped plate with a sticky note on it that read, "Cic, Grandpa and I will be back by dinner. Here's a snack. Call your mom. Love, Grandmother".

She couldn't believe her luck. She ran back out, flinging the front door open, waving Trey inside. He walked up the steps and she gently pushed her lips to his, closing the door with her foot. They headed up the steps to her room, where they'd gone a million times before, but not with butterflies like this. She walked in front of him, holding his hand, pulling him through the doorway. She spun around, wrapping her arms around his neck.

His lips met hers, their tongues dancing around one another, exploring. The intensity deepened, her mouth red and raw from his patchy stubble. She'd never noticed his facial hair before, or his muscular shoulders. Their bodies melded into one, leaning back onto her bed, arms and hands venturing into new territory. They didn't speak, their mouths learning this new form of communication. The few times they came up for air, they gazed into each other's eyes in a way that, a week ago, would have made her want to hurl. Now she couldn't imagine feeling any other way. She needed him next to her, kissing her, maybe more.

As if on cue, her cell phone's shrill ring pierced the air. It was her mom, interrupting them from afar. She sat herself upright on the bed, fixed her hair, and took a deep breath. Trey sat across from her, their legs entangled, panting.

"Hi Mom!"

"Felicity? Where are you?" her mom asked, in what Felicity took as a suspicious tone.

"In my r-room," she said, "Doing homework."

"Is Grandmother there?"

"No."

"Oh. When you see her, will you tell her I need to talk her?"

"Sure," Felicity said. Her earlier conversation with her grandmother came back, along with the memory of the magazine and Airika. She disentangled her legs from Trey's and stood up.

"Mom?"

"Yes?"

"Is everything okay?"

"It will be. Don't worry about it, okay. Your Dad and I are going to work it out."

By the end of the conversation, Felicity felt conflicted on so many levels. She felt bad about lying. She was scared in equal parts that her Mom knew and didn't know about the magazine. She worried it might be true. And she wondered if her Mom could ever forgive *her* for going behind her back and auditioning, not to mention how she'd react when she found out about the biopic via Airika.

Felicity was thrilled to find out she got the part of the young Anya. But now it felt tainted, punishment for being such a heartless daughter. She was mad at her dad for letting it get to this point, while another part of her was doing a happy dance because of how happy she was with Trey. *Does that make me a bad person: being happy when everything else is such a mess?*

"Cici?" Anya called from the living room.

"In here!" She called, double-checking buttons and zippers. Trey zoomed across the room to sit on the dressing stool in the corner, hands visible on his knees.

"Oh, hi Trey. Are you staying for dinner?" Anya said, appearing in the doorway.

"No, I should go home," he said.

"Nonsense. Your mom's at work, right? You can't live on pizza. Stay. I insist. Just call your mom."

"Thank you, Mrs. Jax. I will."

Anya appreciated the chivalry, but couldn't remember the last time he'd called her "Mrs. Jax."

Chapter 43

Despite the win on the publicity front, Alex couldn't relax. He needed to get out of his contract now more than ever, but didn't see how he could pull it off. Just because his boss turned out to be a porn mogul it didn't negate the contract. He needed to find someone—a lawyer—exceptionally skilled at finding and exploiting loopholes. Someone without scruples. One name came to mind, but that meant confronting his jealousy. When he'd exhausted his mental search for another option, he made the call.

"Hey bro," Zach said.

After what-upping back and forth, Alex got to the point.

"Can you get me your dad's lawyer's number? I need some help with a contract."

"Don't you have a lawyer?" Zach asked.

"Yeah but he's too … moral."

"Your lawyer is too moral? You should put him in a fuckin' museum." Zach laughed. "But if you need amoral, then yeah, Dad's is the best of the best. I'll shoot you a text."

"Thanks."

"No problem. I gotta ask, is everything alright?"

"It will be," Alex said.

"Good luck, man. You've got an amazing … family," Zach said.

Seconds after they hung up, as promised, Alex received a text with Ira Stearn's contact info. Despite his earlier misgivings about Zach's motives for helping Jenna get out of town, Alex knew his friend well enough to know he'd never cross that line. And now, all he could do was find out if he had any legal-ish way of walking away from his contract unscathed. It was a long shot, but worth a try. If not, he needed a plan B. Quick.

Ira Stearn, Esq. was not surprised to hear from Alex Anders, not because he expected to, but because nothing surprised him. He didn't see himself as jaded, just realistic. The rich were often more desperate than the poor, paranoid someone would take their money, distrustful of everyone's motives. He made a fortune off encouraging their paranoia and convincing them that yes, someone *was* trying to rip them off, and that only *he* could save them from destitution.

They were so gullible. They all thought he was their best friend. And he enjoyed the perks. He couldn't lie (about that). His ideal day started off with a thick black espresso on the green of an oceanfront golf course from which he conducted his day's business: schmoozing clients, barking orders into his phone, relaxing at the end of the day in an exclusive men's-only clubhouse where he could put up his feet, light up a Cuban indoors, and let a smoky scotch slide down his throat, enjoying its peaty aftertaste.

His ideal day occurred at least three times a week. How many people could say they loved their job? Ira Stearn could.

So when Alex Anders called to talk about retaining his services for review of a contract, he didn't concern himself with petty questions about things like conflict of interest. Not representing one party simply because he represented their opposition didn't flutter the needle on his ethical compass. Ira's only conflict lay in checks not clearing. Ethics were for mere mortals.

Chapter 44

Jackson Jones kept his most prized possession in his Las Vegas office, where he spent the most time. He picked it up, fingers squeaking across the fret board, noodling around with a complicated Phazee Crux rock solo to clear his head before the start of business. The pearly white pick guard gleamed in the morning light, accentuating the Stratocaster's classic sunburst coloring. The Shawn Jax signature guitar was his one big splurge after making his first million. He bought it at a Sotheby's auction for $15,000, a sum equal to his previous year's income. Playing it was the closest to meditation he'd ever come. It represented the sole vestige of his sixteen year-old self. If not for that, Alexander Deshevka—son, brother, Russian immigrant—would cease to exist, replaced on all levels by his alter ego, Jackson Jones, CEO of Flesh, Inc.: fearfully respected business mogul.

His idea of a religious experience was watching the orange pink haze of the desert sun rise below him, sitting atop his empire, looking out on the world famous Strip. The Strip, deserted and lonely at this hour, reminded him of St. Basil's basilica after the Cold War. All these years later, he still thought about his homeland. He had no intention of returning, however. The pain his own people inflicted on him and his family was enough to squelch even the strongest bouts of nostalgia for what his life could have been if they never came to America. His father's funeral hadn't been enough to bring him back, and he doubted anything else would come close. So it existed, like his birth name, only at this early hour, preserved inside a glass case high up on a shelf in his memory, untouchable.

The phone on his desk rang, signaling that his workday had commenced. Flesh, Inc. was his life's work, his baby, and he reveled in its daily challenges. He'd always been a problem solver, never shying from confrontation. It kept his mind sharp and his instincts honed.

His empire began with a simple producer's credit in the film, "Pussy Police Academy" in which he'd discovered its star, Pussy Willows. He rescued her from a couple of drunks outside a strip joint. From there, he and Ms. Willows completed a nine part series, parlaying his role from producer to running his own production company. The age of VHS opened a new market for distribution, which he quickly exploited. Then came DVD, followed by the bane of his existence and source of his fortune: the internet.

So much porn, so little quality. How could he compete with free? He sold memberships and viewing fees to his bread and butter customers, but their insatiable taste for more daring content led him to realize they'd never be satisfied. He sold enough in advertising to build up his empire, but continued transitioning into areas he felt had more long-term growth. He dreamed of bridging the gap between mainstream America and the XXX world by making an Oscar worthy XXX art film (blowing "Deep Throat" out of the water), garnering him credibility in the business world.

Until then, he focused on mainstream soft porn: pop music featuring scantily clad (barely legal) stars; home decorating channels featuring shows where hunky men came in to rescue desperate housewives from their less than handy husbands (the most appealing form of soft porn for women, focus groups showed); and Men's magazines featuring raunchy articles on young girl-next-door types pictured in compromising positions, wearing next to nothing.

His secretary's voice came over the office intercom. "Mr. Walker on line two. Shall I take a message?"

"No, no. I'll take it. Put him through," he rolled the high-backed leather chair away from the window, settling behind his desk, guitar still in hand.

"Simon Walker. Good morning."

"Good morning, sir," Simon waited for a response, and when he didn't get one, continued. "We've had a slight hiccup. Nothing to worry about, mind you, just a small matter."

"You need my help with a small matter?" Jackson Jones asked.

"No, of course not. I wouldn't waste your time. I just …" Simon stuttered.

"Then don't."

Simon gulped. He couldn't end the call fast enough. Jackson Jones hung up, then buzzed his secretary. "Get me Alex Anders' schedule."

Simon Walker was an incompetent, if not a double-crossing scoundrel, and in business he'd learned to always see the important things through himself. Trust no one.

Chapter 45

"Fantastic," Simon said to the dial tone. Jackson Jones' silky charm inspired abject terror in those who crossed him. Escaping him was like avoiding oxygen during an airborne chemical warfare attack.

Not that Simon planned on crossing him, but every day he lost a little more control over his star client. He couldn't understand how his plan could have gone so far awry.

In such moments of doubt, he reminded himself that Alex Anders had no one to blame but himself. For years Simon admired and supported Alex, working for free, booking gigs anywhere that would take them, convincing venues to let them back even after the bass player smashed the speakers, or the drummer sexually harassed the bartender (who happened to be dating the owner). Simon had worked tirelessly promoting Alex's ill-advised venture into alt-country, when he'd gone solo after yet another band broke up. And through all that, Simon had been the one constant. They were family, or so he thought.

When he'd pitched the idea to team up with Shawn, combining a more mainstream rock sound—a sound that broke Phazee Crux to AAA radio (no small feat)—and tacking on a couple of collaborations between Shawn and Alex, he hadn't expected to be ignored completely; and worse, turned into an anecdote. His suggestion was cited as "one of the worst thing he'd ever been asked to do" as Alex told journalists regularly.

Not long after, Jackson Jones presented the opportunity to make good money, catapulting him into a new stratosphere of entrepreneurial possibilities, and Simon jumped.

At first everything went as planned. Everyone seemed happy and Simon was on top of the world, until that Dutch commercial derailed the whole thing. Alex started asking questions and Simon didn't know how to answer. The one stipulation had been that Jackson Jones remained anonymous. When Simon didn't cave, Alex turned on him and they'd been at odds ever since. Alex no longer trusted Simon and vice versa. Simon tried everything to get the situation under control: manipulation, women, endorsements, intimidation. Nothing worked. Alex Anders was a hard nut to crack.

Chapter 46

Ira Stearn took a cursory look over the familiar contract. Alex didn't appreciate the speed at which he flipped through page after page. *There's no way he's reading that fast.* It occurred to him this had been a colossal waste of time and money. It was money that, if he couldn't get out of this contract, would be a lot tighter.

"It's ironclad." Ira stated, settling back in his chair, pushing the contract back to Alex.

"You're sure?"

"Yes. Unless..." Ira leaned his elbows on the desk, eyes gleaming.

"Unless what?" Alex said, sitting up on the edge of his chair. Ira eyed him over horn-rimmed glasses, relaxing into the back of his own much higher, more luxurious chair.

"Unless, you take advantage of clause 7b," Ira said, flipping to page six, indicating a paragraph half way down the page.

"7b?" Alex said, scanning the nonsensical text. "What does it say?"

"It says," Ira smirked, "that you can, after the first year, re-negotiate the terms of the agreement."

"That's good, then. At the end of the tour, the year is up. All I have to do is negotiate to be let out of the contract."

"Well, not exactly. You can renegotiate the terms, not the duration."

"I don't understand."

"You can ask for more royalty points, say. Or a larger advance based on previous success. The finer points."

"But I don't want to renegotiate. I want out."

"Well then, it's ironclad."

Alex's face flushed in anger. He came to Ira Stearn to stop being bullied. To take control. And here he was, compromising himself for this bottom feeder at $1,500 an hour to be told,

Sorry, better luck next time.

"You know, if you'd hired me in the first place I would have negotiated a much better deal." Ira said, sliding back in his chair, removing his glasses and setting them on his desk. Alex made a guttural sound in his throat, disbelieving his ears.

"Thanks, I'll stick with my current representation."

"Tell me you're not still with Frank Fitzsimmons?" Ira said, rolling his eyes in exasperation or pity, Alex couldn't tell which.

"You have a problem with Frank?" Alex asked, feeling defensive.

"No problem, so long as you don't mind losing." Ira smiled, but he shifted in his seat, and Alex could swear he sensed an underlying anger.

"Did you lose to Frank?" Alex goaded. Ira narrowed his eyes at Alex.

"I don't lose to that smug bastard. He thinks he's so superior with his 'high moral standards' but that's just loser-speak for being too chickenshit to play in the big leagues."

Alex had no idea what that meant and didn't really care. His only concern was that he'd flown all this way and paid a bunch of money for nothing. *So that's it.*

He looked out the plane window, watching the country pass by in geometric earthy carvings, like a secret language he'd yet to unlock. He wished they would open up to him, revealing the solution to this gargantuan mess.

His worries didn't include the fact that, if his flight didn't land on time, he would miss tonight's concert in Vegas, breaching his side of the contract. He hated Vegas. It was one of the few places that made him feel like his life didn't turn out the way it should have. As much as he liked to think himself a fairly evolved male, pro gender equality and all that, he couldn't escape the simple fact that he was a man. It wasn't the sex, exactly, that held the power. It was the youthful promise Vegas proffered: a version of life where you didn't have to compromise, where every one of your fantasies could be realized. He'd never been the cheating type and groupies held no interest for him because even if he'd been single, to completely eliminate the chase denied him the opportunity to desire. It just wasn't sexy.

But Vegas—for all its faults (it's many, many, faults)—dangled that potential like a proverbial carrot. It was a place you could get rich, win big, meet someone, live out your sexual fantasies, escape reality, and go home like nothing happened. It was a place that put a crack in his stony façade. The less time he spent there, the better.

Chapter 47

Jenna sighed into the phone. Felicity braced for punishment.

"Why didn't you tell me?" Jenna asked.

She struggled to maintain her previous Zen while the anger and hurt only a teenage daughter could incite bubbled to the surface. She wanted to scream and ground her until she graduated high school, but another part of her had to pat her on the back and congratulate her tenacity. When Felicity wanted something she took a clear efficient path toward that goal. Jenna wished they could swap ... at least until Felicity turned eighteen. Parenting would be a cakewalk if the child were the pushover and the parent the strong stubborn one.

"Because you wouldn't have let me audition."

"You're right," Jenna admitted. "But that's my right. You have to respect me if you want me to trust you. You can disagree, but you can't lie to me."

"But you don't listen!"

"I'm listening now. Tell me. Why should I let you do this?"

"Because I love it. Because it will help me get into an Ivy League college. Because I got the part. And because I'm not going to do the stuff you're afraid I'll do!" Felicity said.

Jenna took a couple calming breaths.

"Okay ... I hear you. And I'm glad you found something you love. I'm proud of you getting the part. I am. But you don't have to be in movies to get into college. And *I* want, no need, to protect your childhood."

Felicity sighed and Jenna heard the wavering in her breathing that meant she was close to tears. Jenna closed her eyes and took another breath, willing herself to get through this. "I know you don't understand, Sweetheart. You feel grown up, and I remember feeling the same. But there's a lot you don't know. And my dream is that you get to hold on to that as long as possible. That's why I can't let you take that role."

"Uaaargh! You don't get it. Just because you screwed up your life you think you can take it out on me. It's so unfair!"

Jenna took another deep breath (her yogi would be so proud of all this conscious breathing), silently counting down from ten. *Nine, eight, seven*, she thought, clenching her jaw, trying to focus her mind. *Three, two....*

"You're right, it is unfair. But life's not fair." Jenna said, hearing the words reverberate inside her head in her mother's (and Noelle's) voice. Then cursed the inescapable fate of womanhood: turning into one's mother.

"Why!" Felicity shouted.

"I'm doing this because I love you."

"Gee, thanks!" Felicity hung up.

Jenna sunk down into the couch, head falling into her hands. *Am I doing the right thing?* She knew Felicity had a good head on her shoulders but couldn't help remembering that she had too. It wasn't always enough.

Yes, she'd done the right thing. Some temptations were too great. They were when she was that age and now there was more of everything. The fact that Felicity didn't realize she was being used to bolster the film's PR made Jenna's point for her. She hated not being liked, but she wanted the best for her only daughter.

Chapter 48

Felicity stomped outside, kicking a chunk of gravel from the driveway into a bird of paradise. She stalked around the side of the house, mumbling to herself down all eighty-four stairs, finally reaching the cool sand, where the crashing waves drowned out her grumblings. *I'm sick of being treated like a child!* She flicked off her sandals, rolled up her jeans and walked along the water's edge, water licking her calves. She dragged her feet through the water, creating a small wake behind her.

By the time she calmed down, her jeans were wet up to the knees, the rolled cuffs dripping down her calves. She plopped down on the dry sand, knees pulled up, hands behind her in the sand. She mentally catalogued every time her mom had held her back, under the guise of "protecting her." It was as if, because *she* messed up, Felicity was preemptively punished for things she didn't get to experience. The white haze of the afternoon sun reflected onto the water. She watched it until the sun dipped down, turning from white to gold to blood-orange before finally disappearing.

She brushed herself off and trekked home, jeans heavy and cold, exfoliating the exposed strip of leg. She thought about what her mom said as she walked up the stairs, still frustrated that her parents didn't trust her judgment. She could handle a lot more than they thought. By the time she closed the sliding glass door behind her, guilt seeped back into her conscience, replacing her anger.

Then she saw Trey. His smiling eyes and scruffy hair made her problems melt away. Her grandpa appeared behind him, grabbing an apple from a bowl on the counter. He patted Trey on the shoulder and walked away without saying a word.

"He knows about us," Trey whispered, checking over his shoulder.

"Did you tell him?"

"No, I think he just figured it out."

"Well, I guess they were going to find out eventually," she said, stepping into his open arms.

"So ... do you want to be my girlfriend?" He said in a tone that was playful yet serious.

"Hmmm ... let me think about it," she said, kissing him. "Okay!"

She snuggled into his shoulder, and he kissed her hair. Then they made their first official appearance as a couple, joining her grandparents in the living room. They held hands and sat down on the couch, side by side. No one said anything. Felicity couldn't hide her disappointment. *Don't they care that I have my first boyfriend?* Her grandmother read a book in an overstuffed armchair, and her grandpa sat at the grand piano in the corner of the room. How anticlimactic.

Out of nowhere, Shawn started to play "Here Comes the Bride," glancing over his shoulder at them, a grin spreading across his face. Felicity felt her cheeks get hot. He played, choppy and over the top. From her soft-spoken Grandpa the juxtaposition struck her as absurd. She got the giggles. Once she started, that was it. Anya let out a big laugh, followed by a quick snort, setting Shawn off, followed closely by Trey. They shook, chortling and crying until their cheeks and sides hurt and no one could remember how it started in the first place.

Chapter 49

Jenna arrived at Noelle's house half an hour after she called. The proofs from the *Vogue* shoot were ready and Jenna was jumping out of her skin in anticipation. For once, a magazine she couldn't wait to read!

"They've already chosen the ones they'll use, but do you want to see the rest?" Noelle asked.

"Yes!"

She spread the images out across her desk. The diffused light shone just right to see details without causing reflections. She stepped back and admired them one at a time, picking them up, running her fingers along the edges as though to remind herself of their tangibility.

"Wow," she said, "look how great they are."

Noelle's face lit up. "I have a surprise for you."

"What?" Jenna said, not taking her eyes off the photos.

"Here's the image for the story cover," Noelle handed Jenna a glossy shot of the model in Jenna's favorite dress of the day: the strapless ivory gown with the ruffled train.

Jenna took a closer look, scrunching her face. *That looks a bit like ...* Yes! She took this shot! She gaped at Noelle, disbelieving. Noelle's grin spread wider as she held out the magazine mock up.

"*Photography by Noelle Enfin and Jenna Jax-Anders.*" Jenna read aloud. "I- Why would you-?" she couldn't get her brain and mouth to cooperate. Noelle patted her on the back, eyes twinkling.

"Why would you do this? I mean ... thank you! Thank you so much! But why?" With her synapses firing again, it sounded too good to be true.

"I am old and successful with nothing left to prove. I have no children. No legacy. You can be my legacy."

"It's too generous. I don't deserve it."

"Pish! Of course you do. *Vogue* chose your images. All I did was give you credit for something you did."

Jenna mulled it over in her head, still gawking at the mock up. She could debate her worthiness or sit back and enjoy it. An ear-to-ear smile split across her face. Her photo was going to be in *Vogue* magazine!

"To you." Noelle produced two champagne flutes and held hers up in the air. Jenna didn't mention that it was eleven am. They clinked glasses and Jenna decided that, for once, she'd give herself permission to enjoy the moment without waiting for her world to crash down around her. And in that very moment, she missed her husband and her best friend. She wished she didn't; but she did.

Chapter 50

The good thing about flying in private jets, apart from ample legroom, was that they were almost never delayed. Alex arrived in Las Vegas well before the concert. He would have time to shower and eat before sound check, he thought.

He got into the car that was waiting for him on the tarmac when he arrived. He didn't give it a second thought until the driver took a side street, the onyx pyramid of the Luxor getting smaller in the distance. He hadn't told anyone of his trip. Who arranged for a car?

"Hey! This is the wrong way. Mandalay Bay is after the Luxor."

The driver gave an indiscernible grunt. They kept going. Something was wrong. The hair on the back of his neck stood up as he realized how vulnerable he was. *Stupid!* He blamed himself for yet again not asking the important questions.

When they pulled into a cavernous parking-garage he looked for clues to his whereabouts. All he saw were numbered spaces and arrows indicating the exit. He felt his cell phone still in his pocket, and relaxed slightly. He wouldn't use it unless he had to, in case the noise gave him away, but he had it if he needed it.

The driver stopped and a security guard opened Alex's door. He was wordlessly ushered into an open elevator. He felt like he was in the second act of an action movie. A voice in his head screamed, *Run!* But he didn't. He couldn't articulate why, but a certain curiosity piqued. Testosterone and adrenaline spurred him on, his inner Bruce Willis ready to throw punches and one-liners.

The elevator dinged on the top floor. Stepping out, he crossed through a private entrance into the largest office he'd ever seen. The spectacular desert view caught his eye first as he stepped forward. A tall, clean-shaven figure stood up from behind a thick desk. The man was dressed in a tailored pin-stripe black and gray suit, with a bold purple tie. Alex hadn't expected his action movie nemesis to be so well groomed and handsome. Maybe he overreacted before.

"Alex! Come. Sit." Jackson Jones said with an easy smile, shaking Alex's hand. He seemed shorter up close, though pretty near Alex's own height. Alex must have looked confused because as he sat down (his chair seemed really short) Jackson Jones made a show of introducing himself, excusing his lackey's poor manners. Everything seemed amiable until Jackson Jones said, "It seems we have an important matter to discuss."

Alex's stomach dropped. He felt like he'd been called to the principal's office. He wracked his brain, not coming up with any plausible reason for Jackson Jones to bring him in.

"It has come to my attention that you wish to renegotiate your contract."

Shit! How could he possibly know about that? His pulse quickened.

"I ... where did you hear that?" Alex stuttered.

"My lawyer."

That backstabbing bastard, I should've known.

"I would like to be released from it, upon completion of the tour." Alex said, hoping he sounded business-like and calm.

"I'm sorry to say that is not possible. However, I would like to ask why you are unhappy with the current terms. Have the accommodations not been adequate?"

"No. Yes. They've been fine." Alex said, flustered by the casual turn. He scoured his brain for reasons, coming up short. The tour support was fantastic, his royalty points more than fair, and the signing bonus had been generously deducted from his recoupable debt (unheard of in the music industry). Why was he unhappy? It was a fair question.

"I, uh, think my demographic could have a problem with ... " *Be careful how you word this.* " ... some of the more conservative fans, I mean … "

"You're afraid your fans are put off by porn money?"

"Er, yes."

"In my experience, rock music fans are some of my best customers."

"Well, also I have a daughter, and a lot of younger fans," Alex said, grasping.

"You're afraid of sending the wrong message? Is that it?"

"Something like that."

"May I ask, Mr. Anders, if you watch porn?"

"That's personal," Alex said. Jackson Jones leaned back in his chair, patiently waiting for his response.

"But yeah, I'm a guy," Alex admitted.

"Are you put off by it?"

"N-no."

"Are you so different from your demographic?"

"I guess not." Alex was starting to feel ridiculous.

"Is this about the commercial in Holland? After you expressed your concerns regarding the subject matter, I respected your wish to pull out of it. Excuse the pun," he laughed.

"I know. And I appreciate that. It's just …" Alex didn't know how to finish the sentence. The more he thought about it, the clearer it seemed. Was he really such a prude? Just because he was a husband and father didn't mean he wasn't also a man. Why *should* it bother him or his fans where his funding came from?

"You still have reservations?"

"Well," Alex started. "My wife wants me to get out of my contract."

"She wants you to give up your dream?"

"No!" Alex said, a little louder than he meant. "It's just been hard . . . spending so much time apart. Her dreams have been on hold while I pursued mine. It's not fair."

"Why didn't you say so? Your wife can join you on tour at any time you like. You could have just asked and saved yourself the trouble."

Alex's forehead wrinkled as he tried to see this conversation through Jenna's eyes. It *would* help if she joined him on tour more often.

"Tell you what. Next time, bring her in. I'm certain we can find a compromise amenable to all. You bring her to Vegas, I'll put you up in a honeymoon suite. You'll take her to a show, to a romantic dinner. It'll be like a second honeymoon. She'll thank you for it."

"Okay. I'm sorry to have disturbed you," Alex said, forgetting for the moment how he got there.

"Well! Now that's settled. I'm trying to figure out how to play 'Paper Money' off your second album and I can't quite get the bridge. Would you mind?" Jackson said, proffering his treasured guitar up from behind the desk. Alex's concerns and confusion drifted away as he, in the most improbable of circumstances, taught the country's biggest porn mogul how to play one of his least known songs. Calling this "surreal" didn't begin to do it justice.

Chapter 51

"Will you be my date for Grandpa's induction ceremony?" Felicity asked Trey over Chinese the next night. They had fallen into an easy weekend pattern of eating, making out, eating, and walking around Silver Lake holding hands. She had never been so happy.

"Hmm ... Let me think about it," he teased.

She glared at him, taking a big bite.

"Okay," he said. They both smiled.

"Do you want to come with me to pick out my dress?"

"I love you, but no. I was gonna play basketball."

"You love me?" She asked in a light tone, in case he didn't mean it.

"I love you," he said again, his eyes serious.

"I love you too." She smiled, feeling shy all of a sudden.

They finished their food in giddy silence. Trey stood, taking her by the hand. She wrapped her arms around his neck, running her hands through his golden hair. He made an "mmmm" noise in his throat and leaned in, pressing his forehead against hers. She closed her eyes. They made their way down the narrow hall to his bedroom.

He slept on a twin bed that still had a Jimmy Neutron sticker on the headboard. Signed concert posters mostly covered the kiddy train wallpaper below. Clothes were strewn around the room, invading the rare space between cables plugged into amps and guitars, leaning against opposite walls. The bed was freshly made.

As they made their way over, he peppered her neck and face in soft kisses. She closed her eyes, reveling in his touch. He took his time, pulling his shirt up over his head before running his hands up her back, relieving her of her own shirt, and struggling to unhook her bra. Her breathing came in quick bursts of anticipation. She tried to undo his jeans but he stopped her, lying her down on the bed.

"Are you sure?" he asked. She nodded, pulling him down to her, feeling his weight on top of her.

After, they lay together happily squished on his little twin bed, still breathing hard.

"Are you okay?" he asked.

"Never better. You?"

"Mmmmm."

"I love you," she said, snuggling into the nook of his collarbone.

"I love you too," he kissed the top of her head.

The next day after school, she stood outside the building with Trey, huddled under the awning. It was mizzling out (somewhere between a mist and a drizzle) as she waited for her ride, not minding the excuse to snuggle up to him. Her grandmother pulled up to the curb and Felicity gave Trey a quick kiss goodbye, missing him already. It was the first afternoon they'd spent apart since they started dating.

An hour later she stood in front of a wall of dresses at some designer's studio her mom sent her to. Her usual aversion to shopping dissolved in her euphoria. Nothing could bring her down now. She didn't even mind that her grandmother bailed to run a few errands.

Karyn C. showed her a couple dresses her mom picked out and asked if she wanted to try them on. The first was a charcoal strapless A-line dress with frayed ruching through the midsection. It was pretty, but the color washed her out. Next she tried a one-shouldered gown, knee length in the front, longer in the back, the same color as Trey's eyes. It had the same charcoal fabric as the first dress around the middle, but was far enough from her face to add interest, allowing the turquoise color to make her blue eyes pop. Flowy and feminine. And unexpected. She felt beautiful—it was perfect.

Out on the cobbled walkway, lost in the clouds, she answered her phone. Her grandmother's voice sounded strange—distant and formal. "Felicity, I need to tell you something."

The rest of the conversation was a blur. At some point, maybe minutes later, maybe hours or even days, she was pulled to her feet by her grandmother and buckled into the back seat of a car, holding her hand as they zipped through the city. Her mind was numb. Time and place drifted away and the world passed her by in a series of undefined colors and shapes.

At the hospital, she saw Trey's mom. She was crying. Anya hugged her and they spoke for a minute. Felicity took it in without comprehension. She stood stock still in the middle of the waiting room, until the two women walked toward her. Inexplicably, she felt an overwhelming urge to back away from them. They sat her down on one of the chairs, flanking her on either side. Whatever they were saying was clearly difficult for them but Felicity didn't understand. They seemed to need her to agree to something. She just wanted them to stop talking. She nodded.

Before she knew it, a doctor swept her off down the hall to a room. The door outside read "ICU." Felicity couldn't remember what the letters stood for. But then she saw him. Trey. His leg was bent at an unnatural angle, and his head was covered in bandages, completely obscuring the top half of his face. The lower half was covered in bandages too so that the only visible skin was the unshaven stubble beneath his nose. She barely noticed the machines hooked to him, beeping and wheezing.

"I'm sorry about your friend, and I know this is difficult for you, but you were the last person to see Trey alive and we need you to identify that this is him. Is this what he was wearing?"

What? She thought, finally comprehending what he asked her to do. *He can't be dead. I just saw him. I can see his chest moving. He loves me.*

"In order for him to donate his organs, we must be able to

identify him. Your friend is brain dead, these machines are only keeping his organs viable."

"Yes." She nodded. Her voice came from outside her body, but as she said it, she returned. The full force of reality thrust itself at her. She felt ... like she was going to throw up. *Uh-oh.* Her insides twisted and clenched as tears ejected themselves from her eyes.

Two nurses escorted her from the room as she sobbed and wretched. They took her to an open room, laying her down on a bed. One of them handed her a box of Kleenex and the other left the room. Her grandmother came in a moment later. Felicity gripped her grandmother's shoulders, sobbing and convulsing.

Chapter 52

"Where are you?" Jenna asked.

"Vegas, getting ready for the show tonight."

"You need to come home."

"Are you home?"

"Trey died. In a motorcycle accident. You need to come home," she repeated.

"Wha- Oh no. Felicity. That's … " he trailed off. "I'll be there soon."

Two hours after receiving the phone call from her mom, Jenna arrived at Bob Hope Airport where a car awaited. The drive to Malibu took longer than the flight, with traffic. She shouted at the driver to go faster.

"It's stopped traffic, ma'am. The Lakers are playing. Nothing I can do."

She couldn't stop fidgeting, or checking her phone. She would never be able to forgive herself not being there when Felicity needed her most. What kind of a mother goes off to "find herself," leaving her poor baby alone? Okay, maybe not alone, but it should have been *her* at the hospital and *her* arms of comfort and *her* voice on the phone. She had failed when it mattered most. *Are we there yet?*

After what felt an age later, they wound their way up the Pacific Coast Highway and down the gravel drive to her parents' house. She flung open her door, making her way into the house before the car came to a stop.

Anya was waiting in the entryway and narrowly avoided being bowled over by Jenna's frantic entrance. Jenna looked around for Felicity, but Anya put a finger to her mouth, indicating quiet, and pointed upstairs to Felicity's bedroom. They padded out to the deck.

"How is she?" Jenna asked, tears pricking her eyes.

"She's okay, I think. It's going to be hard, but she'll be alright."

"I can't believe this. She's too young to deal with something like this," Jenna gripped her face in her hands.

"There's something you need to know," Anya said, looking over her shoulder, lowering her voice.

"What?" Worry etched across Jenna's soft features.

"She loved him."

"I know. They were best friends!" Jenna said, offended her own mother thought she was that out of touch.

"No. They were dating. She was *in* love with him."

Jenna's mind reeled. If that was true, why hadn't Felicity told *her*? What else hadn't she told her? A million questions flooded her brain. Then suddenly, they were quiet. All that mattered was Felicity. *Her* needs. *Her* space. *Her* time.

"What can I do to help her?" Jenna asked.

"Love her. Be gentle. Let her grieve in her own way," Anya said, placing a hand on Jenna's shoulder. Jenna nodded, stifling a sob. She hugged her mom as she hadn't done since childhood.

Opening Felicity's door, she saw the familiar photos on the wall, the vanity from her own childhood and her daughter lying on top of the covers, huddled in the fetal position, staring at the wall. She stepped over the mounds of dirty clothes and books, moving some aside, making room to kneel in front of Felicity's vacant gaze.

"Hey," she said, rubbing a hand along Felicity's back. Felicity didn't say anything and Jenna contemplated leaving her alone. *Let her come out when she's ready.* She pulled her hand back and Felicity grabbed it. Jenna crawled onto the bed and held her.

***

"Family emergency. I'm leaving. Now." Alex said to Simon, bags packed, ready to go.

"What'd someone die?" Simon asked, not looking up from

his text.

"Yes."

"What?" Simon looked up, letting his phone beep at his side.

"Trey died," Alex said.

"Shit, man. Yeah, you go. I'll take care of it."

"Thanks," Alex said, grateful to go without a fight.

He was surprised to get a phone call from Ira Stearn on his way back to his hotel room. He ignored it. It rang again. Again, he ignored it. On the third try, he relented.

"What!" Alex demanded.

"I am calling on behalf of my client to remind you of your contractual obligations."

Is he serious?

"Look, it's a family emergency. Talk to Simon."

"Which family member died?" Ira asked as though he were asking what kind of sandwich Alex preferred.

"Trey." Alex responded, teeth clenched.

"And what is his relation to you?"

"What! Are you serious with this? He's my daughter's best friend. What do you care?"

"It is clearly stated in your contract that a 'family emergency' is defined as a death and/or serious illness of an immediate family member. Therefore, if you do not fulfill your contract, whereby you perform this evening's concert, and have not given sufficient notice to reschedule said date, you will personally reimburse all costs incurred by said absence."

Alex's mouth hung open. After all this time playing by their rules—thinking he could get more bees with honey, or whatever that stupid saying was—they had to play it this way.

"Talk to my lawyer," he seethed, chucking the phone on the bed. It bounced off and fell to the floor with a violent thunk. Anger coursed through his veins as he flung clothes haphazardly into his suitcase.

"Hello?" Airika's voice interrupted his tirade. Alex looked

up from the suitcase, too angry to speak. "Going somewhere?" She asked.

"Home." He said, glaring at the mangled pile of clothes in front of him.

"Everything okay?"

"No," he said. "I gotta go. My flight leaves in less than an hour. You want something?"

"I, uh ... you know, never mind. It can wait," she said.

Alex felt bad taking his anger out on her. For all the things that may have been her fault, this wasn't one of them. He sat on the corner of the bed and looked up at her.

"Are you sure?" he said, checking his phone. He had a couple minutes before the car came to pick him up. He watched her shift her weight from side to side.

"Um, have you talked to Jenna lately?"

"I just got off the phone with her."

"Oh. Well, I know the tour is almost over and I ... before we go back to LA, I was just wondering if you'd thought about what I said before," she said, looking anywhere but at him.

"Which part?" Now that he'd let her get started, he regretted it. He didn't want to have this conversation now.

"The part about me loving you. I wanted to know... you know if you and Jenna decided not to get back together ... I don't know. Would you ever consider being with me?" She stood there, feeling naked, without anything to hide behind.

He sighed and sunk his face into his hands. Thinking about the pain his little girl was in, the mess he'd made of his marriage and his career, he couldn't stand the idea of causing more pain. He could spare a couple minutes to let her down gently, or at least as long as it took the driver to call.

"Look, I don't feel comfortable discussing my marriage with you. Jenna and I have our issues, but I know with absolute certainty that she's the one I want." He looked up at her, watching her cheeks turn pink as she stared at the floor. "Look, you're a beautiful woman. You have incredible confidence, and that's sexy." She looked up at him, a shy smile playing on her lips. "You're ambitious and driven. There's no question you're a catch for any guy with half a brain." She beamed up at him, seemingly forgetting about the rejection. He backtracked. "If you'd just rely on those things and stop manipulating people, I think you'd be surprised by the guys who would take interest."

He watched as her gaze strayed from his face back down to her feet. Her cheeks flushed pink again and he thought he could see tears forming in the corners of her eyes. *Shit, don't cry*, he thought. He stood up and gave her an awkward hug. She cried into his shoulder as he shushed her the way he used to do with Felicity as a baby to calm her down. Eventually, she pulled herself together and pulled back a little. Her blonde hair fell around her shoulders, creating a small cave of space between their faces. She kissed him softly on the mouth, with all the rarely surfacing tenderness she possessed. He let her kiss him but pulled back, his hands on her shoulders. He looked intently into her face.

"I have to go now. Okay?"

She nodded. He picked up his stuff and left the room.

It wasn't until he sat down on the plane that he finally had a chance to process what was happening—with his poor little girl, his family, marriage, career. It was all such a mess. He leaned back in his seat, his heart aching to comfort Felicity, and cried.

Jackson Jones and Ira Stearn were a separate problem—heartless bastards, all of them—but they could wait. He felt gutted that he couldn't keep his daughter from pain, but at least he could be there for her, whatever she needed.

Chapter 53

The memorial was beautiful, somber. Jenna and Alex sat on either side of Felicity near the front of the church auditorium. Jenna had never been inside a Unitarian church. Its old world façade, though spectacular, seemed out of place in downtown LA. The packed auditorium felt spacious with its high windows and sky-high ceilings.

The Reverend gave a heartfelt eulogy, reflective rather than preachy. As he spoke, her mind wandered to Mrs. Parker and the excruciating pain she must be in. For self-preservation purposes, Jenna couldn't put herself in those shoes. The unimaginable cruelty of losing a child was unbearable—it defied the laws of nature. She knew it did—had—happened, but it felt surreal. Her heart constricted.

She'd never met Mr. Parker but she'd heard enough stories to know he hadn't been particularly present in Trey's life. If she remembered correctly, he'd given Trey that motorcycle in the first place. She hoped Mrs. Parker had consented, for both their sakes.

When the Reverend finished, he asked if anyone else would like to speak. Trey had been well liked by everyone, judging by the turnout. Jenna was looking around for hands that didn't go up when she saw Felicity stand. Instinctively, as she watched her daughter walk up the aisle to the podium she grabbed Alex's hand. This was their first physical contact since she'd left. This wasn't how she'd imagined it.

Actually, she hadn't really pictured it. She supposed she thought he would apologize and that she may eventually forgive him, but hadn't allowed herself to imagine it in any detail, not trusting herself to stay strong. Alex locked eyes with her and squeezed her hand. They looked on, worried and awed by their daughter's confidence, helpless.

"Trey was my best friend. He was the most amazing person I've ever known. He could always make me laugh … " she sniffed, "no matter my mood. He was fun. He always thought of the most random, greatest things to do." She tried to steady her shaking hands. She smoothed the crumpled speech on the podium and gasped for breath. "He challenged me and listened to me and … loved me." Felicity smiled into the distance, breaking Jenna's heart. She wanted to jump up to comfort her, but Alex held her back, squeezing her shoulders.

"He inspired me to be a better version of myself, leading by example. He would have done anything for his friends without asking anything in return. He was the least judgmental person I've ever met. I will miss his generosity of spirit and sweet, laid-back nature. He was the kind of guy every girl wishes she had in her life. There was no one better. I am grateful to have known him."

Jenna looked over at Alex, who dabbed a tear from the corner of his eye. She didn't bother trying to temper the tears streaking her cheeks. She looked on helplessly while Felicity choked up, opening her mouth like she had more to say. Nothing came out as heaving sobs took over. Jenna moved to get up but Alex kept his arm around her in a firm embrace. Felicity stepped down, hugging Mrs. Parker for a long time, their shoulders shuddering quietly.

Jenna couldn't wrap her head around the whole event. She watched her daughter sit with her boyfriend's mother, going through the most terrible time of her life, unable to help. And Alex was here with her, holding her. It was all so Dali-esque.

After the service, they went back to Anya and Shawn's house. Felicity stayed with Mrs. Parker to attend the smaller gathering of family at her house. Jenna hated not staying by her side, but how could she deny her that closeness to his family? At least it would give her and Alex a chance to talk, out of Felicity's earshot.

"Man," Alex said, slumping into the overstuffed armchair

in the living room, throwing his feet up on the ottoman. Jenna took the couch next to him, tucking her legs beneath her, head leaned back against the padding.

"You know the worst part?" Alex said.

"Hmm?"

"All I could think was, 'I'm so glad it wasn't Felicity.' Isn't that awful?"

"It is. But it's impossible not to put yourself in Mrs. Parker's shoes. I can't imagine … "

They settled into silence, lost in their own thoughts. Finally, Jenna delved into the unavoidable.

"What are we going to do?" she asked, emphasizing "we."

"You know what I want."

"We can't just go back to how it was," she said.

"Can't we just say, we screwed it up but let's start over?" He leaned forward, taking her hands in his.

"Hang on. What do you mean, 'we'?" She tilted her head to one side, eyes wide.

"Just … I mean, come on. Don't I deserve the benefit of the doubt? Yes, I screwed up in high school and I can understand that finding out when you did was hard. I get that." He said, holding his hands up in a "hear me out" gesture. "But I've always been faithful. I have always loved and supported you."

"*You* supported my supporting you. My staying home to raise our daughter. You didn't support my return to modeling. Or encourage me to have any dreams at all. That's great you didn't cheat on me … after we were married. That's my silver lining?" Jenna stood, hands shaking with rage.

"You never had dreams for me to support. That's not my fault! And you hated modeling; you told me how superficial it was and how bitchy they were. I'm sorry that I thought you were happy. You didn't tell me, so how the fuck was I supposed to know?" Alex stood, facing Jenna, chest heaving.

"I shouldn't have to tell you," she said, crossing her arms.

"Like you didn't tell me you were going off to Tahoe with

Zach," he said, not quite under his breath.

"What?"

"You heard me. You didn't waste any time finding a guy to fawn over you. Did you sleep with him?"

"Wow," Jenna said, "I can't believe you have the gall to ask that."

"That's not an answer."

"Here's an answer? Go fuck yourself!" she spat, storming out of the room.

Chapter 54

Sitting in front of the computer, Jenna stared at the screen, replaying the fight with Alex in her head. Their issues were so much deeper than she'd realized. She couldn't come up with a solution. And if they couldn't reconcile, was she ready to divorce him?

Her long practiced habit of procrastination kicked in, forcing her hand to click on unopened emails. *It can't hurt.*

Junk. Junk. Junk. *No, I don't need my massive penis to claim my million dollars* ... Delete. *Oh! Here's one from Noelle.* Open.

From: Noelle Enfin <nephoto@nephoto.com>
To: Jenna Jax-Anders <jja94@gmail.com>
Subject: Photos???
Dear Jenna,
Zach told me you left due to a family emergency. I hope everything is okay and that you are well. I wanted to remind you about your daily photo challenge. I think, given the circumstances, it may be more insightful than a written journal. Life happens. It distracts. Don't lose sight. Make yourself a priority.
Ta Ta,
Noelle

Jenna sighed. She couldn't help Felicity, her marriage was over, and she hadn't even begun to think about what she was going to do with the rest of her life. Her moment of clarity and purpose, so clear a week ago, felt like another lifetime. And being in the next room listening to her daughter sobbing only reminded Jenna how powerless she was.

The sobbing tore at her heartstrings and she couldn't sit idly by. She had to get out. She hefted her camera from its padded case and headed out for a walk. The beach this time of morning was quiet, all pastel blues and pinks. She saw glassy waves and soft tweets of seagulls, saving their energy for scavenging later when the crowds came bringing with them a cornucopia of leftovers. Remembering Noelle's challenge to see things in light and shadow, Jenna looked for subjects with both.

A seashell, stranded by the low tide, wore white ruffles on one side, dark sand on the other. A strip of wet sand, darkened from the receding water, reflected the cloudless sky. A lifeguard tower stood, abandoned this time of year, its dark windows contrasting with the gleaming white watch deck.

Click. Click. Adjust aperture. Click. Check preview. Out of focus. Adjust shutter speed. Click. Better. An hour passed, marked by tiny increments of clicking and checking until the sun rose higher, shadows becoming more pronounced, and Jenna's thoughts tuned in to the moment.

The world in black and white seemed like it should be clear, but there were always shades of gray. The contrast pulled certain things into focus, and left others muddled together in the background.

Nearing the house, she noticed Felicity sitting on the bottom step. *What is she doing?* Jenna trained the lens toward her parents' staircase. Click.

When she checked it, her heart broke. The girl in the photo stared vacantly out at the ocean, a tear glistening in the late morning light. Forlorn. That's the word that came to mind. The girl in the photo couldn't possibly be her baby girl. The girl in the photo was a woman of the world, a woman who'd experienced love and loss.

Was it possible that in the time it took Jenna to find her self, her daughter had grown into a young woman? The heart-wrenching curse and greatest joy of being a parent embodied in a single image: watching her child grow up to become a beautiful young woman while her sweet little baby disappeared, relegated to her memory. Cliché though it was, she couldn't help thinking it went by too fast.

Chapter 55

Airika waited for Alex to disappear around the corner toward the green room, before spinning on her heel, cornering Simon.

"What's going on?" she demanded.

"With you and me, love?" Simon said.

"No, idiot, with Alex," she could hardly contain her disgust. Short and bald was *so* not her type. She only slept with him again because he caught her in a moment of weakness.

After her phone conversation with Jenna, she'd experienced a new feeling: guilt (a first, for her). She didn't like it. Simon happened to be lurking in the lobby bar after she left Alex's room (where he rejected her naked emotional plea). Guilt and jealousy overloaded her senses and, if she'd been that kind of girl, she would have cried. Instead, she healed through sex. Again. *Ugh!* She thought, cursing her vulnerable slip. *This is why one-night stands are perfect. No muss, no fuss, no seeing them the next day.*

"Aw, come on, you don't still want him, do you?"

"He's acting weird," she said, more to herself than him.

"He's fine. Back where he belongs: on the road."

"I don't buy it." She knew something was amiss and that Simon was too stupid to figure it out on his own. Perhaps she could turn his lust to her advantage. At least then it wouldn't have been a total waste.

"How 'bout you 'n me, nick off to my room? Whaddya say?" he wiggled his eyebrows at her. "I can't stop thinking about you." He reached out to ensnare her waist but she stepped away, evading his grasp.

"Fine. Ten minutes."

Luckily, he wasn't one of those guys whose ego needed to be stroked. In the mating and dating hierarchy, she towered above him, and he was smart enough to be grateful. *As well he should be!* She wished Alex felt the same. She looked around one more time, hoping to see him.

Ten minutes later, she lay naked and panting in Simon's bed. He whistled in the shower, annoying her, and she hated to admit that he was actually a great lay. She'd never realized that the benefit of dating a guy from a lower rung of the dating ladder was the extra effort he made to please her, auditioning for another night's performance. He didn't even seem concerned with what she did to him. Narcissism satisfied, she spread out, stretching across the bed like a snow angel in the sheets. Obviously, she wouldn't let Simon see her so pleased.

He opened the bathroom door, steam billowing out into the stale air-conditioned room. She pulled the sheet over herself, his naked body reminding her of her own exposure.

"MmMmmMmmm," he said, shaking his head. "I love seeing a beautiful creature in my bed."

"Lie back down, then," she said, evoking her huskiest tone. She patted the empty bed next to her, strategically allowing the sheet to slip off her leg. He did as he was told. She straddled him, letting the sheet slip away, revealing her naked form.

"So," she said, kissing his neck. "What is it that's got Alex so ... " she grinded on him. "Worked up?"

"Mmmm," he moaned, defenseless. "I dunno. Mmmm, yeah, like that."

"He's been so tense," she said, massaging his chest, running her hands down his torso to his thighs.

"Ohhh, yeah ... " he closed his eyes. "He's just wound up tight. Mmmm ... Not yet," he lifted her under the arms, flipping her onto her back, taking control. She moaned as he ran his tongue across her nipples and down further to her ... *Ooh!*

Twenty minutes later they lay, for a second time, breathing heavily. He slipped his arm behind her neck and she flung her leg over him. *He's a cuddly little leprechaun,* she thought.

"Was there something you wanted to ask me, love?"

"What do you mean?"

"You think I'm stupid? I know that wasn't for nothin'. I'll pay up," he said without opening his eyes. She turned on an elbow to face him.

"What happened? Alex was so angry and then all of a sudden he can't wait to do as he's told?"

"I dunno. Sensitive artist type, I guess," he folded an arm across his face, shaking his head.

"Sensitive about what?"

"He owes the label a film. Jackson Jones isn't a man to give up ... " Simon's eyes shot open, horrified by his own stupidity.

"Are you talking about a porn?" She sat up straight, covering herself again with the sheet.

"Shit. You ain't supposed to know who it's for. But yeah, he wants it to win fucking Oscars. Break down barriers about sex in America or some shit."

"Alex doesn't know, does he?"

Simon shrugged in answer and leant over to kiss her collarbone. She felt dazed. She laid her head back down on the pillow; her straight hair stuck out at all angles, like a lion's mane. Her mind swam with possibilities. There were a lot of things celebrities got used to, including being asked to take their clothes off, but this really crossed a line. Jenna would freak if she found out.

Airika couldn't tell if Simon told her to distract her or as a sort of confessional. Alex Anders: Porn Star? Not likely.

Alex, along with a large percentage of Airika's clients, was a serial relationship whore. Most artists were insecure, seeking validation at every turn. Being alone did nothing to assuage their feelings of inadequacy—something she couldn't understand. She preferred self-sufficiency sprinkled with one-night stands. *Relationships always disappoint.*

"You know," Simon said, caressing Airika's naked shoulder with his forefinger. "I'm starting to fancy you." He kissed her neck. "Maybe we can do this again?"

She slid off the bed, scoffing at him, giving him a look to put him in his place. "Not likely."

Chapter 56

Jenna was the first up the next morning. She made coffee and went outside to get the paper. It was a banal ritual to pass the quiet time before confronting the problems she desperately wished were a nightmare from which she'd wake up.

She checked the mailbox and grabbed the dewy newspaper bag. She saw a package addressed to her and ripped back the plastic, revealing a note from the editor.

J-

Great work! Noelle added your photo credit. Here's the final copy. Good luck in the future. Let's work together again!

-Henrietta

Wow. Jenna stood, transfixed, heart thumping in anticipation. She ripped off the sticky note, revealing the glossy cover beneath. She flicked past pages and pages of advertisements, finally finding the table of contents. There she saw the thumbnail version of *her* photo. She stared, overwhelmed and elated. It was the single most satisfying moment of her life. She wanted to stay wrapped in the warmth of its embrace forever.

She ripped through the pages to their spread. Her name! In *Vogue* magazine! Her photo! *Wait a second*, she thought. She recognized the framing, the angle, the light hitting the side of the model's face, gleaming against the bustling fabric, but … something was different. She couldn't put a finger on it. It was definitely her photo, but not. What happened? She looked through the rest of the layout. Same thing.

Back in the kitchen, she sat in front of her laptop, magazine splayed open in front of her. Noelle had emailed her the photos to add to her growing portfolio. She found the email, scrutinizing one image then the other. Something was amiss. She zoomed in on the computer image and got her mom's magnifying glass for the magazine. Inch by inch she scanned the image and adjusted the zoom. It took a full ten minutes of careful scrutiny. Was the model skinnier? Her nose smaller? Her neck longer? *Yes!*

Jenna knew about airbrushing, of course, and previously considered it one of her generation's greatest achievements. But she'd thought it was about smoothing blemishes and removing unflattering shadows. Changing the features of an already stunning model was taking it far outside her comfort zone. She didn't remember this happening when she was a model. *Did they do it to me without my realizing?*

Her head spun with questions and doubts. Her elation dissolved as she closed the magazine, getting up to pour herself a cup of coffee. She slid open the glass door to the deck, grasping the warm mug with two hands as she stepped into the cool morning air.

The railing was wet with dew as she leaned on it. The mixture of salty sea air and earthy coffee calmed her. Why couldn't anything be simple? Or look the way she'd imagined? All she wanted was to feel purpose, be a good mother, have a happy marriage, and maybe lose those pesky five pounds that seemed to have taken permanent position on her once-flat belly (in a non-digital way, of course). Was that too much to ask?

"Yes!" an obnoxious voice in her head shouted. She pushed it away. Every woman wanted that. Surely it was achievable. Plenty of women had it all. Look at Oprah, for instance: sense of purpose, check; happy relationship, check; good mother, not applicable; pesky pounds? Okay, maybe even the woman who had it all had her battles too.

Ooh, what about Sandra Bullock? Sense of purpose, check; happy relationship, not so much; good mother, check; pesky weight, not a problem! Okay, so two women with nearly everything. There must be someone who had it all. *Hmmmm.* Julia Roberts: sense of purpose, check; happy relationship, check; good mother, check; pesky weight, not even when she was pregnant! *See! If Julia can have it all, so can we all.*

"Mornin'," Shawn said, sliding the door closed behind him, joining Jenna on the deck.

"Good morning. I made coffee."

"Ta." He said, holding up his own cup in a one-sided cheers gesture.

They watched the morning rituals of the seagulls flying out over the ocean, searching for breakfast, dipping and diving across the cloudless horizon.

"How ya goin'?" he asked.

"Fine."

"Why do you American Sheilas always say 'fine'? If things aren't shite, they're great. It's one or the other."

"Shite," she said, chuckling. Leave it to her dad to say something insightful while lumping women into a pejorative generality.

"What's the matter?"

"Everything. Felicity. I feel so helpless ... Alex ... My life in general." She sighed, not wanting to go into detail.

"Shite," he said, nudging her shoulder with his. She smiled. "Sometimes you just have to let go," he said, patting her on the back and heading inside.

Instinctively, she wanted to argue. She couldn't let go of her marriage, child, and budding career! Absurd! The little devil on her shoulder said, "So what if you did? What then?"

Inside the house life continued as usual. Shawn prepared his world famous flapjacks while Anya squeezed fresh-picked oranges from the tree out front, humming along to a familiar tune by Doris Day. *What's that song?* Jenna smiled when she remembered: "Que Sera, Sera." Of course.

Jenna watched Felicity come down the stairs, into the kitchen, picking up a plate of pancakes. Anya handed her a glass of juice and Felicity smiled. Jenna's heart warmed, her worries dissipating like the early morning marine layer.

Chapter 57

Jean-Pierre had been Anya's personal stylist for as long as Jenna could remember. Once a regular fixture in the Jax household, now he only came by before a big event, like this Hall of Fame induction. Originally from Paris, he'd spent the last forty years in the States, which had done nothing to dampen his accent. Jenna used to think he put it on to seem more exotic. Maybe it was JP's way of keeping his identity, she mused. She could appreciate that.

"Allo, mon amour!" he trilled, kissing Anya on both cheeks twice. She obliged, grinning.

"Ça va?" She asked.

"Oui, ça va bien, now I see you again! You look beautiful, as always."

"You remember Jenna ... and my granddaughter, Felicity?" Anya said, waving an arm toward them.

For the most part, Anya and Shawn lived a modest existence, but this—the 15 by 20 foot spare room turned closet—was Anya's big splurge. The walls were lined in neat rectangles and cubes, separating evening wear from day wear, heels from flats, and a myriad of accessories. Off to one side, the closet opened up into a large bathroom complete with a vanity and salon chair, water closet, and a fully stocked wine fridge. Jenna spent countless hours in this closet as a child, playing out every little girl's dress-up fantasies.

"Voilà, zhese are straight from Bryant Park, as you requested. You will be ze first to wear zem," he said, pointing to a chrome rack of garments, all in Anya's size, all age appropriate. He waved a hand over two more racks, eyes raised in glee. "Zhese ... are for you!" He said to Jenna with the flourish of a magician, his gaze quickly falling on Felicity.

She looked thinner, slightly gaunt. It had been two weeks

since Trey died, and grief had taken its toll on her daughter. Jean-Pierre seemed to think otherwise, visibly thrilled to be dressing a tall, thin, beautiful young woman.

"Zhis is for you," he said to Felicity. He reached for a pale aquamarine dress, with charcoal ruching that looked perfect for her. As soon as he pulled it off the rack, Felicity burst into tears and fled.

Jenna followed her down the hall to her room. "What's the matter, Sweetie?"

"I was supposed to go with Trey. He was going to be my date to the ceremony. I picked it out because it matched his eyes." Felicity sniffed. Jenna's throat choked up as she listened, wishing she'd known. Felicity lay on the bed, staring at the wall.

"Oh, Sweetheart, I'm sorry. I had no idea," she rubbed Felicity's back.

"'S okay," Felicity murmured.

"You know, if you don't want to go, we don't have to. I'll stay with you; take you to a museum or anywhere you want. Just say the word."

"No. I want to go." Felicity forced a smile. "But thanks for offering."

"Okay, but you wear anything you want. Sweats, even." Jenna kissed the top of her head and stood up. She paused in the doorway, then made her way back down the hall to the closet.

"Everything okay?" Anya asked.

"I think it was just too much too soon," Jenna said. Anya nodded.

"Zis one will look fabulous on you!" Jean-Pierre said.

Jenna welcomed the distraction. He held out a delicate 1920's inspired sheath dress, mid-thigh length, feathers lining the hem, exactly what she would have picked out for herself. She reached for it, but out of the corner of her eye, another dress caught her attention.

Bold, she thought, *but I like it.* The black and white striped print crissed and crossed, bending and swirling at impossible angles, creating beauty from chaos.

The dress was short. Tight. Simple. It struck a perfect balance between strong and feminine. She tried it on. There would be no lingering in the shadows in a dress like this.

"Perfect! Ooooh, try zhese too!" Jean-Pierre said, shoving an exquisite pair of shocking red open-toe booties at her. She slid them on, twirling in front of the mirror like a five-year old playing dress up. Jean-Pierre clapped. Jenna looked to Anya, whose brows furrowed in a noncommittal look.

"It's different ... " Anya said. *Uh-oh, here we go.* "But also kind of ... perfect."

"Really?" Jenna beamed.

Jean-Pierre and Anya nodded as she swirled back around, admiring herself in the mirror. Suddenly, inspiration struck. She knew how to help Felicity.

"Mom, do you still have that dress you wore to Dad's first Grammy's?" She asked, rummaging the evening wear section of the closet. Anya reached to Jenna's left, and produced a black jumpsuit with sheer gold mesh across the bust, leaving the impression of metallic skin.

"I thought you liked the one you have on."

"I do. It's not for me. Can Felicity wear this?"

"Yes, of course. If she wants," Anya said. "Do you really think she'd wear this awful thing?"

"I'm not sure. We'll find out." Jenna said, eyes twinkling.

Chapter 58

"Knock, knock. Can I come in?" Jenna danced from foot to foot in the open doorway, unable to stand still. Felicity didn't respond, but her eyes flit over to Jenna's general direction. Jenna held the jumpsuit behind her back, crinkling in its plastic shell.

"What's that?" Felicity said, sitting up on the bed.

"I've been thinking," Jenna said. Felicity made a face that said "uh-oh," but held her tongue. "And I realized something." Jenna sat down on the edge of the bed. "You were right." Now she had Felicity's attention. "You have an incredible opportunity, and even though I'm afraid of letting you go and letting you get hurt, I realize I need to step back and trust you. I can't stop you from experiencing pain." They both stiffened and Jenna took a moment to recover. "I don't want to stop you from becoming the fullest version of yourself. So," she said, holding the jumpsuit in front of her with a Vanna White flourish, "This is for you!"

"What is it?" Felicity asked, scrunching her nose.

"It's the outfit your grandmother wore to the Grammys the first year Grandpa was nominated, in 1970."

"Really? She wore that?" Awe and disgust intermingled on her face.

"Yep. And I thought maybe you'd like to wear it when you announce your acting debut."

"Really? I can do the movie?" Felicity bounced up to her knees, throwing her arms around her mom's neck. Jenna nodded into Felicity's shoulder.

"Thank you!"

"I'm proud of you," Jenna said, holding her at arm's length so she could look her in the eye.

"Thank you." A tear glistened in the corner of Felicity's

eye. "Erm, do I have to wear this hideous outfit?" She asked.

Jenna let the suspense linger as long as she could. "What, the golden granny disco look is so hot right now."

They broke into a fit of laughter, collapsing on the bed, delirious giggles overtaking them.

When their manic burst was over, they lay on the bed, cheeks aching, chestnut and caramel hair splayed everywhere.

"Mom?"

"Mmm?"

"I'm glad you're back."

"Me too."

Jenna sat up and scooted to the edge of the bed, carefully putting her feet over the trunk at the foot of the bed. Something caught her eye, poking out of Felicity's messenger bag.

"What's this?"

"Wha-? Oh, that? Nothing."

"It's not 'nothing', it's a magazine." Jenna slid it out, unrolling it, and saw her husband's (slightly) airbrushed face looking back at her. *Why don't men have to meet the same standards of beauty as women?* She shook her head and redirected her attention to the article. Felicity squirmed beside her. Jenna read, her mouth tightening.

"Where did you get this? And when?"

"A girl at school gave it to me a couple weeks ago." Felicity said, not looking up.

"Who?" Jenna demanded.

"Sadie."

"Did you read it?" Jenna asked, more worried than upset.

"No." Felicity responded, somewhat truthfully.

"Good. Don't." Jenna said, holding the offending thing in a death grip.

Jealousy and rage flooded her system like a drug. It was one thing for Airika and Alex to have caused *her* pain, but this? Burdening Felicity with this added pain and worry pushed her over the edge. There was no excuse not to have this situation under control.

Fuming, she stormed out to her car, still parked in the driveway. She slammed the door shut and dialed Alex's number.

Chapter 59

No way, no how. Alex couldn't believe his ears. Jackson Jones, his not-so-anonymous backer, and Simon Walker, his long-time manager, sat together, calm as could be. He sat opposite them in the white leather love seat in his hotel room, hands on his knees, unsure if he should storm out, laugh, or cackle demonically. *They're not serious,* he decided. He kept a neutral face while they stared him down. Minutes passed. *Oh God, they're waiting for a response.* Alex was a fox in a trap. They knew it and he knew it.

He saw his worst fears realized. The fine print he so pointedly ignored while signing the too-good-to-be-true contract, magnified and highlighted his stupidity in bold.

He recalled mention of something about starring in a motion picture, produced by his label's parent company. He didn't think anything of it. Cross-promotion. Nothing wrong with that, he'd thought. In fact, he'd harbored a secret fantasy of trying his hand at acting. But not this way. How did they phrase it? Behind-the-scenes art film with unrestricted access? Translation: glorified porn.

Time slowed as Jackson Jones explained that Alex had been filmed in his hotel rooms, backstage at shows, during meetings, etc. And although the final climax scene (pun intended) wasn't what they'd hoped for (with Airika) their female audience may prefer him ending up with his wife, anyway.

"Wait. What? The behind-the-scenes DVD footage? They've been filming me in my room? Having sex with my wife?" Alex hadn't asked all the right questions, but surely his contract couldn't justify filming with hidden cameras. And they couldn't use footage of him having sex without his permission. Right? He could only imagine what (apparently legal) hidden cameras had captured of his band mates' escapades. Or, more horrifying, was what their footage of he and Jenna, and he and

Airika might be edited to look like.

"Listen, mate ... " Simon started, an unusual feeling taking hold of his innards, forcing him to explain himself.

Jackson Jones went into damage control mode. He'd known Simon's weakness for Alex all along, and how to exploit it. Convenient to his endgame, guilt was not an emotion with which he bothered.

"Alex. I understand your hesitance," Jackson Jones said, sounding the part of the Russian porn mogul who watched too many American gangster movies. "I understand your fears. I think, however, if you'll let me, I can allay those fears. You're a reasonable man, no? I am a reasonable man too. Let us two reasonable men come to a compromise."

"What kind of compromise?"

"The film has been in production for six months on four continents. It follows the lives of six people, shot docudrama style. Their love lives intertwine with their careers, friends, and various activities. Think of it as a romantic comedy, with a little more truth."

"By truth, you mean sex," Alex said, memories of cameras following him throughout the tour, on meet and greets, photo shoots, and onstage surfacing in his mind. He couldn't shake the images. That couldn't have been what they were filming. Someone would have told him. Simon would have told him.

Despite their recent antagonism, Simon had always looked out for his best interests. Beneath the gruff exterior, he was a good guy. Sure, they'd had their share of fights, but they'd been together for so long. They were like family.

Alex's denial halted as soon as he looked over at his manager—hunched and tiny, as though the chair were swallowing him whole. He looked ... guilty. Simon's bravado vaporized in the wake of this bomb dropping.

It was a sham. The whole damn thing. Alex had been betrayed. The weight of the lie bore down on him, rendering him immobile.

"You have a unique opportunity right now," Jackson Jones continued, unfazed, "to join the ranks of many of your musical peers, to appeal to a female base in a new way. Most women prefer adult films with plot and character development. They love reality television. We can give that to them. A combination of reality TV, celebrity, and sex. Your sales will be through the roof, as they say. Just think of your idols. How many were controversial figures? Think about it. The Beatles had long hair, Elvis swiveled his hips, Madonna groped herself in lingerie in front of burning crosses. Alex Anders can show women what it's like to have sex with a rock star! And if it's not with you, it will be with the next up-and-coming rock star because the world is ready. People are hungry for it. You have a chance to be great, Alex."

Alex didn't speak. He didn't think. The lines of reality bulged and bubbled, twisted and morphed until all that was left was a single palette, mixing colors and sound into a brown blob. Indistinguishable.

He paused outside the door processing everything he'd heard. Simon came out, putting a hand on Alex's shoulder. He opened his mouth, but before he could say anything, Alex cut him off: "You're an asshole." He walked away without a backward glance.

Chapter 60

"I can't believe I'm leaving you another message. Pick up your damn phone! Call me back." Jenna demanded, hanging up and chucking the phone at the passenger seat as though Alex would feel the pain. Jenna ran her fingers across her temples, grabbing handfuls of hair in tight fists. The pain felt good. She'd never understood people who physically hurt themselves in order to relieve their emotional pain, but in this moment, she felt a sudden insight.

She read the article. Start to finish. She read all about how Alex had "suspected her feelings" but that the "timing hadn't been right" to do anything about it. That they were "in love" (Airika's words) and "enjoying each other's company and emotional support on tour." How "things at home had been rough for a while" and that it was "just a matter of time before the truth came out."

What a bunch of blatant, unadulterated bullshit! The article itself was very much what Alex told her it was. She found it harder to read in print, but on its own, not unexpected. The part she was unprepared for was one line at the bottom, that read "If you're dying to know more about Alex and Airika, just wait until the film comes out this Spring—it's reality meets celebrity meets sex scandal. Stay tuned."

A funny thing happened when she finished reading. She felt nothing, not because she suddenly became an emotional ice queen, but because it was all so transparent. It was like watching reality TV and realizing they shoot "reality" over multiple takes from different angles, after people have signed waivers to appear on camera. Their cracked cover exposed a crevasse of Grand Canyon proportions separating reality from television—or in this case, print.

It was so easy to get wrapped up in the details of fame and

tabloids and this alternate version of reality. There was the constant threat of information being used against her, the fear of saying or doing something that could ruin her husband's career. And there was the suspicion she felt meeting new people, never sure if they wanted to be friends with her or her famous last name. *What a ruse!* A silly little mask, underneath which was an inanely simple explanation behind the "scandal." The reality was that someone had been fed information and published lies. The real question was, to what end?

Without a second thought, she called their attorney, Frank, alerting him to the article's allusion to the film, and asking him to review Alex's contract, and advise their next step, ASAP.

Her priorities aligned, Jenna got proactive. Alex was a talented musician, married to a woman with a famous last name. He'd always been too trusting of people and it was easy to see how he ended up in this position.

Jenna never realized how prominently she factored into his career until now. She steered him away from untrustworthy people, leading him in better directions. Without her, he didn't always know the difference. And now she was reclaiming her power and eliminating the hangers on who'd gotten too close as of late.

After these past weeks, watching Felicity endure unimaginable pain, Jenna had been reminded that life was about moments. As a family, they'd had many wonderful moments. There wasn't a thing in the world worth giving that up for. She had to preserve those moments for Felicity's sake. She had displayed grace and maturity through her grief. Jenna aspired to learn from her example. Felicity was so wise. Jenna realized she was lucky to be able to confront those who caused her pain, and find closure.

Inside the house Anya and Felicity were tense, awaiting her reaction. That made her sad. She didn't want to be a person who caused her loved ones to worry. She could control that.

"Anyone want to go for a walk?" She asked.

"I do." Felicity said.

"Sounds lovely." Anya said, visibly relieved.

Three generations of Jax women rolled up their pant legs, raked their bare toes through the damp sand, collecting small treasures, smiling in the golden afternoon light. Jenna snapped pictures of Anya inspecting a sand dollar, Felicity kicking a wave, the two of them inspecting a pile of seaweed, a carefree Felicity jumping from rock to rock while Anya worried about her falling. The last shot wasn't hand held. Jenna balanced the camera on a flat-ish rock, set the timer and posed for a touristy shot with her mom and daughter on either side of her. Click. A photograph of the way she felt, in this particular moment in time.

There was more to life than keeping up commercial-perfect appearances; and now she was living it, enjoying her own reality. When they returned home, disgorging their treasures, Jenna rinsed the salty sea from her skin. Her phone vibrated on top of the duvet as she toweled off. She let her wet hair fall limp down her back, soaking her t-shirt as she picked up the phone. It reminded her that Alex's make-up show in Vegas was tonight. *And still, no messages.*

Chapter 61

Driving to Vegas seemed like a good idea when she started out, four and a half hours ago. Jenna wanted to stay proactive and it seemed better than flying. Sitting in traffic on I-10, however, reminded her why people hated driving in L.A. She hadn't even made it out of the county yet.

She needed to see Alex and have it out in person. If there was enough footage of he and Airika to be called a sex scandal, she'd rather confront it privately now rather than waiting for an audience at the Hall of Fame induction.

She scanned through radio stations, hoping for a little audio courage to inspire her sagging energy. Spanish, Christian, Country, Mexican Country, ad, ad, ad, Spanish, *ooh*, drums! Guitar! She left it on. She laughed, recognizing the riff even before her dad's voice sung lyrics literally written for her.

"The world's wrapped around your finger, Little Lady/ You're my world too, Little Lady/ Don't do what they tell you/ You just do what you do/ Little Lady's on her way/ Shining brighter than the stars someday/ Yeah, she will, shine on my Little Lady."

As the song ended, the station announcer gave a traffic update. "Westbound I-10 is closed due to a propane tanker crash, but the East bound direction will remain open and should return to speed shortly." It was a sign. She nudged her way over three lanes, with a minimum of hand gestures and honking.

Defying all logic and self-preservation, L.A. drivers felt entitled to block any other car from changing lanes, ever. As though under personal assault, they took dangerous measures to prevent anyone from following through on their indicator. This explained why so few used them.

As the fast lane opened up and traffic moved faster, she rolled down the windows, letting the wind blow through her hair. Choking on smog and feeling something fly into her hair, she remembered she was in LA and rolled them up again. Despite her newfound sense of purpose, it wasn't quite like the movies, after all.

***

Meanwhile, Alex's lawyer paid a visit to Shawn and Anya.

"Frank?" Anya said, walking up to him, hand outstretched.

"Mrs. Jax." He shook her hand, tipping his head in a formal nod. They'd known each other for at least ten years but his greeting remained unchanged from their first encounter.

"Is everything okay?" She asked.

"Pardon the intrusion, but do you know where I might find Mr. or Mrs. Anders?"

"Jenna just left to meet Alex in Vegas. Is everything okay?"

"No, it's rather urgent I speak to Mr. Anders."

"May I ask what this is regarding?" Anya said.

"This is highly unusual, and I fear I can't give you specific details, but I can tell you we are on a tight timeline. I have just discovered a rather significant loophole regarding an ongoing issue," he said, nearly tipping his mouth into a smile.

Anya didn't know what to think, but didn't hesitate to give Frank the details of Alex's whereabouts and call for a jet. Despite recent months' events, she still had faith in Alex and Jenna and hoped they'd work things out.

***

Two hours later, Frank knocked on the hotel room Anya directed him to, briefcase in hand. So when Airika, wearing nothing but an oversized men's shirt answered the door, he wasn't quite sure what to do. He double-checked his notepad.

"Do you know where I might find Mr. Alex Anders?"

"Yeah. He's across the hall. We switched rooms."

"Thank you, Ms. Thomas."

Airika winked at him, amused by his formality. Simon called out from the bed, trying to coerce her into coming back to join him. She closed the door and Frank walked across the hall to knock on Alex's door.

"Thanks to a tip from your wife, I reviewed your entire contract. There is reference to a behind-the-scenes film, starring you, featuring appearances by other band members." He looked at Alex to make sure he was following. Alex nodded. "I had changed a particular phrase, 'unrestricted access' to 'restricted access, as defined in Appendix B'." But see here," he pointed to the bottom of the page, "you never signed this form, meaning they never had your permission to be filmed."

"Really?" Alex asked, grabbing the contract to see for himself. As he did, a loose page fell out. He picked it up, and, with a flash of recognition, his heart sank. He remembered Simon handing him a page just like this one, saying, "Here's the new waiver. Sign it so we can get back to work."

He hadn't thought anything of it at the time. He'd trusted his manager. But, where in the unsigned copy it read "restricted access, as defined in Appendix B," the one with his signature on it still read "unrestricted access." He'd been duped. Frank's eyes widened as he realized what happened.

"Jackson Jones told me what they've been shooting. I haven't seen it, but I'm pretty sure they have footage of Jenna and me," Alex cleared his throat. "We can't let them do this," he said, hanging his head.

"There may be a way." Frank said, his brown eyes gleaming. "I never saw mention of Jenna. Unless she signed a separate waiver, they cannot use the footage of her."

Alex looked up, anxiety and hope in his expression.

"If, as you say, you only had intercourse with your wife, and they cannot use the footage of her, then they would not have their 'money-shot," as I believe it's called. That being the case, it would no longer qualify as pornography, nor even an interesting sex scandal." Any other time, formal Frank's usage of the term "money-shot" would have cracked him up. Right now, he felt like kissing the man.

"Thank you." Alex said, surprising Frank by pulling him into a big hug. This wasn't a Man Hug (closed fist, one arm style), but a real, two-arm open-handed hug. Frank cleared his throat, pulling away and nodded stiffly, turning to leave.

Chapter 62

Jenna knocked on Alex's door, resigned to the inevitable confrontation. She wouldn't take being lied to, given their history, and she wasn't about to be made a fool of in public, especially not at Felicity's expense. Reconciliation may not be possible, but they could at least get closure and present a united front for Felicity.

She needed to know if anything had happened between he and Airika at any point on the tour. The only explanation she could imagine for his distance and demeanor was guilt. If she was right she'd rather confront it now, in private, rather than waiting for the movie to see it play out.

She took a deep breath, telling herself now was the time for her to face it and make peace (if necessary), before New York when they'd have to break the news to Felicity.

The door flung open, revealing Airika, pale-faced and wide-eyed, still only partially clothed. Her worst fears realized, Jenna couldn't think of what to say. If she didn't know better, she would have said Airika looked scared. The situation seemed less clear, more variables clouding her judgment. Her arguments, along with their friendship, flushed down the drain of Unsaid Things.

"Can I come in?" Jenna asked.

"Sure." Airika showed her in, letting the door close behind. They sat, as they would have before, on the bed, legs crossed under them. It struck her as forced and awkward, like their conversation.

When they were little, entire nights of sleep were lost to endless storytelling and gossip sessions. They talked about everything—relationships, family, school, crushes, celebrities, fashion, how they were going to be big stars. It was the quin-tessence of their friendship. Its absence left a giant crevasse in plain sight. Their polite conversation danced around the void, neither willing to address it.

"Look, Air. I just don't know what to say." Jenna started.

"I wanted to call so many times," Airika said, relief washing over her perfect complexion. "I know I shouldn't have done what I did. I miss having you in my life."

"It's been awful, all the way around." Jenna agreed, looking around the room, trying to be the bigger person, and not think about the fact that Airika wasn't fully clothed.

"I know. Let's just put it behind us. Go back to how it used to be," Airika said.

"You can't be-," Jenna stopped herself, taking a breath and thinking about what was best for Felicity. "I would like to move on."

"Oh Jenna, I'm so happy to hear you say that," Airika said, jumping up to hug her.

Jenna backed away, putting ample space between them. "Are you even sorry?"

"J, I've already apologized, like, a thousand times. But if you have to hear it again, fine."

Jenna waited. And waited. *There,* she thought.

"No. You've never actually apologized. Ever. And that wasn't an apology either. It was an implied apology. Not the same thing."

"God, why are you being like this? I said I wanted to make up," Airika said, put out by this unexpected attitude.

"But the thing is … the thing is—it's not up to you. You kissed my husband," Jenna said, standing up, "and after I caught you, you continued to pursue him," she closed the gap between them, motioning to Airika's attire. "You told Rose!" She hovered inches from Airika's stricken face. "And you don't even have the decency to be sorry!" Her heart thumped wildly in her chest.

"What I gave up for you should count for something too," Airika said. "I'd say we're even, so let's just call it good."

Jenna's eyebrows shot up to her hairline, horrified as much by what Airika said as by her obvious sincerity. All the years of not standing up for herself fueled her outrage, and she slapped Airika hard across the face. She couldn't believe she did it. Airika stared at her, mouth agape. She looked like she might cry.

Jenna clenched and unclenched her jaw, as though at any moment another tirade may tumble out, or worse—an apology. She closed her mouth and left, slamming the door behind her.

Chapter 63

Alex heard a door slam and cautiously opened his own. Jenna saw him and inhaled sharply.

"But I thought ... " she started, confused, pointing across the hall to Airika's room.

Alex's eyes widened as recognition dawned. "No, we switched rooms," he said. She was so relieved that she felt her knees give out, heavy from the burden she'd been carrying. She was so flustered from her encounter she'd completely forgotten why she drove to Vegas in the first place.

"Did you think-?" Alex's forehead crinkled in frustration at the implied accusation.

"Yeah," she murmured, collapsing in his arms.

It felt so good to hold her after all that time apart. He wanted to tell her how much he loved her, how he'd missed her, how all he wanted was for them to go back to normal. Instead, he held her, feeling her chest heave up and down in big oversized breaths. Annoyance fluttered in the pit of his stomach knowing she still didn't trust him and he wanted to ask what happened across the hall, but didn't think it prudent when he was still keeping a secret from her.

Her hair smelled of the beach, like coconut. He loved her smell. He kissed the top of her head. She squeezed her arms tighter around his torso. She was shaking.

"You okay?" He asked.

"Mmmhmm," she mumbled into his chest. When she finally pulled away, she looked up at him and said, "I love you." Grateful relief washed over him, rendering him inarticulate.

"I love you too," he said, "more than you know."

"Do you think we can make this work?" She asked.

"I hope so. I'll do whatever it takes."

"Hmmm. Me too," she said, though her face said something else he couldn't read through her sad expression.

"How can I trust you like I used to?" She thought aloud.

He was pretty sure her question was rhetorical.

"I can't *forget* the whole Airika debacle. And I'm not going back to who I was—just a housewife. Turns out, there's more to me than shopping and working out." She made a face that said "who knew?"

"And I feel like every time I get a handle on things, something new and terrible tests my resolve," she said, her eyes glazed over in thought.

He knew she was referring to Felicity. That was too much to handle right now. He addressed the easier subject.

"You've never been 'just a housewife,' you've renovated every room in our house, making it a home. You're an amazing mother, especially given how young we were. You take care of everyone around you. We couldn't survive without you."

"But, how do I trust you when I know you're keeping things from me?" She lifted her eyebrows, daring him to argue. "What do you know about this film coming out?"

He sighed. "First, there won't be a film. Or at least not like they wanted."

"Like who wanted?" She asked.

"Jackson Jones," he said, gauging her reaction.

"The porn guy?" She asked. He nodded. She ran a hand through her hair and sat back, ready to hear whatever he had to say.

"He's my anonymous backer," Alex started, explaining all about the favors and Simon's betrayal and finally, the porn they were trying to make. She listened, as though caught in the headlights, not saying anything.

"So they have footage of us having sex?" She said, finally.

"Yes, but I've already talked to Frank and he says that as long as you didn't sign a waiver, they cannot use any footage of you."

"I never signed anything. But," Jenna said, trying to wrap

her brain around all this new information. "If they have the footage, what's to stop them from leaking it?"

Alex hadn't thought of that. They needed some kind of insurance.

"Hang on, you said Ira Stearn represented Jackson Jones?" Jenna asked. Alex nodded. Jenna scooted forward on the bed and looked into Alex's eyes. "You need to ask Airika to help. If she really loves you, and I believe she does, tell her this is her chance to make things right. I don't know all the specifics but I know she's been hoarding evidence against her father and Ira for years, in case they ever crossed her. Get her to talk to Frank."

Alex couldn't believe it. There was a way out. And again, Jenna figured it out. If he didn't do everything in his power to hold on to her, he was an absolute fool.

"Airika," he said, holding the phone in one hand and Jenna's hand in his other, "I need a favor."

Chapter 64

They arrived at the famed Waldorf Astoria hotel on Friday morning, the crisp New York air smelling faintly of spring. A West Coast Girl through and through, Jenna still got a thrill being in Manhattan. It felt like being in one of her favorite movies. From their hotel room, she could see the Chrysler building, glinting in the sunlight.

After all the recent drama she thought it would be great for she, Felicity and Alex to rent bikes and ride through Central Park, then have a picnic lunch. Enjoy being tourists. To her surprise, they were happy to oblige.

They cruised along the winding paths of the park. Jenna cruised, anyway. Felicity and Alex raced along, intermittently slamming the brakes when confronted with oncoming pedestrian traffic. She watched them zip and zoom around, while she basked in the view of ducks swimming in the pond, the shock of color blooming against the green wall of foliage, couples holding hands on benches. She catalogued how she felt in this moment: happy, content, whole. She felt like herself.

The afternoon was a blur. They ate their way back to the hotel, trying something from every street vendor they passed. Jenna took photos of Felicity eating roasted cashews, of Alex's scrunched face as he stuffed a giant hot dog in his mouth, complete with ketchup mustache. She asked the porter to take a photo of the three of them outside the hotel. They looked idyllic. It was a perfect day.

*****

She and Felicity left Alex to get ready for the ceremony and they headed to Anya and Shawn's suite. Jean-Pierre was there, along with Anya's hair and make-up stylists, ready to work wonders on them, making them look ten years younger and ten pounds lighter. She noticed a melancholic turn in Felicity's mood. She ached to be able to help. She'd learned that Felicity would talk about it if she wanted, and otherwise, the best thing was to give her space.

Two hours later, three generations of Jax women emerged, glowing in their immaculately coiffed beauty. Jenna's chestnut hair had been swept into a loose up-do, with plenty of stray curls making their way down her back. Her smoky eyes and red velvet lips juxtaposed the geometric black and white dress.

Anya wore a maroon silk jacket and skirt—understated and elegant. Her blonde hair was pinned back in a classic French twist. The only thing over the top about her was the swirling diamond cuff she wore on her right wrist. Jenna marveled at her grace. She was mesmerizing.

"Wow!" she gasped, seeing Felicity.

Her tan skin brought out the almost-not-even-there turquoise of her dress, accentuating her big blue eyes. Her sun-kissed hair fell in pretty tendrils around her shoulders. She looked like the beautiful young woman she was. Jenna, taken aback, was overwhelmed with love and pride. She stood in awe of this beautiful creature before her. She didn't deserve any of the credit. Felicity was her own person.

They found Shawn and Alex in the VIP lobby, where they'd been enjoying a drink (or two). Without all the primping, guys had the advantage, time-wise. Given the choice, however, Jenna preferred women's fashion options to a boring suit or tux any day.

They posed on the red carpet, flash bulbs ablaze. Questions about music were directed to Shawn and Alex; "Who are you wearing?" to Anya and Jenna. And Felicity. Word had already gotten out about the biopic.

Jenna watched, as her sixteen-year old daughter answered questions with the poise of someone twice her age. It took every ounce of willpower for Jenna not to start blubbering "My little girl's all grown up!" She couldn't risk ruining her makeup. Not to mention, Felicity would kill her.

They made their way inside the ballroom, with its opera house seating and crystal chandeliers. Mindy, Alex's publicist, was waiting to take him backstage. As a presenter, he had a variety of duties, and a lot of backstage schmoozing to do. He squeezed Jenna's hand before Mindy swept him off, while an usher directed she and Felicity to their seats. Anya and Shawn were no longer behind them, stopped by old friends and famous faces.

They sat down at a table near the front of the stage. Jenna took a sip of champagne. Felicity sipped her water. They looked around to see who else was there. The table to their left was empty but Jenna noticed a place card indicating that the seat directly behind hers was reserved for Eric Clapton. The next table represented the other Aussie and Kiwi bands that had been up-and-comers along with Shawn back in the 70's. Jenna smiled at Marta, the wife of Shawn's ex-drummer. She turned back to Felicity to ask her a question about the woman next to Marta when something—someone, rather—caught her eye, the words never making it out.

Felicity turned around to see what was so interesting. When she saw who it was, she stood up and gave Simon Walker a hug. He'd been like an uncle to her all these years. Next to Simon sat a man Jenna didn't immediately recognize. He was tall and dressed in an Armani suit, his salt and pepper hair skimming the top of the expensive fabric. He was deep in conversation with the bimbo to his left, whose fake boobs were a hiccup away from the next Nipple Gate scandal.

"Excuse me, Jenna?" Mindy appeared out of nowhere.

"Yes?"

"Would you mind coming with me? It'll only take a minute."

Jenna stood, following Mindy through the maze of tables off to a quiet corner near the stage.

"What's going on?" Jenna asked.

"You need to see this," Mindy said, pulling a phone from

her pocket, pressing play on a video pre-loaded on the screen.

Jenna looked on in horror as a montage of video clips of she and Alex flashed in front of her, first eating and walking together, then her, chest down in the lingerie she recognized buying on their anniversary. Her heart sank as she saw Airika come in, first confronting Jenna, then enjoying a romantic meal with Alex. Then it sped up, cutting to clips of naked skin, hotel rooms, pieced together in a flesh orgy, finally showing Airika on top of a faceless man with thick dark hair on his arms in a hotel room, then splayed out, post-coital, tangled in his sheets, nude. It ended with a clip of Alex sneaking out of his room, then finally onstage, under the lights. The nauseating blend of romance and tawdriness made it look like a trailer for a high-budget porn. She looked on in disbelief.

"Why are you showing me this?" Jenna said.

"Alex asked me to show you before Mr. Jones did," Mindy said, gesturing to the mystery man next to Simon.

"I thought they couldn't use the footage?"

"I'll let Alex explain, but the long and short of it is that Simon and Mr. Jones are exploiting a loophole about newsworthiness to use footage without your permission. Alex thought Frank took care of it but we have yet to hear from him, and Alex didn't want you taken off-guard."

Jenna didn't know what to say. She hadn't heard from Frank yet either, although he was supposed to be here tonight. She'd assumed Rose McKenna had exaggerated the scandalous footage, especially since *Rolling Stone* fired her and killed the story. She staggered back to her table, looking on in disgust as The Bimbo cackled, her nipple making its long-awaited escape.

"Let me help you with that." Jackson Jones said, leaning in to slide her top back in place.

Jenna tried to stem the nausea and compose herself, wanting to act normal for Felicity's sake. Her mind reeled with questions and she desperately wanted to talk to Alex, but he'd be onstage any minute.

She no longer needed to catch a glimpse of his place card to know who he was: Jackson Jones. She assumed a man who insisted on being an anonymous boss hadn't received an invitation to this evening's event. *So why is he here?*

Simon continued talking to Felicity, and caught a glimpse of Jenna, baring his teeth in a smile. She tried to wipe the glare off her face to smile, but it came across as more of a sneer. She took another sip of champagne. She looked around for Alex, but he was nowhere to be seen. Then she turned back to Simon. He took off his jacket and hung it around his chair. He rolled up the cuffs on his shirt. He was sweating. *Good, he should sweat.* She thought, cataloguing all the ways he'd betrayed Alex. She noticed the hair on his arms—thick and dark.

Before Jenna could fit all the pieces together conclusively, Anya and Shawn showed up, bringing along an entourage of industry people, all smiles. Jenna tried to relax, there was nothing she could do now.

"Do you remember that gig in San Francisco?" A tall man in a suit jacket and jeans (clearly from back in his heyday) with a crazy mop of gray hair was saying. "When we were supposed to open for Patti Smith and the club wouldn't let us in without our passports? We stood in the rain like complete wankers and missed our set!" His anecdote received loud guffaws and slaps on the back.

Jenna needed to speak to Frank. *Where is he?*

Chapter 65

Backstage, Mindy briefed Alex on the details of montage sequences, performance order, and all manner of minutia relating to the minute by minute planning of the night's event. Of course, special consideration was being made for the cameras and commercial breaks, blah, blah, blah. He wasn't paying attention. He nodded and hmm'd at all the right times, but his mind was a million miles away—or wherever Frank was.

Frank had tried to call earlier, but bad reception dropped the call before he could find out what was going on. When Alex rang him back, it went straight to voicemail. He paced the holding area, biting his nails to the quick.

"Stop fidgeting!" Mindy commanded, getting his attention. "Have you listened to a word I've said?"

"I have!" He shouted, immediately regretting it. "Sorry, Min. Really, you don't need to worry. It'll be fine." He gave a weak smile. She rolled her eyes.

"What'd she say when you showed her?" he asked.

"Not much. I think she needs a minute to process." Mindy said, trying to keep things as light as possible. She looked down at her clipboard, something else catching her attention and off she went, chasing a PA, asking about changes to the tele-prompter script. Alex hated making her his messenger but when he saw Jackson Jones at the table next to Jenna, he'd felt backed into a corner. He'd had to make sure she heard it from him, not Jackson Jones. He resumed pacing, and spun around, colliding with Frank, who seemingly materialized in front of him.

"Omph! Sorry!" he said, then saw who it was.

"Alex," he said. "Good luck tonight." Frank clapped him on the shoulder, grinning. Alex stared at him.

"Frank! What happened? Did you get my messages? Did

you get what you needed from Airika?" Alex said.

"No, my phone was off. And I haven't spoken to Ms. Thomas. What did I need from her?" Frank said, bewildered.

Alex swallowed, in disbelief that he'd fallen for Airika's lies again. *She didn't call him?*

"Have you seen the trailer?" Alex asked. The color drained from Frank's face. He shook his head. Alex tipped his head back. "Jackson Jones just showed me the trailer. Apparently there's some newsworthiness loophole that allows him to use footage of Jenna shot in public spaces. And they can use everything else as long as they don't show her face. Is it true, can they do that?"

Jenna saw Frank walk backstage and turned to Felicity. "I'll be back in just a minute." She followed him around the seating area, toward a long hall that lead backstage. She saw Frank and Alex talking, and from the looks on their faces, they were in trouble.

"So?" she asked, not bothering with pleasantries.

Frank shook his head. "It doesn't look good. Our options are limited. We could claim defamation, but they could release it anyway and wait for us to sue. By then the damage would already be done. Our best option right now is to hope Ms. Thomas didn't sign a waiver and won't allow her likeness used."

Jenna didn't know what to say. Alex put his arms around her, letting her head sink into his chest. She would have started bawling if she hadn't heard the clickety clack of high heels getting nearer. She looked up to see Airika striding toward them, flanked by Simon and Jackson Jones. Jenna gasped and felt Alex's hands clench into fists.

"Fitzy, mate. Sorry I didn't get back to you the other day. How's that contract workin' out for ya?" Simon said, eyeing Alex.

"Airika, you promised," Alex said.

Simon cut him off. "You kids are gonna be big stars," he said, directing his attention to Airika and Alex, holding up a document, presumably the waiver in question. "What a handsome couple you are! No offense, Jenna. You know, just business and all that."

"You wouldn't," Jenna said to Airika. Despite everything that lead up to this moment, she would never have imagined Airika capable of such evil.

Airika stared Jenna down, revealing no emotion. She didn't get a chance to answer as Simon barreled on. He turned to Alex.

"My job is to make you money. That's what I'm doing. The wife and kid thing doesn't make money. A famous father-in-law you refuse to collaborate with and this all-about-the-music purism don't pay the bills. Scandals pay the rent. Sex pays off the mortgage. Combine them and you've got a fucking empire!"

Alex fumed. "So you just lied to me? After all these years?"

"All these years of not making my rent, you mean?" he said, stunning Alex into silence. "Your ball and chain was holding you back. You were unhappy. Anyone could see that. I did you a favor." Simon said. "You should be thanking me. You will be soon." Alex's eyes widened and the vein in his forehead pulsed.

Airika smiled at Simon. "What's in it for me?" she asked, running her finger down his arm.

"Doll, you'll be a superstar. Women will love to hate you and men will want to fuck you. You'll be on the cover of every magazine, the headline of every news story. This is your big break. You'll never need to work again."

"And if I don't sign?" she asked, ever-so-sweetly. Jenna wanted to puke at her tone. She didn't buy that act for a second.

Jackson Jones, who had been quiet until now, interjected. "You want to consider your options carefully," he said to Airika. "If you do this, it can be as Mr. Walker described." Airika raised her eyebrows as if to say "go on." He continued,

"If you choose not to … I have it on good authority that your trust fund payments, which I believe afford you a certain lifestyle, will be suddenly suspended. It would be a shame, no?"

Airika narrowed her eyes at Jackson Jones. She kept her mouth shut, motioning for Simon to hand her the paper. "Good girl," Simon said. Alex and Jenna looked on, helpless and dumbfounded. Frank shifted from one foot to the other, like he was standing on hot coals.

"I knew this one wasn't just a fine piece of ass," Simon said, leering. "You should've hit that when you had the chance, again."

Alex stepped around Airika and punched Simon, landing with a loud crack across the left cheekbone. Simon smiled maniacally. "You hit like a girl."

Airika chuckled, and threw a right cross, leveling Simon to the floor.

"Get off me!" Jackson Jones shouted at the two men in navy blue jackets and caps that read "FBI." The one on the right nodded to Airika.

As one, they turned to look at her, mouths agape. "In my head, I was just going to say 'you're welcome', but you all look like orphaned puppies wondering what that blood on the road is. So let me illuminate you. Mr. Jones was just arrested by the FBI. His attorney's office—files, bills, notes, computers, probably even some lists of off-shore bank accounts—are all being seized. I'm not sure if anyone is at Flesh, Inc. to watch the same thing happen there, but I'd guess there's security footage, if you wanted to see it later. Probably the only footage that won't be confiscated, actually." Airika looked down at Simon, nearly impaling him with her stiletto. "See, you thought you were manipulating me with sex, but you had no idea who you were dealing with. Ira Stearn and I go way back. I spent all yesterday afternoon reminiscing about the good old days with he and my father at the FBI. They were such good listeners." She turned to Jenna, Alex and Frank.

"You're welcome," she said, stomping off down the hall and out through the emergency exit.

Jenna and Alex stared at each other, not sure what to say.

"Two minute warning!" Mindy shouted from around the corner. Alex stepped over Simon's prostrate body. "You're fired," he said and kissed his wife.

Alex stepped into the spotlight, and up to the podium. He looked out at the audience, full of musicians, managers, producers, friends and family. He smiled. The teleprompter sprang up with introductory dialogue. He ignored it.

"I am honored to be here, presenting my father-in-law with this prestigious honor. I know I'm supposed to give a big speech right now listing his many, many accomplishments and detailing his legacy to the world of music—which itself could take up the allotted time. Instead, with his permission, I'd like to invite him up here to perform a song with me."

He could barely see Shawn's face in the audience, but knew that he was smiling that cheeky smile of his. Shawn had pushed for them to perform together for so many years, and even after co-writing a song that Alex loved, he'd resisted.

He may have been thick-headed, but Alex finally figured it out. Or at least he hoped he had. Music was about having fun and expressing something real. Nothing was more real than family, and tonight seemed like the right time to enjoy his.

Alex summarized a few of Shawn's career highlights as stage-hands scrambled around, setting up guitars and microphones as Shawn walked up to the stage. The audience stood in ovation, cheering the anarchic moment. Shawn signaled his old band mates from backstage to come on up and sit in.

As they re-organized the stage, Jenna found her table and sat in the empty chair next to Felicity. Frank joined them moments later. Jenna squeezed Felicity's shoulders, taking her by surprise.

Alex saw Jenna in the audience and relaxed seeing the joy

on her face. As he stood to greet his father-in-law, Shawn hugged him, saying, "I'm proud of you," into his shoulder.

He picked up a guitar, raising his hands to the indulgent audience, and sat down in front of the mic. "We'll play a song we wrote together in just a minute. First, I have a request for my son-in-law." Shawn leaned in to Alex, setting his guitar to the side. Alex took the mic and said, "This was written for my wife, for our anniversary."

He played the never-before-heard song—in front of a thousand-person live audience and an international broadcast—as though it were a private concert just for Jenna.

By the end of the song, she was in tears (along with half the audience). Mindy was elated—it was publicity gold. Felicity didn't bother to wipe the tears as she clasped Jenna's hand, happy that some semblance of normality had crept back into their lives.

Shawn took up his guitar and played the first few chords of his biggest hit. The crowd erupted in cheers and many musicians he'd played with through the years joined in on the jam. In that moment—if only that one—they were just a bunch of musicians playing for the hell of it. Playing like no one was watching. Free.

By the end of the set, Alex resolved to take Shawn up on his offer to tour together. His definition of selling out had been flipped on its head, and he realized that sticking with his family, despite their fame and his pride, was more fulfilling than anything he could do on his own. Every choice came with a price.

Chapter 67 (Epilogue)

Vanity Fair, *October*

After a controversial year of press, the Jax family is set to release the biopic about its patriarch, Shawn Jax. For all you readers of the less journalistic fare (Ahem! That's you, tabloids), you may be familiar with the controversy surrounding Alex Anders and Jenna Jax-Anders' separation and scandal. But for those who aren't, all we can say (due to the pending court case involving known porn mogul, Jackson Jones) is that the rumors of an affair between Alex and Jenna's best friend, Airika, proved false and, more than that, she turned out to be fighting from their corner, when she tipped off Rolling Stone *to the egregious misstep they narrowly avoided when they fired the writer, Rose McKenna for trying to print a fabricated story fed to her by the advertiser, Flesh, Inc. (owned by one Jackson Jones).*

Airika is also slated to testify against the attorney, Ira Stearn, in the case against he and Mr. Jones on fifty counts of fraud, including one count against Alex Anders. Though none of that is in the upcoming film, it's clear the Jaxes are no ordinary family.

I'm sitting here on the Vanity Fair *cover shoot set with Shawn Jax's granddaughter, Felicity Jax-Anders, who plays his wife Anya (not opposite her grandpa!) in the film. This is her first feature film and, while many have called it nepotism, she assures me she had to audition like everyone else. The Oscar buzz surrounding not only the film, but her performance, gives credence to that claim. Her unassuming nature and intellectualism (when I arrived she was reading 'Anna Karenina'), not to mention personal insight into the role, make it easy to see why she was chosen.*

VF: "So how was it playing your own grandmother in this film? Did it feel bizarre or did you feel like you got to know her better?"

FJ-A: "It was illuminating, definitely. But honestly, I approached it like I would have any other role. It is based on real events, but the script takes creative liberties where needed. I couldn't show up on set thinking about myself as Felicity, the granddaughter. I had to think like a young Anya—see the world through her eyes."

VF: "Does it bother you when people say you only got the part because they knew it would garner more publicity for the film?"

FJ-A: (laughs) "No, not really. If I've learned anything this past year, it's to not take other people's opinions too seriously. Whether we earn every opportunity we get or are lucky enough to have it handed to us, we still have to know what to do with it. My hope is that when people see the film, they'll be able to tell I'm serious about the craft of acting. I did the best job I could with the experience and skill I have, and feel honored to have had the opportunity."

VF: "You seem incredibly mature for someone who just turned eighteen. How do you stay so grounded when so many of your generation fall victim to temptation?"

FJ-A: "Well, I've had a lot more life experience in the past year than many of my contemporaries (pauses) and I'm just lucky to have such a loving, supportive family. They made me who I am."

VF: "Yes, there has been a lot written about your parents in the last year. How are they doing now that the separation rumors have abated?"

FJ-A: "They're great. I make fun of them, saying they act like a couple of teenagers dating, but it's cute. My dad is taking some time off touring to help my mom with the launch of her new line of home décor. She designed every piece and even photographed them for the catalogue. Proceeds from every sale will go to a charity that provides no-interest loans to low-income women starting their own businesses."

VF: "Wow, it seems like you've got the perfect Hollywood fairytale."

FJ-A: *(chuckles) "If life were perfect it wouldn't be half as interesting. Appearances only account for part of the story. But right now I'm in a great place. I feel lucky."*

VF: *"Lucky and talented. Thanks for talking to me, Felicity. I wish you the best for the upcoming award season. I have a feeling this is just the beginning for you."*